SPIRIT CROSSING

ALSO BY WILLIAM KENT KRUEGER

SPIRIT CROSSING

A Novel

William Kent Krueger

ATRIA BOOKS

New York   London   Toronto   Sydney   New Delhi

ATRIA
BOOKS

An Imprint of Simon & Schuster, LLC
1230 Avenue of the Americas
New York, NY 10020

First Atria Books hardcover edition August 2024

ATRIA B O O K S and colophon are trademarks of Simon & Schuster, LLC

Simon & Schuster: Celebrating 100 Years of Publishing in 2024

For information about special discounts for bulk purchases, please contact Simon & Schuster Special Sales at 1-866-506-1949 or business@simonandschuster.com.

The Simon & Schuster Speakers Bureau can bring authors to your live event. For more information or to book an event, contact the Simon & Schuster Speakers Bureau at 1-866-248-3049 or visit our website at www.simonspeakers.com.

Manufactured in the United States of America

1 3 5 7 9 10 8 6 4 2

Library of Congress Cataloging-in-Publication Data is available.

ISBN 978-1-9821-7924-3
ISBN 978-1-9821-7926-7 (ebook)

To the far too many who have
been murdered or are still missing.
Let them never be forgotten.

Sometimes dreams are wiser than waking.

—Black Elk

SPIRIT CROSSING

CHAPTER 1

She built the fire at twilight, and by the time the sky had filled with stars, a welcome blaze lit the campsite. For a long time, the two young women didn't talk but sat together, staring into the flames.

"Are you sorry you came back?" This woman had long hair, night-sky black, and spoke with the accent of someone whose first language was Spanish.

"No, but it's going to be rough." The second woman, the one who'd built the fire, had red hair cut short, and she spoke with a flat Midwest accent. "My life has been about so much that hasn't included them."

"This is your home. They are your family."

The redhead took her companion's hand and kissed it gently. "You're my family now. My home."

"You need to tell them."

"I will. When the time is right." She saw that her companion was hugging herself. "Cold?"

"I am used to hot and humid."

"This is hot for Minnesota. Here, let me help." She wrapped her arms tenderly around her companion.

"You told them I was coming?" the black-haired woman asked.

"A friend. That's all I said."

"What? Not even 'a good friend'?"

"This isn't about me. My brother's getting married. I don't want to steal his thunder."

"We could make it a double wedding ceremony."

"How many times do I have to tell you no?" the red-haired woman said.

"You don't love me?"

"You know I do. And you know why we can't marry."

"I will love you always."

"And I you."

Again they were quiet.

"What did you call this place?" the black-haired woman asked.

"Bizaan. It's an Ojibwe word that means at peace. The white folks call it Still Island. I used to come here whenever I needed to figure things out."

"And the lake?"

"Iron Lake."

"When we went swimming today, it didn't feel like hard water." The black-haired woman smiled. "When will we go to your family?"

"Tomorrow. I wanted today to be just for us. After this, things could get complicated."

"They are your family. They will understand."

"In time."

As the fire died, they laid out the blankets they'd brought on a bed of soft pine needles. The red-haired young woman stared up at the sky. Although the night was warm, the stars seemed to shiver. She'd known the night skies in Minnesota well as a child. In Guatemala, there were constellations and stars she'd never seen before. In the years since she'd left Tamarack County, Annie O'Connor's world had expanded in ways she'd never dreamed possible. But now she was back, and although she knew she would be welcomed with open arms, there was something inside her that was alien, that would hurt the people she loved, that would, in its way, come to threaten them all.

CHAPTER 2

"Can I eat some while I fill my bucket?" Waaboo asked.

"A few," his father, Daniel, said. "But leave some for the rest of us."

"And for the animals," his uncle Stephen added.

Waaboo looked confused.

"Always leave plenty of blueberries on the bushes for the other creatures we share the forest with," Cork, who was his grandfather, explained.

They were driving down an old logging road just south of the Iron Lake Reservation, heading toward the patch that had been the locale of wild blueberry picking for the O'Connor family since before Cork was born. Many families in Tamarack County, Minnesota, had secret places for picking, patches whose locations were passed down as part of the heritage from one generation to the next. This outing was for the men of the O'Connor clan: Cork, the patriarch; Stephen, his twenty-three-old son; Daniel English, Cork's son-in-law; and Waaboo, Cork's seven-year-old grandson. The little boy's real name was Aaron Smalldog

O'Connor. It was Stephen who, long ago, had given him the nickname Waaboo, which in the language of the Ojibwe people meant little rabbit.

"What eats blueberries besides us?" Waaboo asked.

"Bears and skunks and deer. And other waaboos," Daniel said, ruffling his son's hair.

"And lots of birds," Stephen said.

Waaboo's little brow furrowed in concern. "Maybe they've eaten them all by now."

"Don't worry," Cork assured him. "Our blueberry patch has always produced enough for the animals and for us."

It was mid-July of a summer that had so far been ideal. The morning air was sharp with the clean scent of pine. The sky was an arch of pure blue. Cork's heart was full of gratitude. Stephen had been gone for two years, or mostly gone, finishing his degree at the University of Minnesota. Although he'd returned for brief visits, his focus was on his education. And on his girlfriend, now fiancée.

"Nervous at all about the wedding?" Daniel asked. "Still six weeks to change your mind."

"Belle's the best thing that ever happened to me," Stephen said. "Besides, all the arrangements have been made."

"If you ever decide to leave this family," Cork said, "we keep Belle."

"Leave?" Waaboo said.

"Just kidding, little guy," Cork said. "And here we are."

They'd circumnavigated a bog area and Cork parked on solid ground among a stand of birch. The men and the boy got out and grabbed their pails from the back of Cork's Expedition.

"Where are the blueberries?" Waaboo said. "I don't see any."

"We have to walk a little," Cork told him. "We don't want anybody passing by to see where our patch is."

"Nobody's here," Waaboo pointed out.

"You never know who might be watching," Daniel said with a wink. "A good blueberry patch is worth more than gold."

They skirted the bog, following a path almost impossible to see because it was trod only in July, when the blueberries of the North Country had ripened. As they walked, Cork studied the ground with growing concern.

"Somebody's been here," he said quietly.

"How do you know?" Waaboo asked.

"See all those broken plants?" Cork pointed toward a growth of rattlesnake ferns in front of them. "Somebody's trampled their way through. And there." He pointed toward a footprint in soft dirt.

Waaboo looked up at his grandfather. "Were they after our blueberries?"

"We'll know soon enough," Cork said.

The patch lay on the far side of the bog. When they arrived, Cork and the others stood staring at the ravaged bushes.

"They picked everything," Stephen said.

"Didn't even leave something for the animals," Daniel said.

Waaboo looked devastated. "Who were they?"

"Hard to say," Cork replied. "Six-one-twoers, I'm guessing. Folks from around here would be more respectful."

"Six-one-twoers?" Waaboo asked.

"It used to be the only area code for the Twin Cities," Cork explained. "Not true anymore, little guy, but up here we still call them that, the people who come up from the Cities and trample everything."

"No blueberries," Waaboo said, clearly distraught.

"We'll get blueberries, don't worry," Cork assured him. "I know another place."

In dismal silence, they returned to the Expedition and Cork started back toward Iron Lake.

"Where to now, Dad?" Stephen asked.

"You remember an old Finn named Erno Paavola?"

"Not well."

"I did a little bit of PI work for him, three or four years ago. He couldn't pay in money, so he brought me three full buckets of blueberries, the biggest I've seen around here. He was a man who liked his liquor, and he was a little drunk when he gave me the buckets. He told me they'd come from his own private blueberry patch near his cabin. He passed away not long after I did the work for him. He had no family left around here, so I figure it's up for grabs."

"Where is it?" Daniel asked.

"A few miles southeast."

"What if somebody already picked everything?" Waaboo said.

"Don't worry," Cork assured him. "Erno told me his patch was protected by gnomes."

"Gnomes?" Waaboo said.

"You know about Irish leprechauns, right? Gnomes are kind of like Scandinavian leprechauns."

Cork drove the county road south, then east two miles on gravel, and finally turned in to the ruts of a dirt lane that cut through a stand of mixed pine and spruce as it mounted a hill. In a clearing near the top of the rise, a cabin stood amid tall wild grass.

"Paavola's place," Cork said.

"Looks run-down," Daniel said. "Abandoned?"

"As far as I know. But it looked pretty run-down when Erno lived here."

Daniel nodded toward a little structure off to the side of the cabin. "An outhouse?"

"Erno lived off the grid," Cork said. "Kept things primitive. He was sure the end of the world was just around the corner, and only those who were prepared to live without all the modern crap, as he put it, would survive."

"Where are the blueberries?" Waaboo asked.

"I'm guessing we might have to walk a bit," Cork said.

"There better be blueberries," Waaboo warned.

Cork led the way to the rear of the cabin, where the wild grass ran another thirty yards to the forest edge. He stood a moment, scanning the trees.

"What are you looking for?" Stephen asked.

"The gnomes," Cork said.

"You've got to be kidding me," Daniel said.

"Erno seemed pretty serious."

"I'll find them." Waaboo ran ahead, bounding through the tall grass.

"Spread out," Cork said.

The men fanned out, but before they'd taken more than a few steps, Waaboo cried, "Here they are!"

At the edge of the tree line stood two little gnomes, each four feet high, carved from the stumps of a couple of hardwood trees cut down long ago. They'd been brightly painted at one time but now wore only the faintest tatters of color.

"And there's the path," Cork said.

"Not much of a path," Stephen noted.

"Let's go." Waaboo started quickly ahead.

They followed the little boy along the faint trace of a trail through the evergreens. A few minutes later, they came to another clearing, where the sun smiled down on a field of scrub under-growth, a mix of pine seedlings and June grass and lupines. Among the other wild flora were squat green bushes on which berries hung like tiny bulbs on Christmas trees.

"Blueberries!" Waaboo said.

"Move carefully," Daniel cautioned. "We don't want to destroy any of the plants."

"I'll be careful," Waaboo promised and wandered into the patch.

"Quite a find," Stephen noted.

Cork grinned. "Wouldn't have known where to look except for those gnomes."

"And a drunk and cash-strapped Finn," Stephen said.

They'd picked for a few minutes when Cork noticed Waaboo, who was a dozen yards away, kneeling on the ground beside his bucket, staring straight ahead, his lips moving as if he were talking with someone. Then the little boy stood and came to his father, who was not far from Cork.

"Daddy, she's lost," Waaboo said.

"Who?" Daniel replied.

Waaboo pointed to where he'd been picking. "The lady. She's lost and she's sad."

They were alone in the clearing, the men and the boy.

"Wait here." Daniel walked to where Waaboo had left his bucket, looked around a bit, then down at the ground. In a voice that spoke trouble, he said, "Cork, you need to see this."

Cork joined him, and Stephen came, too. The men stood at the edge of a small, mounded area that was almost clean of vegetation. The mound was five feet long and a couple of feet wide.

"Is that what I think it is?" Daniel said.

A few moments of silence passed, then Stephen ventured, "Olivia Hamilton?"

Cork slowly scanned the blueberry patch and the clearing, then the azure arch of the sky above. It was such a lovely scene, so peaceful, at least on the surface. He forced himself to look again at the mounding of earth at his feet.

"We won't know until we dig," he said. "I'd best call our sheriff."

CHAPTER 3

Olivia Hamilton came from money. Her father was a state senator, a politician in a long line of Minnesota legislators. His family's wealth originated in the early days of mining as a result of shipping ore from the Iron Range across Lake Superior on carriers out of Two Harbors or Duluth. Olivia had grown up with money. Spoiled, most folks would have called it, but because she was a Hamilton, they more often used the less pejorative term, *privileged*. By the time she entered her teens, she'd been expelled from a number of private schools, both in the Twin Cities and out of state. In the spring, she'd gotten into some trouble driving with a suspended license and while intoxicated. A deal had been struck that forced her to spend the summer as a counselor at a youth camp near Aurora, the hope being that time in the great Northwoods and responsibility for others might shape her a bit more into the good girl her family, particularly her father, needed her to be.

But a few weeks into her "sentence," as she termed it in text messages to her friends, she had sneaked away from the camp one night with another counselor, a kid named Harvey Green, who had a motorcycle. They'd gone to Yellow Lake, a community south of Aurora with a reputation for being on the rough side. Using fake IDs, they settled into a bar there, a place called the Howling Wolf, which was a notorious gathering spot for hard-drinking men— bikers, loggers, construction workers, and often the kinds of individuals who, except for their need to drink and carouse, typically opted to remain off the grid.

That night, there'd been a bunch of bikers hanging out at the Howling Wolf, the Kings, a group out of Fargo, on their way to a motorcycle rally in Duluth. There was also a local biker club, the Axemen, all of them loggers. In the course of a night of drinking, things got said and a fight broke out in the street in front of the bar. The Tamarack County Sheriff's Department responded. No serious injuries were reported, and no one was arrested. But a lot of names were taken.

Because of his own drinking, which, he claimed, had put him in a bit of an alcoholic haze, Harvey Green lost track of Olivia when the fight broke out. When he decided it was time to head back to the camp, she was nowhere to be found.

The next day, camp authorities reported her disappearance. A huge hunt was launched, involving Tamarack County Sheriff's personnel, the state patrol, Minnesota's Bureau of Criminal Apprehension, and, because of the Kings' Fargo connection and the possibility that the girl had been abducted and taken out of state, the FBI. Everyone who could be identified in the bar the night the girl went missing, particularly the members of the two gangs, was hauled in and relentlessly questioned, to no avail. The bar had no security cameras, so no record of comings and goings. The town of Yellow Lake was turned upside down in the search for clues, evidence of what might have occurred.

There was hope of a ransom demand, but when nothing materialized, the family offered a reward of $50,000 for information that led to finding their daughter. Every call that resulted, and there were hundreds, was followed up but led nowhere.

The search had been ongoing for two weeks. They'd pinged her cell phone location, checked phone records, her text messages, social media posts. Everything ended the night she'd disappeared. They'd grilled Harvey Green and once again grilled everyone they could identify as having been in the bar that night. But until Waaboo stumbled upon a grave as he picked blueberries, there'd been no progress.

While Cork remained in the clearing, Daniel English took Waaboo and Stephen home, where he planned to call the situation in to the Tamarack County Sheriff's Department. The drive took only half an hour, but because his son was unusually quiet, it felt like forever to Daniel.

"She must have been looking at the sun," Waaboo finally said. "Her eyes looked hurt."

"Nothing hurts her now," Stephen said. "She's walking the Path of Souls."

Waaboo shook his head. "Not yet. She's still lost." And he was quiet again.

"What did she look like?" Daniel asked.

"Like you and me."

"Ojibwe?"

Waaboo nodded.

At the house on Gooseberry Lane, Jenny O'Connor and Rainy Bisonette were painting the railing and front porch posts. Jenny was Waaboo's mother, Rainy his grandmother. They waved as Daniel pulled into the drive, but when they saw the empty hands of the men and the boy, who approached them across the lawn, Jenny said, "No blueberries? What happened?"

Before Daniel could respond, Waaboo said, "I saw a dead woman."

Jenny had been holding a brush filled with paint. Daniel saw that her clothes and her face were spattered with spots like white freckles. She gave him a dark look of concern and puzzlement.

"Waaboo, I think your grandma has some cold lemonade for you inside." Daniel looked hopefully at Rainy, his aunt.

"Of course," Rainy said. "And there are fresh chocolate chip cookies in the jar."

"She can't find the Path of Souls," Waaboo said.

Rainy held out her hand to the boy. "*Ondaas*," she said, using the Anishinaabe word that meant *Come*. Waaboo went with his grandmother into the house.

Jenny set the brush in the pan of white paint. "A dead woman?"

"What we believe is a grave," Daniel said. "But our son saw her spirit."

"Oh, god. Where?"

"In a blueberry patch."

"Ours?" She looked doubly horrified.

"No," Stephen put in quickly. "Somebody picked our patch clean. This one belonged to an old Finn Dad did some PI work for a while back, a guy named Erno Paavola. He paid in blueberries, and Dad had an idea about where the patch might be. We found it. And then Waaboo found the grave."

"And saw her spirit?" Jenny put paint-stained fingers to her forehead as if trying to press an understanding into her brain. "He said she couldn't find the Path of Souls."

"We'll figure out what he meant," Daniel said. "Right now, I need to call the sheriff's department. Then I'll go back and guide them down to the patch. Your dad's waiting there."

"I'll come, too," Stephen said.

"No," Jenny said. "I need you here, Stephen. I have so many questions."

"Stay," Daniel told his brother-in-law. "Cork and I have got this."

It was noon now. Daniel stood with Cork and Sheriff Marsha Dross beside the grave Waaboo had found. The sun was directly overhead, creating dark pools of shadow under Daniel and the other two. Daniel stared at his own shadow, wondering how the day, which had begun with his son on such a bright note, could end so darkly.

"It might be Olivia Hamilton," Dross said. "We can't really say how old this grave is."

"To me, those shoots coming up look like they might be thimbleweed," Cork said, nodding toward a bit of green showing through the dirt on the mounding. "It would take more than a couple of weeks for seed to have taken root."

"You're not an expert on burials," Dross said. "Or thimble-weed."

"No," Cork admitted.

Dross looked down at the grave. "I'd hoped she would call home, or just show up, maybe ashamed, or full of guilt and scared of what her parents might say. Something befitting a teenager who simply made a bad choice."

"Two weeks is a long time for shame or guilt to keep her dis-appeared," Cork said.

"She'd run away before and had come back. I was hoping it might be how this played out." Dross gave her head a single, hopeless shake.

"She had a wild streak, Marsha, that was clear."

"What teenager doesn't rebel a bit?"

"You sound like you're making excuses for her."

"I was kind of wild as a teenager," Dross said.

Daniel asked. "Did you ever run away?"

"Threatened it a few times."

"Olivia Hamilton was last seen drinking with a bunch of bikers and loggers. Did you go out drinking with bikers and loggers?"

"Some lumberjacks. But I knew them."

Cork said, "This girl, if it is Olivia Hamilton, didn't know those loggers and bikers."

"It's not Olivia Hamilton," Daniel said.

Cork and Dross both gave him a puzzled look.

"Waaboo told me she looked Ojibwe. It could be Crystal Two Knives. She's still missing."

Dross's puzzled look morphed into one of deep skepticism. "I'm not basing any assumptions on what a seven-year-old boy believes he's seen in a vision."

"Stephen had visions when he was that young," Cork reminded her. "There have been times when those visions have proved very helpful to you. There's a whole lot more to this world than you'll find in a textbook on law enforcement, Marsha. And like I said, the grave does look older than two weeks."

"Doesn't do any good speculating," Dross said. "We won't know a thing until we exhume a body."

Deputy George Azevedo came down the trail that led from Erno Paavola's cabin to the clearing and the blueberry patch. "BCA is on their way. They want us to make sure nothing's disturbed."

"Of course nothing's being disturbed," Dross shot back. "Do they think we're rubes?"

"Just telling you what they said, Sheriff."

"Go on back to the road. When they arrive, show them the way down here."

"Sure thing, Sheriff." Azevedo headed away.

Dross took a deep breath and let out a long sigh. "This is going to be a shitstorm."

"Everybody cares about Olivia Hamilton," Daniel said. "There was no shitstorm when Crystal Two Knives went missing."

"That was different."

"Because she's Indian?" Daniel's words fell like stones from his mouth.

"Because Crystal is a troubled kid with a long history of running away. We've picked her up a number of times for underage drinking, shoplifting, driving without a license, you name it."

Daniel felt his blood begin to rise. "So, when she went missing it was easy just to blame it on her own reckless behavior?"

"On a history that told me she'd show up again. She owned a vehicle, Daniel. She just drove away one day. There's been no report of her car being found anywhere. At the moment, there's no reason to believe that she's been the victim of any kind of violence, no reason to pursue an investigation any further than we have already," Dross said sharply.

"No reason except a grandmother who worries herself sick every night."

"Let it go, Daniel," Cork said.

Daniel's jaw went tight as he bit back the words of an old argument born from an old inequity. He understood Cork's quiet advice. If this was a grave—and he was almost certain it was—it didn't matter who was buried here. This wasn't the time or place to argue the issue. Instead, he looked at the pines that walled off the clearing. "Somebody knew about this blueberry patch but must have figured that no one else did. Burying a body here probably seemed safe."

"What do you know about Erno Paavola, Cork?" Dross asked.

"That he was dead long before this grave was dug."

"I mean, any relatives that you're aware of, someone who might know this place?"

"The PI work I did for him was to track down a niece and a nephew."

"Where?"

"Cloquet."

"Why?"

"Erno didn't say."

"You didn't ask?"

"He hired me to find them, that was all. He paid me in blueberries. Told me they came from his secret patch, which was guarded by gnomes. You saw them."

"I wonder who else he might have told," Daniel said.

"You've got your work cut out for you, Marsha," Cork said, then added, "I don't envy you. A lot of press coverage already around Olivia Hamilton. Until we know who's buried here, the media'll be dogging you every step of the way."

Another deputy approached from the direction of Paavola's cabin.

"What is it, Foster?" Dross said.

"New communication from BCA. The Feds are on their way, too. And they don't want you making any statements to the press before they have a chance to work the scene."

Daniel eyed Dross, whose face seemed to have grown a decade older in the past half hour. "And so the shitstorm begins," he said.

CHAPTER 4

Cork and Daniel left before the other agencies descended. They would want to interview him, Cork knew, and Stephen and Daniel, and even little Waaboo. But he would make them come to him. In his time as sheriff of Tamarack County years ago, Cork had worked with every possible iteration of law enforcement. Although things could sometimes progress smoothly, more often, toes were stepped on and jurisdictional issues created a good deal of tension, especially in a high-profile case like the disappearance of Olivia Hamilton.

Since leaving the blueberry patch, Daniel had been particularly quiet.

"Sorry I cut you off back there," Cork said.

Daniel let a moment pass, then said, "I get it. Wasn't the time or place to argue about a missing Ojibwe girl. Still . . ." He shook his head. "It's not right."

"Crystal Two Knives is still missing," Cork said. "There's still hope."

"Maybe not. If what Waaboo told us is true, that the girl in the grave looks Ojibwe, it could be Crystal. And even if it's not, there will still be nobody looking for her. Not like Olivia Hamilton. She's white and her parents are rich. So, everybody's looking."

He was right, Cork knew, and he understood the bitterness that spilled from his full-blood Ojibwe son-in-law.

They reached home and went into the house through the front door, crossing the porch where the paint job Jenny and Rainy had started that morning was still unfinished. Inside, Cork heard voices coming from the kitchen, and he and Daniel headed that way.

The moment Cork stepped into the kitchen, his eyes lit on Annie, who was sitting at the table. He'd been expecting his beloved daughter home sometime before the wedding, though not quite this soon. Although she'd been working in Guatemala for almost seven years, she's been back several times, usually for Christmas. But her last visit was more than two years ago.

"Hey, kiddo!" he cried. Annie stood, and he took her into his arms and held her a long time. "God, it's good to see you."

"Good to be home, Dad."

He released her, stepped back, and looked at her companion, who, along with Rainy and Jenny, was sitting at the kitchen table. She was about Annie's age, thirtyish, with long hair black and shiny as a raven's wing, a broad, calm face, and dark eyes that, as she regarded him, seemed inviting rather than mysterious.

Cork smiled at her. "You must be Maria."

"Maria Cocum Lopez," Annie said, casting a sweet smile toward her companion. "Cocum is Mayan for listener. It fits her perfectly."

"I'm Cork O'Connor," he said and took Maria's hand warmly in his. "Annie's father."

"I know," she replied with a Spanish accent. "Annie has told me all about you."

"And Annie talks about you all the time in her emails. *Boozhoo*," he said.

"*Miigwech*," she replied, offering an Ojibwe thank-you to his Ojibwe greeting, which impressed Cork. "Annie's taught me a little," she explained.

"I'm so happy you're here. It just adds more joy to the wedding." As he looked at the others around the table, however, joy wasn't what Cork saw on their faces. "What's wrong?"

Rainy said, "We've been talking about the grave Waaboo found."

"Where is Waaboo?" Daniel asked.

"Stephen took him to the lake for a swim," Jenny said. "It was what Waaboo wanted. You know him and the lake. He's like an otter. I think he needed to process things and wanted to do it in the water. And Stephen wanted to talk to him about his visions, give him some comfort and guidance. If there's anybody who understands, it's Stephen. Or," she added, "Henry Meloux."

"Maybe I should go," Daniel said.

"He'll be fine with Stephen," Jenny said. "We'll talk to him later."

"I am so sorry for the woman in that grave," Maria said.

"We're not entirely certain it is a grave," Cork said.

"Waaboo saw her spirit," Daniel said firmly.

"And I am sorry for your little boy, to see such a thing," Maria said.

"Waaboo is nothing if not resilient," Jenny said. "Remember, when he was just a baby, I found him under a rock."

Which was a long story, and true. And after she'd found the child, Jenny had adopted him.

"So Annie has told me," Maria said. "Scary, but beautiful in the end."

"Sit," Rainy said to the two men and lifted a pitcher from the middle of the table. "Some ice water? It's hot out there."

Cork and Daniel joined the women, accepting the offer of water and taking the last of the empty chairs.

"You flew into Duluth?" Cork asked.

"Yes."

"Why didn't you call us? We'd have come down to get you."

"It was easier to Uber here," Annie told him.

Cork sipped his ice water. He hadn't realized how thirsty he'd become, and the water ran down his throat in a long, cooling stream. "So, you got in this morning?"

Annie exchanged a look with her companion. "Actually, yesterday. I rented a canoe from Sorley's Outfitters, and Maria and I spent the night on Still Island. I wanted it to be her introduction to Minnesota."

"It was a very beautiful place," Maria said. "Very calming."

"You're Guatemalan, yes?" Cork said.

"My people are Mayan," Maria replied with a note of pride.

"And how did you two become friends?"

It wasn't the question Cork really wanted to ask. Growing up, Annie O'Connor had aspired to be two things: (1) the first female pitcher starting for a professional baseball team and (2) a nun. She'd been a star athlete in high school and after that had become a postulant with the Sisters of Notre Dame de Namur. In a period of personal and spiritual crisis, she'd stepped away from the formal pathway to becoming a part of the order and had gone to Guatemala to work in a school run by the Sisters there. Cork had thought at first that it was a form of running away. He knew his daughter was struggling to accept that she was what the Ojibwe called a two-spirit person. She'd fallen in love with another young woman, and it had ended badly. But as Annie had continued to communicate from a distance, it had become obvious that in

Guatemala she'd found two significant things—purpose in her service to the poor there and a special person. Still, she'd always been a little circumspect when she mentioned Maria. Although he wondered about the depth of his daughter's relationship, Cork wasn't about to pry.

"I met Maria at a clinic where I'd taken an injured child. Maria's a nurse."

Cork said to Maria, "Rainy's also a nurse."

"Yes, and a Mide, as well, I understand," Maria added. "An Ojibwe healer." She smiled at Rainy. "We have healers in the Mayan culture. We call them *curanderos.*"

"We also have missing women in Guatemala," Annie said, shifting the timbre of the conversation with dramatic suddenness. "And we also have buried bodies, so many of them."

"Annie," Maria said. *"Este no es el momento ni el lugar."*

"She's telling me this isn't the time or place for this discussion."

"Perhaps she's right," Rainy said.

"We keep talking about Olivia Hamilton," Daniel said. "Have we already forgotten Crystal Two Knives?"

"Crystal Two Knives?" Annie said. "Is she any relation to Cece Two Knives?"

"Her granddaughter," Daniel said.

"How long has she been missing?"

"Almost six months."

Annie considered that, then asked, "How about Olivia Hamilton?"

"Two weeks. The search has been pretty intensive."

"The authorities in Guatemala don't do much searching when a Mayan woman is reported missing," Annie said.

"It's the same here with Ojibwe women." Daniel's words carried the identical acid note Cork had heard in Annie's voice.

"Could we talk about something else?" Jenny said. "Like maybe Stephen and Belle's wedding. That's what's brought Annie and Maria here."

Cork saw a look pass between his daughter and her friend, the kind of look that made him wonder if the wedding was the only reason they'd come.

CHAPTER 5

Two agents showed up that evening. One was federal, FBI. The other was state, Bureau of Criminal Apprehension. They were hard to distinguish from one another. White shirts, ties, dark suits, shiny shoes. Cork figured they hadn't been to the blueberry patch. They were just grunts with names of people to question. In his time as sheriff, Cork had worked significantly with both agencies, and he'd come to know men he respected. These two were new to him and seemed too young and too officious. And they didn't play well together either. They stumbled over each other in their questioning, and the looks that often passed between them were less than collegial. Mostly they were interested in Cork's knowledge about the location of the blueberry patch. He explained about Paavola and being hired to find his niece and nephew. Then he explained about the payment in blueberries.

"Blueberries?" the FBI agent said. "Seriously?" He gave a chuckle, not humorously but derisively, as if this kind of rural barter was unbelievably backward.

The BCA agent asked about the niece and nephew.

"I have their information at my office," Cork said.

"And where would that be?"

He told them that he operated out of Sam's Place.

"Sam's Place?"

He explained about the hamburger joint he owned, which was housed in an old Quonset hut in Aurora. That brought smirks to both agents' faces. He offered to supply them with the information, but they assured him they would find it on their own. Stephen and Daniel couldn't add much. In the end, the agents asked for the shoes the men and boy had been wearing that morning in order to use Sirchie impression cards to help eliminate them from consideration of any prints found at the scene. Cork and Daniel had already anticipated this and had the shoes ready.

"Have they exhumed a body?" Cork asked.

"They're excavating the site now," the BCA agent said. "That's all we know."

Cork saw them to the door. As the agents descended the porch steps, he heard one of them say, "Blueberries." And both men laughed.

After they'd gone, Rainy said, "That didn't seem to get us anywhere. Anyone want coffee, decaf?"

Cork said, "I think I'll have a beer. We got any Leinie's?"

Shortly after the agents had arrived and it had become obvious that they considered the possibility of a vision unlikely, if not downright ridiculous, Jenny had taken Waaboo upstairs. After the men had gone, Daniel headed up to join her in Waaboo's bedroom. From the hallway, he could hear his son's laughter. Daniel thought it odd that his son should be so lighthearted after what he'd discovered in the blueberry patch that day. But he knew that Stephen had talked to Waaboo about visions and had, perhaps, helped the little boy understand what he'd seen.

"Everything okay?" he asked, stepping through the door.

Jenny and Waaboo sat together on the bed, their backs against the headboard. Waaboo was smiling broadly. In her hands Jenny held a book, *James and the Giant Peach.*

"The giant peach just squashed the mean aunts' house," Waaboo said with delight. "Now it's rolling away."

"Have they gone?" Jenny asked.

Daniel nodded. "If there'd been one more of them, they could have done a pretty good imitation of the Three Stooges."

"Just doing their jobs, I suppose," Jenny said. Then she asked Waaboo, "What did she look like? The woman you saw in the patch."

"Not like you. Her hair was black. And she wasn't old."

Daniel couldn't help smiling. "Your mother is young, little rabbit. And beautiful."

Jenny nodded her thanks.

"She looked like you and me," Waaboo said to his father.

"Ojibwe," Daniel said. "Did she say anything?"

"Only that she was lost, too. She wanted us to find her. And she wanted to walk the Path of Souls. She said the other spirit did, too."

"Other spirit?" Daniel sat on the bed beside his son. "What other spirit?"

Waaboo shrugged.

That day wasn't the first time Waaboo had seen things others could not. In that way he was like Stephen, who'd had visions all his life. Daniel English was full-blood Anishinaabe. That some people were given visions was a truth he accepted easily. He himself had never had what he identified as visions. And before he married Jenny and settled in Aurora, he'd never known another person who claimed to have had them. But he knew about Stephen's visions, and those of the old Mide Henry Meloux as well. And now little Waaboo. Stephen, when he talked about his own ability, spoke as if it was a burden, an onerous responsibility, one that, if he could, he would gladly relinquish. "But," he would always say, "these things are up to the Creator."

Waaboo saw dead people. And Daniel couldn't help wondering what in the hell the Creator was thinking, saddling a child with a thing like that.

"Were you afraid?" Jenny asked.

Waaboo shook his head. "I just felt bad for her. Her eyes looked hurt, like she was staring at the sun."

Jenny glanced at Daniel for an explanation.

Because he didn't want to go into gruesome details, he said simply, "May point to cause of death." Then he asked Waaboo, "Was she afraid?"

Again the boy shook his head. "She was just lost. I told her we would find her. Well, I told her that Daddy would. It's what he does."

Daniel had a thought and took out his cell phone. He tapped on the photo app, scrolled through the pictures, found the photo he was looking for, and held it out for his son to see.

"Was that the woman you saw in the blueberry patch?"

Waaboo looked at the photograph, then shook his head.

Jenny turned the phone so that she could see the photo as well. "Crystal?"

Daniel nodded. "Worth a try. But maybe she's the other spirit."

That night as he lay in bed beside Rainy, Cork stared up at the dark ceiling. A light breeze came through the window, cooler than anything that had blown across Tamarack County all day.

"Trouble sleeping?" Rainy finally asked.

"A lot on my mind."

"Thinking about Waaboo and his vision?"

"Thinking how hard it's been on Stephen all his life. I know he's talked to Waaboo, and maybe that's helped some, but I can't help wondering why God settles this kind of burden on any child's shoulders."

"Maybe Uncle Henry could offer some insight," Rainy suggested. "Maybe he should talk to Waaboo."

Cork liked the idea. "Couldn't hurt. And Henry might be able to help him understand more about the vision, everything that passed between him and the spirit he saw. Waaboo said she was Native. If that's true, then it's not Olivia Hamilton in that grave. Maybe there's more to Waaboo's vision that might help us understand who she is."

"So, anything else troubling you?"

Cork hesitated, then confessed, "Annie."

"It's good to have her home, even if it's just for a little while, for the wedding. And Maria's such a nice surprise."

Cork made a sound in his throat that was meant to convey his agreement, but it came out as more of a growl.

"What?"

"It's clear they're a couple, so why doesn't she just say that? Does she think we won't understand or accept?"

"I'm sure she has her reasons. Is that really what's troubling you?"

"I get the feeling she's not really here. Not that she doesn't want to be here, but there's something holding her back."

"Any ideas?"

He shook his head, even though in the dark it was a gesture Rainy couldn't see. After another long period of silence, he said, "She feels haunted to me."

"What do you mean?"

"Like something's happened that she can't let go of. Maybe something in Guatemala."

"Like what?"

"I don't know. But whatever it is, maybe it's so awful she can't share it."

"You could always ask her."

"I'd rather she tell me in her own time and in her own way."

"Whatever you think is best."

Cork wished he were certain what that was. But like so much in his life, past and present, he was just stumbling along, worrying, hoping, praying that somehow in the end, in the darkness of all his self-doubt and concern, a light would shine and illuminate the right path.

Annie couldn't sleep either. She and Maria had been given the attic room. When Annie was growing up, this had been the bedroom of Aunt Rose, her mother's sister. Aunt Rose had helped raise all the O'Connor children, then had fallen in love, married, and gone off to begin a family of her own.

Annie stood at the attic window, staring at the elm in the front yard, which was dimly illuminated by a streetlamp. That tree, like so much about the house on Gooseberry Lane, was woven into all her memories. The night before, while Maria slept, Annie had stood at the edge of the island, staring across the dark water of Iron Lake at the distant lights of town, knowing that she should feel pleasure in coming home but feeling instead apprehension. Could they understand? Could they accept?

She'd almost told Jenny the truth that day. They'd finally had a moment alone, sitting on the front porch swing, and despite the dramatic events of the morning, they'd shared memories in the way of sisters.

"I've missed you so much," Jenny had said. "But I'm proud of what you're doing in Guatemala, what you've become. I always thought you'd be the first woman to pitch for the Twins. Instead, you've become our own Mother Teresa."

"Give me a break, I'm no saint."

"True. I can remember lots of times that Irish temper of yours got you into trouble."

She'd taken Annie's hand. "I like Maria. She's a good soul. You make a good couple. We all think so."

"I should have come right out and told everyone."

"No need. It's pretty clear."

"She's been a gift. We've done so much together. I hate thinking I won't be able . . ."

She'd stopped herself before the revelation spilled from her.

"Won't be able?"

"Able to help for a while, I mean," she'd stumbled. "In Guatemala. I'm not sure when I'll go back."

"You might stick around after the wedding? That's terrific news."

Jenny had given her sister a hug from the heart. It felt wonderful, but it also brought on a wave of guilt for holding back a truth she could not share, not even with her beloved sister.

Now, in the night, she felt Maria's hand on her shoulder. "We cannot control what life delivers to us. It does no good to worry."

"How do I tell them?"

"You will find a way," Maria said.

Annie hoped she was right. Together they returned to bed.

CHAPTER 6

Henry Meloux had lived in his cabin on Crow Point for nearly a century. It was rustic by any standard. His water was hand-pumped. His cabin was heated in winter with an old potbellied stove. He did his bodily business in an outhouse.

There was another, newer cabin only steps away from Meloux's. It had been built to house a woman named Leah Duhling, a Lac Courte Oreilles Anishinaabe elder who, several years earlier, had come to live on Crow Point to help care for the old man. Leah had passed away peacefully almost two years earlier. Now the cabin was occupied by a man who called himself Prophet. Although Meloux was past his century mark, he still walked a good deal in his beloved wilderness, still dipped his ancient body in the cold water of Iron Lake when it wasn't frozen over, and still never turned away anyone who made the trek to Crow Point seeking his advice or help.

On this morning, it was Daniel, Jenny, and Waaboo who came. They'd left the house early and had driven the graveled county road northeast to the place where a double-trunk birch marked the beginning of the two-mile path that led to Crow Point. Waaboo danced ahead of them. The moment they left the cover of the trees and entered the clearing on the point where the cabins stood, the little boy broke into a run. When Daniel and Jenny reached Meloux's cabin, Waaboo was already seated beside the old man on the wooden bench outside the front door.

The ancient Mide smiled at them and tousled the hair on the little boy's head. "*Nigigwaadizi*," he said. It meant "acts like an otter" and was the spirit name the old man had given the boy in the naming ceremony.

"Look!" Waaboo said, opening his palm toward his parents. A dozen wild blueberries were nestled there. Waaboo popped the berries into his mouth.

"Prophet and I picked them yesterday," Meloux said.

"We tried to pick some," Waaboo told him through blue-stained lips.

"So I heard," the old man said and eyed Daniel.

Prophet stepped from the newer cabin, where white smoke poured out of the stove pipe jutting from the roof. He was in his midthirties, tall and lean. There was something about him that was like a wolf, watchful and powerful. And dangerous if threatened. But he held a broad smile on his lips that morning, and he called out, "I'm making blueberry pancakes if anyone is interested."

"Me!" Waaboo jumped up from the bench, then hesitated a moment, glancing at his mother.

"Go on," Jenny said. "But don't be greedy."

Meloux sat in full morning sunlight, his long hair aglow as if it were a flow of white fire. Beneath a multitude of wrinkles, his face was a landscape of calm. His eyes were heavy-lidded, his irises dark almond. He regarded the two people who stood before him.

"Sit," he finally said.

Jenny seated herself on one side of Meloux, Daniel on the other.

"I have been told that the boy found more than blueberries yesterday," Meloux said.

Daniel wasn't surprised that Meloux knew about the incident. The rez telegraph.

"He found a lost soul," Daniel said.

"Tell me about that."

Daniel described how he'd seen Waaboo kneeling on the ground and talking as if to someone who stood before him.

"He said she was lost and sad and that she was Ojibwe."

"Crystal Two Knives?" the old man asked.

"I showed him a photo of Crystal," Daniel said. "It wasn't her."

"There's something else," Jenny said. "This woman spirit told him there was another lost soul."

"The missing white girl?"

"He didn't know," Daniel said.

"What else did he say?"

"Not much. But he told us he wasn't afraid."

The old man thought awhile, then said, "What is it that you need?"

"Would you talk to him, help him see if there's more to his vision?" Daniel said. "If it wasn't Crystal Two Knives he saw in the blueberry patch, then who was it? And who is this other lost soul?"

Meloux considered the request and gave a single nod. "I will spend the morning with him. We will pick blueberries and we will talk."

"*Chi miigwech*," Jenny said. She stood up and Daniel stood with her.

"One thing," the old man said before they turned to leave.

"Yes?" Jenny said.

"When you return, bring your sister."

* * *

Daniel dropped Jenny off at the house on Gooseberry Lane, then headed to work.

The Iron Lake Ojibwe Tribal Police Department was located in a structure newly built in anticipation of the reservation receiving final approval to begin its law enforcement operation. In 1953, with the passage of a piece of legislation titled Public Law 280, criminal jurisdiction on the reservation had been transferred from the federal level to the state, and the Tamarack County Sheriff's Department had begun offering its services to the reservation. The result had always been questionable. Cork, when he'd been hired as a deputy, was the first officer on the force with any Native American blood in him. Which had helped some. But because he was of mixed heritage, he was still viewed with skepticism by many on the rez. Things didn't improve much after he'd been elected sheriff. For years the tribal council had discussed creating its own policing body. As with all things bureaucratic, the process had taken time. But the Ojibwe knew how to be patient and persistent.

Six months before Olivia Hamilton was reported missing, the department began operation. A man named Monte Bonhomme had been brought on as chief of police. Bonhomme had a long law enforcement background with the Mille Lacs Band of Ojibwe in the central part of the state and so possessed a good deal of experience with the confusing labyrinth of jurisdictional issues involved in law enforcement on a reservation. Daniel English, who'd been a conservation officer for the Iron Lake Ojibwe Department of Natural Resources, had been his first hire.

Monte Bonhomme was at his desk when Daniel walked in. The chief glanced up from some papers and said, "Take a day off to pick blueberries and you find a grave instead. Good work, I suppose."

"Dumb luck. Have they finished exhuming the body?"

"They have."

"Were you there?"

"I was. In keeping with our cooperative agreement with the sheriff's department."

"And?"

"The buried girl wasn't blond and had been in that grave a lot longer than two weeks. When it became clear that it wasn't Olivia Hamilton, the Feds and BCA lost interest. More or less they turned the case over to Sheriff Dross. The body's at the morgue. Long black hair and she was wearing a beautifully beaded bracelet, so reasonable evidence she might be Native. Which means it'll be a while before a good postmortem is done. Olivia Hamilton will continue to get all the attention."

"I think I can tell you what the ME will find." Daniel explained what Waaboo had said about the eyes of the woman, that they were open and looked hurt, as if she'd been staring at the sun. "If that's true, I'd say she was strangled to death."

"That's a detail you didn't tell me when you called yesterday," Monte said. "Go over it all again. And this time, don't leave anything out."

Daniel sat down and related the events of the previous day. He added something else he'd neglected to tell Monte the day before. He related what Waaboo had said about another lost spirit.

"Olivia Hamilton?" Monte asked.

"Maybe. Or maybe Crystal Two Knives. Waaboo couldn't say."

Monte opened a drawer in his desk and took out a folded document. "Come here."

As Daniel approached, Monte unfolded the paper and laid it out. It was a map of the Iron Lake Reservation. Daniel wasn't surprised to see that it looked like a patchwork quilt of holdings—land held in trust by the tribe, land held by individual tribal members, land owned by white people or white entities, and land whose ownership was in dispute because of conflicting interpretations of treaty language. As with many other reservations across the country, there was an ongoing effort to purchase the land not currently owned by the Ojibwe in order to consolidate the Iron Lake Reservation and, as much as possible, re-create its original configuration.

"Check this out," Monte said.

He put his finger on a large section of land that abutted the reservation on the southeast. It was nearly sixteen thousand acres the county had laid claim to on the basis of a disputed interpretation of the treaty agreement 150 years before. The long-held position of Tamarack County was that the reservation was subsequently diminished or disestablished by the Nelson Act of 1889 and other federal actions, and the Iron Lake Band of Ojibwe's sovereignty was limited to lands held in trust by the federal government pursuant to the Indian Reorganization Act of 1934.

Daniel considered it all legal gobbledygook. Like most folks on the reservation, he understood that the move was driven by private interest in the mineral reserves beneath the surface. The Iron Lake Ojibwe had been battling for years to secure rightful dominion, and the case was still making its laborious way through the court system. Erno Paavola's cabin and its surroundings lay in what most folks in the county now referred to as the Contested Section.

"If the female in the grave was Ojibwe, I think we have a legitimate claim to jurisdiction in this case," Monte said. "Or concurrent jurisdiction at least, per our cooperative agreement with the Tamarack County sheriff."

While the case was being litigated, the Tamarack County Sheriff's Department and the newly instituted Iron Lake Ojibwe Tribal Police Department had reached an agreement to share responsibility for law enforcement in the Contested Section. In truth, because of the remoteness, it was almost always more expedient for a tribal police officer to respond to disturbances. The area was sparsely populated, and so far, there'd been no major incidents to test the strength of this loose agreement.

The department door opened and LuJean Desjardins strolled in. Officer Desjardins was large. Not heavy, but big-boned and powerful-looking. Her face was solid, as if cut from a block of old-growth maple. Her cheeks still held the pocks that told of serious adolescent acne. When she was confronting a miscreant, her eyes became two dark holes of impending justice. But among her fellow officers, she was a wealth of jokes and funny stories. She was the only officer on the force who was Iron Lake Ojibwe. The other officer was Anthony Zuppardo, whom they all called Zippy. He'd grown up on the Leech Lake Reservation, where his mother was a teacher at the Bug-O-Nay-Ge-Shig School. Although he was white, he had reliable common sense when it came to reservation issues.

"Almost shot a thief this morning," LuJean said.

"How's that?" Monte asked.

"A raccoon's been raiding my garbage bin. I've tried every-thing, but it's one smart critter. Caught it in the act this morning. I had my Mossberg to my shoulder, ready to squeeze off a shot." She lifted her arms in pantomime and sighted with one eye shut. "Then two little raccoon heads popped up beside her. Momma just feeding her babies. What could I do?"

"A Mossberg? Really?" Monte said.

"I was thinking of using a grenade, but I didn't want to disturb the neighbors so early in the day." She looked at Daniel. "*Boozhoo,* and congratulations. If that's appropriate given the circumstances. Heard about you finding a grave instead of blueberries. Olivia Hamilton?"

"They exhumed the body," Monte told her. "Pretty clear it wasn't the Hamilton girl."

"Crystal Two Knives?"

"Not her either," Daniel said.

Monte said, "I was just pointing out to Daniel that the girl's body was found on land that is arguably within our jurisdiction."

"The Contested Section?"

"Exactly. Every other law enforcement agency is still focused on the Hamilton girl. I think we ought to take on this investigation ourselves. It might lead us to Crystal. Or maybe even the Hamilton girl."

Daniel glanced at Desjardins. It was clear they were all in perfect agreement. Which was not always an easy achievement when it came to almost any issue in the Native community.

CHAPTER 7

Cork walked into the office of Sheriff Marsha Dross, who was sitting at her desk looking grim.

Nearly two decades earlier, when Cork had occupied the office and had sat in the chair behind the desk, he'd hired Dross as the first female officer for the Tamarack County Sheriff's Department. Now, looking at Dross, who was bent like a wilted flower, he didn't miss the job or wearing the badge one bit.

"Feeling stepped on?" he asked.

Dross was in her early forties, her hair just beginning to show a hint of gray. Usually, she was upbeat, a woman who enjoyed cross-country skiing and snowshoeing in the winter and, in the summer, canoeing the Boundary Waters. She was fond of line dancing. On karaoke nights at the Four Seasons hotel, she exhibited a fondness for songs by Tina Turner, Joan Jett, and Blondie. She had a pretty fine voice herself.

"Bastards," she said.

"FBI? BCA?"

"Take your pick."

Cork sat down in the chair on the other side of the desk. "I worked with some pretty decent agents back in the day."

"These guys are barely old enough to shave. And, God help us, they think they know it all."

"Don't play well with others?"

"BCA has officially told us to stand down from the Olivia Hamilton investigation. It's out of our hands."

"BCA usually just assists."

"The governor's people have decided otherwise. Olivia Hamilton's family's influence, I'm sure. From the get-go, they didn't trust our competence."

"What about the body they exhumed?"

"Pretty clear it's Native. And that grave in the blueberry patch was the final straw, I guess. Blamed me for taking precious time and resources away from finding the Hamilton girl."

"It could be Crystal Two Knives, although when Daniel showed a photograph of Crystal to Waaboo last night, he said it wasn't her."

"I'm reserving judgment on the supposed vision of a seven-year-old boy, but I've asked Theresa Lee to be there when the ME does the postmortem. She might be able to help with identification."

Theresa Lee taught forensic anthropology and archaeology at Tamarack Community College. She was of mixed heritage, a licensed professional archaeologist, and one of only two licensed forensic anthropologists in the entire state. She'd been in charge of a number of high-profile excavations of archaeological sites across Minnesota and the upper Midwest, as well as exhumations of graves when it was thought that they might be Native.

"When will that be?" Cork asked.

"Not for a couple of days at least."

"So, in the meantime, you're just going to sit there and fume?"

"Back off," Dross warned him.

"Here's something you might want to chew on. Last night, Waaboo said that the spirit of the woman in the grave told him there was another lost soul out there somewhere."

"Cork, I've got to tell you, I'm taking all this Waaboo business with even less than a grain of salt. I didn't tell the other investigators about your grandson's talk with a dead woman. You can understand why."

"Just bear with me for a minute. Suppose what Waaboo says is true, just suppose. Could it be Olivia Hamilton?"

Everything about Dross's demeanor began to change. She slowly sat up. Her look of skepticism was gradually replaced with one of piqued interest.

"Have you told anybody else?" she asked.

"Two agents interviewed us last night. But it was before Waaboo told us about the other spirit."

"BCA or FBI?"

"One from each."

"A little odd."

Cork nodded. "But I suppose in a case like this they want to make sure nothing's miscommunicated. They were a bit of a mismatched team, though, and didn't spend much time. To them, we're just the folks who happened to stumble onto the grave. I told them about the work I'd done for Paavola and that he'd paid me with blueberries. They thought that was hilarious. They asked if he'd told me where the patch was. I said no. They asked how did I find it then? I told them it's what I'm good at, finding things. I said if they wanted my help finding Olivia Hamilton, I'd be happy to give it. Their response was basically 'The last thing we need, Mr. O'Connor, is some meddling bumpkin who gets paid in blueberries.' But there's one thing they didn't ask about."

"What?"

"Who else might know about that blueberry patch."

A fire came into Dross's eyes. "Paavola's niece and nephew, the people he hired you to find."

"Exactly. And now that they know the woman in that grave was Native, the Feds and BCA probably don't care."

Dross swiveled in her chair and stared at her office wall. Her eyes seemed focused on a personally inscribed photograph of Ann Bancroft, a Minnesotan who was one of the world's premier polar explorers and who'd accomplished many firsts for a woman in the polar regions.

"What would be the connection between the body in the grave and Olivia Hamilton's disappearance?"

"Maybe there isn't one. But I've always believed that if you pull one thread, it sometimes loosens others," Cork said. "You told me that you were a bit like Olivia Hamilton when you were a teenager. On the rebellious side. And I know that you would like very much to find her alive, if that's still possible. Maybe you can. But if she isn't alive, maybe you can find out what happened to her. I don't know that the grave in the blueberry patch is relevant, but what if it is?"

Dross gave a slow nod, her eyes still on the image of the explorer. "We'd have to tread carefully."

"We?"

Dross swung her chair back around to face Cork. "We."

Cork couldn't help smiling. "Count me in."

Ever since he'd taken off the sheriff's badge, Cork's primary source of income had been Sam's Place, the old Quonset hut on the shore of Iron Lake, where burgers, shakes, hot dogs, and fries were served through two take-out windows. When they were growing up, every O'Connor child had been required to work at Sam's Place and, when old enough, to take the reins of management. But Annie had been gone forever. Stephen had left two years ago to complete his college work in the Twin Cities. Jenny still sometimes helped out, but she was busy raising Waaboo. She was also gaining a reputation as a novelist, and her research and speaking engagements often kept her unavailable.

Cork had considered selling Sam's Place. He'd had lots of offers over the years. But in the end, his heart was bound too firmly to the business that his good friend Sam Winter Moon had bequeathed him. Instead, he'd hired and trained good managers, often kids from the Iron Lake Reservation. For many, it was their first employment. Cork did his best to guide them with a firm but gentle hand.

After he left Marsha Dross, he dropped by Sam's Place to check on things. That was one reason. The other was that he still conducted his private investigation business out of his office in the rear of the Quonset hut. That morning, he wanted to look at the file he'd created in his work for Erno Paavola.

Cork arrived at ten. Sam's Place opened at eleven. Sylvia Villebrun was in charge that day and was busy getting things organized.

"*Boozhoo*, Sylvia," Cork greeted her when he stepped into the serving area. "Beautiful day today. Going to be busy. Who's on the schedule?"

Sylvia glanced up from where she was filling the deep-fry well with oil. She was nineteen, tall and willowy. Her long black hair was done in a braid that she'd curled under the net on her head. She'd worked for Cork every summer in high school. After graduation, she'd headed to the University of Minnesota, Duluth, with the intention of becoming a speech therapist. She'd returned at the beginning of the summer and was working for Cork again, putting away college money.

"Cass and Augie until three. Megan and Erica from three until closing." She didn't look up from her work. "Augie was supposed to help me set up. Running late. Again."

"Want me to have a word with him?"

"I'll take care of it."

Sylvia set down the big jug of fry oil and looked at Cork. Her eyes were the color of polished maple wood. "I heard about the grave in the blueberry patch."

"Yeah," Cork said.

"Do they know anything?"

"Not yet."

"Was it Olivia Hamilton?"

"It was a Native woman."

"Crystal?"

"It'll be a while before anyone knows for sure."

Sylvia shook her head. "Two girls missing; it makes you wonder if any of us are safe."

The summer before, Crystal Two Knives was one of the kids Cork had hired for Sam's Place. She hadn't come with high recommendations. In fact, Crystal's caseworker warned Cork that the girl was trouble and would probably not be his best choice. Cork knew she'd been involved in an abusive relationship with an older man, a Shinnob named Red LaGrange, a punk Cork knew well and disliked immensely. But Crystal swore to him she was done with LaGrange. She wanted a different life for herself. So he'd given her a chance.

It was true that Crystal wasn't particularly customer friendly. When she worked a serving window, she could be curt if faced with someone who grilled her about every menu item or hemmed and hawed in their choices. Mostly Cork had her working in back, preparing the food, which she turned out to be very good at. She knew her job well, didn't waste a lot of time, and the orders were filled quickly. Cork often complimented her on the quality of her work, which, he had a sense, was more meaningful to her than the money she earned, though the money was important. She'd bought herself a car. A junker, it was true. But it was hers, and she was proud of herself for having accomplished that. Even when high school started again in the fall, she'd worked late afternoons or evenings until Cork had closed up Sam's Place at the end of the season, earning, she said, gas money to last her the winter. Three months later, she'd gone missing.

Cork left Sylvia to her work and went to the file cabinets in his office area. He pulled out the file he'd kept during his investigation for Erno Paavola and wrote down the address he'd finally found for the man's niece. It was in Cloquet, an hour and a half south of Aurora, near Duluth. He'd driven down to confirm his finding, had spoken briefly with the niece, and discovered that her brother was a welder and working a construction job somewhere on the North Shore. The niece hadn't seemed much interested in her uncle, but Cork didn't dig any deeper. His job was simply to locate them. He'd passed along the information to Paavola.

He said goodbye to Sylvia, but when he opened the door to leave, he was nearly bowled over as Augie Treuer rushed in.

"Sorry, Mr. O'Connor," the kid said.

"Running late, are we?" Cork said.

"I got stopped. A ticket. Operating a motorcycle without an endorsement on my license."

"Why don't you have an endorsement?"

"It's not my motorcycle. Belongs to my cousin. He lets me use it to get to work."

Augie lived on the Iron Lake Reservation. Cork knew the money he earned went, in large measure, to help support the family.

Cork put a hand on the kid's shoulder. "Tell you what. You

work on getting that endorsement on your license, and in the meantime, I'll have a talk with our sheriff, see if we can't cut you a little slack."

"Thanks, Mr. O'Connor. Thanks a lot."

"Go on," Cork said and gently urged the kid toward the serving area.

"You and the sheriff?" Rainy said.

"I'll be back in time for supper," Cork assured her.

"You really think it might have some connection to the Hamilton girl's disappearance?"

"We won't know unless we pursue it."

"Thin ice," she said. "The Hamilton girl's disappearance isn't your job or Marsha's jurisdiction anymore."

"Those monkeys that the FBI and BCA have working the case are still all focused on the customers in the Howling Wolf bar the night Olivia Hamilton went missing."

"Doesn't that make sense?"

"They've grilled every one of those guys mercilessly and, as far as I know, don't have anything yet."

Rainy sat on the sofa in the living room, folding laundry. Most days, she was either busy helping watch her grandson or spending time on Crow Point with her great-uncle Henry, or volunteering at the health clinic in Allouette on the reservation.

"I don't know that I'll bail you out if they throw you in the hoosegow," she told Cork.

"A rap on the knuckles is the worst we'll get. And we might come up with a lead." Cork cocked his head, noticing the quiet in the house. "Where is everybody?"

"Belle came this morning after you left. She and Stephen went to have coffee at the Broiler and talk over wedding plans. Annie and Jenny are giving Maria the grand tour of Tamarack County. Then they're heading to Crow Point to pick up Waaboo."

"I didn't see Annie this morning. How does she seem?"

Rainy put down the bath towel she'd been folding. "Distant."

Cork said, "Like she doesn't really want to be here."

"Talk to her," Rainy said.

Cork gave a nod. "When I come back."

As he turned to leave, Rainy said, "I wasn't kidding. I'm not wasting a nickel to bail you out of jail."

CHAPTER 8

Not much had changed in Tamarack County in the years since Annie O'Connor had left. She'd left initially to attend college and to prepare to become a nun. Life had altered her direction, and she'd ended up in Guatemala, working with the Indigenous Mayan people displaced by gang- or drug-related violence or by the long civil war in the years before she'd arrived. It had been, in a way, a flight during a time when she was terribly confused about who she was.

When she met Maria, it was as if her life finally found its meaning.

Maria loved monarch butterflies. She'd been raised in the mountains of Guatemala, one of the places where those beautiful creatures migrated from North America to winter. She grew up poor, as did so many native Mayans. But she had riches, she told Annie. The butterflies, for one. Her family, for another. Her small village. Her mother was a midwife, and Maria learned those skills from her. But her mother wanted more for her daughter, and with the help of a charitable organization called the Maya Educational Foundation, Maria went to the University of San

Carlos in Guatemala City to study medicine and become a nurse. Because of the poverty she saw in the barrios of that city and the lack of basic medical services, she chose to stay to work among the urban poor.

"You're too good to be true," Annie told her often. It was said with love but also with a note of envy. Because Maria seemed so at ease with who she was and what she wanted and what, it appeared, God wanted of her. Annie struggled with all these things.

Maria wasn't perfect. She couldn't hit a softball to save her soul. American football confused her no end. Her literary tastes leaned toward gothic romances. And she had an inexplicable penchant for Peeps marshmallow Easter chicks. Still, Annie loved her with all her heart.

"How're you doing back there?" Jenny asked as she drove her sister and Maria toward Crow Point. "You've been awfully quiet."

Annie came out of a fog of confusing thoughts. "Sorry." She'd wanted Jenny to give Maria the grand tour, so she'd sat alone in the backseat. She leaned forward now and touched Maria's shoulder. "What do you think?"

"I think this is a beautiful place. It seems to me a good place to have grown up."

"It was," Annie said.

Although the North Country offered enormous beauty and tranquility, she knew there was another aspect to everything in life, a darkness that no place, no matter how beautiful or tranquil, could prepare you for.

They parked at the familiar double-trunk birch and began to walk down the long path that led to Crow Point. The day was summer warm, the trail lined with wildflowers, the air filled with the hum of insects, the trees alive with the voices of birds. Jenny and Maria walked ahead. Annie was content to drift along behind them.

"It is magical," Maria said. "So beautiful and so alive."

"Wait until you meet Henry," Jenny said. "He's like no one else."

"Annie has told me a lot about him. In my country, among my people, we also have those who possess great wisdom. We call them *rishis*."

It had been years since Annie had stepped into the clearing on Crow Point, but the moment she did, she felt the power of the place. So many good memories here, so many lovely moments in the comfort of Meloux's company.

Prophet greeted the women. Annie had been told about this enigmatic man who, two years earlier, had been hired to lead a group of deadly mercenaries into the Boundary Waters in pursuit of Henry Meloux and Rainy and a woman they were protecting. In the end, like so many others, he'd become a follower and defender of the ancient Mide. Prophet was not his real name. It was the name he'd been given in a dream. Annie knew that before he met Meloux, he'd gone by the name LeLoup. Wolf, in French. She felt immediately the restrained power in the man. But there was no sense of threat. Rather he gave off the feel of a guardian spirit.

"Waaboo and Henry are still gathering blueberries," Prophet said. "But I expect them back any moment. Would you like something to eat or drink?"

"*Miigwech*, Prophet," Jenny said. "But we're fine."

"Momma!"

They turned at the sound of Waaboo's voice and watched him run across the clearing ahead of the old man. A bucket swayed back and forth in his hand. "We got a ton of blueberries!"

When he reached them, he proudly held out his bucket, which was three-quarters full of the small berries.

"Did you pick all the blueberries?" Jenny asked.

"Unh-uh. Mishomis made sure we left some for the other animals," Waaboo replied, using the Ojibwe word for grandfather to indicate Meloux.

The old Mide came slowly, walking with the help of a staff. Annie saw that the head of the staff had been carved into the shape of an eagle's head.

"*Boozhoo*," Jenny greeted him. "And *chi miigwech*. Our little Waaboo has quite a prize."

"He is well named. He hopped among the bushes like a rabbit." The old man's eyes took in Maria. "I do not know you."

"Maria," she said and gave the old man a respectful nod. "A friend of Annie."

Now Annie felt the weight of the old man's gaze fall upon her.

"You have grown," he said. "In many ways. It is good to see you again."

Prophet said, "What do you say we wash those berries, Little Rabbit? And then maybe eat a few?"

When Waaboo had gone, Meloux sat on the wooden bench outside his cabin, bathed in sunlight. He beckoned Jenny to sit beside him and indicated the ground in front of him for Annie and Maria.

"Did you talk to him?" Jenny asked.

The old man was quiet for a time, then spoke slowly. "All things possess a spirit of their own, but there is a greater spirit that runs through all things. We are separate but we are connected. Do you see?"

"I think so," Jenny said.

"When your child knelt among the blueberry bushes, the ground he touched connected him with the spirit beneath, I believe. He spoke with this spirit. She told him that she was lost and sad and looking for the way to the next world. She also told him that there was another lost spirit. I believe that spirit must be nearby."

"We were hoping you might help him understand a bit more about who these spirits are."

"He told me that the spirit who spoke with him was called Tacicala."

"Tacicala?" Jenny said.

"In the language of the Lakota, it means Fawn," the old man said.

"Why Lakota?"

"Not all Indians are Anishinaabe."

"And the other spirit?" Annie said.

The old man shook his head. "This was not revealed to him."

"You should be careful about all this," Maria said.

"What do you mean?" Jenny asked.

"I knew a girl in Guatemala," Maria said. "In the time of our civil war, when so many loved ones disappeared. People came to her, because if she held a thing of value from the missing person, she could tell that person's fate. It was a heavy burden for her."

"What happened to her?"

Maria hesitated, then said, "Men came to her village. They took her away. She became one of the many who just disappeared."

"That can't happen here," Jenny said fiercely. "This isn't Guatemala." To Meloux, she said, "Is there something we should do?"

"What is given to us by the Great Mystery we do not always understand or accept. Waaboo does not yet understand the full truth of what he has been given. Someday he will." The old man smiled. "But he is not afraid, your little rabbit."

"Mom!" Waaboo called from the doorway of Prophet's cabin. "Come quick!"

"What is it?"

"You'll see. Come on."

Jenny rose. "Thank you, Henry."

When Jenny had gone, Maria said, "I did not mean to upset her. But in my experience, special people are often at great risk."

"Tell me about your experience," the old man said.

"I have been a nurse for many years and visited many places in my country. People with gifts—of kindness, of wisdom, of special sight, of deep spiritual belief—these are the ones that those who are bent on oppressing target first. That is the truth of things. At least, where I come from."

"It is the truth everywhere," the old man said.

"Is Waaboo in danger?" Annie asked.

"He is surrounded by love. There is no better protection. But . . ." Meloux looked toward Prophet's cabin. "He should be watched over carefully." The old man turned his face to Annie. In the sunlight, he seemed to glow like the filament in a light bulb. "You have not come home."

Annie looked at him with confusion. "I'm here."

"Your heart is not."

"There's a lot going on."

The old man looked from Annie to Maria and spoke to them both.

"The path through life is difficult enough to walk as one spirit. To walk this path as a person of two spirits, that can be a great challenge. But if you want the path you walk to lead you to *ninoododadiwin*"—he smiled at Maria—"in our language, it means harmony. If you want to walk the path toward *ninoododadiwin*, there is only one way. That is the way of love."

He let silence follow his words, which Annie had heard as a blessing, and she loved the old man for it.

"But there is something else to talk about," the old man said. "Yes?"

His eyes settled on Annie, and she felt as if he were looking all the way down into her soul and could see the darkness there. She hardened, told her herself not to yield, and held to silence.

At last, Meloux nodded. "Very well. But I am always here."

Waaboo rushed from Prophet's cabin, bringing with him two bowls. He handed one to Meloux. "For you, Mishomis." The other he gave to Annie. "Mom says you two can share."

In each bowl was a bit of freshly made blueberry maple syrup and a spoon.

"Prophet wants you to tell me if you like it."

Maria took the first taste, closed her eyes, and said, "Heavenly."

Annie took a bit of the mixture and agreed, though in truth she was so distracted that she barely tasted it.

They returned to Jenny's car along the trail through the forest, Waaboo dancing ahead and Jenny hurrying to keep up with him. Annie and Maria lagged behind.

"He is a remarkable man," Maria said. "Why didn't you tell him?"

"Because I don't want anyone to know."

"But I know."

"And it weighs on you."

"Your burden is mine." She took Annie's hand. "We are connected by the great spirit that runs through all things." She bumped Annie's hip playfully with her own. "And more."

They walked awhile that way, hand in hand. Then Maria said, "You should have told him. I believe he would understand."

"Let it go," Annie said.

But why hadn't she told Meloux everything? Because Annie had the sense that somehow he already knew. And that he wanted nothing less than to crack her open and have it all spill out for everyone to see, the whole horrible truth.

CHAPTER 9

Daniel was sitting at the kitchen table when Jenny returned along with Annie, Maria, and Waaboo. She'd called as soon as she had cell phone reception, and Daniel had promised to meet her at the house on Gooseberry Lane.

"We picked blueberries, Daddy," Waaboo said as he ran to his father. "And we brought home some syrup Prophet made." He held out a small jar filled with a thick blue liquid.

"Looks delicious, little guy."

"Where is everyone?" Annie asked.

"Stephen just left a few minutes ago. Belle called. There's been more trouble at the Spirit Crossing protest. Some arrests. He went to help."

"What can he do? He hasn't even started law school yet."

"Sometimes, he runs errands for Belle and the others who are working on the legal side of things," Daniel explained. "But he's often on the front line, using his cell phone to document what's going on and reporting back to Belle. He says that's where he prefers to be."

Rainy stepped into the kitchen, holding the medical bag she used in her work as a public health nurse.

"You're going, too?" Annie asked.

Rainy nodded. "Belle said there might have been some injuries. I've been helping out when I can. I'm usually there when a big demonstration has been planned. But sometimes things just flare up."

"We should go with you," Annie said. "Maria's a nurse."

"What are the protests about?" Maria asked.

"An oil pipeline," Waaboo said. "It's a bad thing. It'll pollute Mother Earth."

"I am all for saving Mother Earth," Maria said.

"Come, then," Rainy said. "But we have to leave now."

"Can I come?" Waaboo asked.

"Another time," Jenny said.

The boy looked disappointed, and Daniel said, "I have an important job for you here."

"What?"

"Go ride your bike for a while and when you come back, I'll tell you."

Waaboo set the jar on a kitchen counter and took off out the back door along with Rainy and the other two women. Jenny sat down at the table with her husband as the spring on the mudroom screen door gave a loud squeal, then slapped shut with a bang.

"God, I hate that pipeline," she said.

"We all do. Give me the lowdown on our son. What did Meloux say?"

Jenny recounted her conversation with the old Mide.

"So, the buried girl has a name. Tacicala."

"Fawn in Lakota," Jenny said.

Daniel nodded, pleased with this information. "The identity of the second spirit is still a mystery, but Henry believes the second spirit must be near her grave?"

"That's what he thinks. But didn't the FBI and BCA go over that whole area?"

"Monte told me that after it was evident the girl in the grave wasn't Olivia, they pretty much took off. They certainly weren't looking for a second grave. But that second spirit could be Crystal Two Knives. Or, I suppose, Olivia Hamilton." Daniel looked toward the mudroom where Waaboo had gone. "How's our little guy handling all this?"

"Pretty well, all things considered," Jenny replied. Then she seemed to get the true intention behind her husband's question. "You're thinking of taking him back there, aren't you? You can't be serious."

"You said yourself that he appears to be doing well."

"He's a seven-year-old boy, Daniel, not some scientific instrument of law enforcement investigation."

"If there's another girl buried out there, don't you think we should do everything we can to locate her body?"

"There must be some other way. Cadaver dogs?"

"If Waaboo senses something more concrete now, we'll get the cadaver dogs out there or whatever we need. Look, Jenny, the spirit of a young girl is begging for help. How can we deny her that?"

Jenny's lips went into a hard line, and she was silent a long time. "All right," she finally agreed. "But I go, too."

Waaboo's only question had been "Can we pick blueberries?"

Now he sat in the rear seat of Jenny's Subaru Forester, singing softly to himself. Daniel, who was driving, recognized the tune, "Jambalaya," which Waaboo often requested when Daniel brought out his accordion for an evening singsong at the O'Connor house. In the rearview mirror, he watched his son's head bob up and down as he sang very softly "me-oh-my-oh."

They were still a couple of miles from the turnoff to Erno

Paavola's cabin. Daniel had called Monte Bonhomme on his cell phone and explained what he was doing. Monte said he would meet them.

"Dad," Waaboo said.

"Yes?"

"Why don't you play the accordion like you used to?"

"What do you mean?"

"You haven't played it in a long time. I like it. You smile when you play and you make me smile and want to dance."

"Glad to hear that. I'll keep it in mind."

Waaboo went back to singing to himself, and a few minutes later, Daniel pulled to a stop at Paavola's cabin on the hilltop. He lowered the windows and turned off the engine. It was early afternoon and hot, not a breath of wind blowing through the trees.

"Erno Paavola was living in that?" Jenny said. "It looks like a good kick would knock it over."

"Cork said nobody's lived there since Paavola died."

"It looks haunted," Waaboo said.

They sat quietly for a couple of minutes, the only sound the buzz of insects in the still summer air.

"I'm bored," Waaboo said. "Can we go pick blueberries now?"

"You picked blueberries all morning with Henry Meloux," Jenny said.

"It's fun. I could pick blueberries all day."

"We wait here for Monte," Daniel said.

"Then can I at least look at the haunted cabin?"

"All right," Jenny said. "But just look. And stay where we can see you."

Waaboo jumped from the car and ran toward the dilapidated structure.

"He's right, you know," Jenny said.

"Waaboo? About what?"

"You don't play your accordion anymore. And you haven't written a line of poetry in forever."

"Not inspired, I guess."

"It's been that way since you joined the tribal police."

"Not an easy job," Daniel said with a shrug.

"Talk to me," Jenny said.

Daniel gathered himself, trying to give voice to something he'd wrestled with for a while. "When I was a tribal conservation officer, folks appreciated what I did. Preserving the rez resources, keeping our waters clean, catching white poachers. Now I give those same folks tickets or arrest their relatives or break up fights where neither side is happy with me."

"That's not everyone on the rez."

"Maybe not." Daniel kept his eye on Waaboo, who'd stopped short of the cabin and now stood staring at it. "But sometimes I feel so limited in what I can do. Besides just get folks riled up at me."

"Is this about Crystal?" Jenny said. "You did the best you could."

"And she's still missing."

The disappearance of Crystal Two Knives had been the first official investigation Daniel had undertaken as an officer on the tribal police force. He'd followed every lead, spoken with every person who knew her, had leaned hard on Red LaGrange, her abusive ex-boyfriend. When he sought the help of the Tamarack County Sheriff's Department, he got what felt to him like a runaround. He'd searched NamUs, the National Missing and Unidentified Persons System, and the Minnesota Missing and Unidentified Persons Clearinghouse, and had contacted the BIA Missing and Murdered Unit. Nothing. Crystal Two Knives, like so many Native women, had simply vanished.

Waaboo backed away from the cabin slowly, as if afraid it might be about to bite him. He came back and stood by Daniel's opened window, his face pale.

"What is it, Waaboo?"

"*Maji-manidoog,*" the boy said.

"Devils?" Daniel translated.

"That place is evil, Daddy."

Daniel heard the approach of another vehicle. He glanced in his rearview mirror and saw Monte Bonhomme's Tahoe coming up the rutted dirt lane.

"Blueberry picking time," he said to his son. But Waaboo's face didn't brighten.

Monte was accompanied by LuJean Desjardins and another woman. Daniel knew her, Theresa Lee, a forensic archaeologist and anthropologist who taught at Tamarack Community College. She was small, her hair pulled back in a graying ponytail, her eyes dark brown, the features of her face and her skin color clearly showing her Native heritage, Fond du Lac Ojibwe. Monte had told Daniel earlier that, because of her expertise, he was going to ask Lee to join them in the search for another grave. A black duffel bag hung from a strap over one of her shoulders.

"*Boozhoo,* Theresa," Daniel greeted her.

"*Boozhoo,*" she replied. She smiled at Jenny and then at Waaboo. "This must be your little rabbit. Hello, Waaboo. My name is Theresa."

LuJean eyed Waaboo's ashen face and said to Daniel, "You sure about this?"

Jenny knelt and put her hand on her son's shoulder. "Are you okay going back to the blueberry patch?"

He nodded.

Jenny stood up. "We do this very carefully."

"Understood." Daniel grabbed a bucket from the backseat and took his son's hand. "Let's go, little guy."

Waaboo's mood seemed to brighten as they left the cabin behind and walked through the wild grass toward the trail that led to the clearing and the blueberry patch.

"Mom, here are the gnomes." He broke from his father's grip and tapped one of the carved figures. "They're like Finnish leprechauns. Come on. The blueberries are this way."

He started ahead of them down the path.

"Waaboo!" Jenny called. But the boy danced on.

"So, we may have a name for the deceased," Monte said. "Tacicala or Fawn."

"And we know this how?" Theresa Lee asked.

Monte scratched his jaw and glanced at Daniel.

"Part of Waaboo's vision," Daniel said.

"Ah, the vision." From the way she said it, Daniel understood that Theresa Lee, like any good professional, was not wholly embracing of this kind of lead. "That's not much to go on."

"It's more than we had before," Monte said.

"Are you going to let Dross know about the name?" Daniel asked.

"We have no real proof of anything yet," Monte said.

"So, any further word on the search for Olivia Hamilton?"

"As I understand it, the Feds and BCA are hauling in the Howling Wolf customers again."

"Didn't get them anywhere before," LuJean said.

Monte shrugged. "I guess it's the only avenue they've got at the moment."

Waaboo reached the clearing before the others. When they caught up with him, he was standing still, his little shoulders slumped in devastation.

"What happened?" he asked.

Much of the clearing—the blueberry bushes and the other vegetation—had been trampled, crushed, torn up.

"Why?" Waaboo said.

Daniel put a hand on his son's shoulder. "I suppose they were looking for evidence, Waaboo."

"They didn't have to kill everything."

"No," Monte said. "They didn't."

Lee scanned the clearing and shook her head. "Who was in charge here?"

"It was kind of a pissing contest," Monte said. "No clear winner as far as I could tell. We weren't involved. The grave is over there."

Jenny and Waaboo hung back, but the others walked slowly to the oblong hole where the body of the girl named Fawn had been buried and then exhumed.

"Pretty shallow. Whoever buried her did a poor job of it," Lee said. "Either they were in a hurry or they just didn't care."

"Maybe they thought this was such a safe place they didn't have to be careful," LuJean said.

"How would someone know about this blueberry patch?" Lee looked at Daniel. "How did you know?"

He explained about Cork and Erno Paavola and the payment in blueberries.

"That's how you knew. But what about whoever buried this girl here? How would they know? Is that something the FBI or BCA are looking into?"

"Excellent question," Monte said. "But one I can't answer."

"They haven't communicated with you?"

"To them, we're bumbling reservation cops. We just get in the way. But I suspect they aren't looking into it. They're way too focused on finding the Hamilton girl."

"Come on," Daniel heard Jenny say. "Let's see if we can still find a few berries." He looked back and saw Jenny take their son's hand. But Waaboo held back.

"I want to go home," Waaboo said. "I don't like it here."

Daniel came back to his wife and son. "How about we just walk around a little bit?"

Waaboo shook his head. "I want to go home."

"Then we'll go," Jenny said firmly.

"Wait—" Daniel said, but Jenny cut him off.

"We're leaving. Now. Waaboo and me. You can stay if you want to."

She took her son's hand, and they left together, walking back toward the path that led to Paavola's cabin. Daniel watched them go but made no move to join them.

"Go on," Monte said. "I don't want you sleeping on the couch tonight. We'll go over the area. If we find anything, I'll let you know."

Daniel shook his head. "This is important enough to risk a night on the couch. Let's do it."

LuJean scanned the destroyed clearing. "What a shame. This was a lovely patch."

"It will be again," Monte said. "That's one of the things I love about Mother Earth. She heals. All right, Theresa. How should we do this?"

"Let's start with a line search. We're looking for a sudden depression or a sudden mounding or an absence of vegetation, anything that strikes you as unusual. If we find something, we'll flag it." She reached into her duffel bag and pulled out a small yellow flag on a long wire stem. "Then we'll move on. When we've completed the search, we'll come back and investigate each site carefully. Ready?"

And so they began.

CHAPTER 10

It was almost two hours south to Cloquet. Dross drove her cruiser.
On the way Cork filled her in on the investigation he'd done for
Erno Paavola several years earlier.

"It wasn't easy. Paavola knew his niece, Irene, had married but
didn't know her new last name. Like Paavola, his nephew seemed
to be living off the grid, so no good recent information on him.
I searched the public records for a marriage license but came up
with zip. Paavola told me his sister had passed away, but he had
an old address for her in Aitkin. I went down there. The place
was a shabby rental, falling apart. A woman across the street remembered the family. She didn't remember a husband ever being
around, but Paavola's sister was apparently something else. Kind
of a terror. Always threatening to sue over trivial things. She remembered the kids fled pretty early and Paavola's sister more or
less drank herself to death."

"So how'd you track down the kids?"

"Lucked out, actually. I went back and searched the marriage
licenses again. Paavola is a good Finnish name up here, but I've
seen it misspelled. That double *a* in the middle can be tricky. So I

checked variations. Bingo. There was a marriage license issued for an Irene Pavola—single *a*—and William Boyle in Aitkin County. A few more clicks on my computer and I found her. A social worker for Saint Louis County."

"So, you talked to her?"

"I did. Drove to Cloquet. Found out that she was divorced from Boyle and that her brother, one Mathias Paavola, had lived with her for a while."

"Did you talk to him?"

"He was away, working a construction job. She said she'd let him know that their uncle Erno was looking for them."

"Did she ask why her uncle was interested in tracking them down?"

"Of course. Told her I didn't know."

"Did she say anything about Paavola?"

"I didn't ask. My job was to find them. I did tell her that I was going to pass along her contact information to him."

"And she was fine with that?"

"Didn't seem excited but also didn't voice any objection."

"Did you ask about the name difference on her marriage license?"

"She was surprised. But she told me she and her husband were big drinkers back then, drunk when they got married, so that might have explained it. She stopped drinking. He didn't. One of the reasons they divorced."

"Did you find out anything else?"

"That was pretty much it." Cork had the sense that Dross was disappointed in his inquiry. "No reason to go any deeper then."

"We'll go deeper now," Dross said.

Irene Boyle had a small, neat-looking rambler on the outskirts of Cloquet. It sat on a plot of land that sloped toward the Saint Louis River, which was visible beyond a line of trees. A new housing development was going up a couple of hundred yards to the east, and a few other homes were within hailing distance, but Irene Boyle's little rambler was a bit isolated. Dross pulled into the driveway and parked next to a red Camry. It was Saturday, and when they stepped from the cruiser, Cork heard the drone of a power mower at a house down the road. The sidewalk from the drive to the front door of Irene Boyle's home was lined with bright marigolds. On the porch were two tall terra-cotta planters, each holding an eruption of red geraniums.

Dross pressed the doorbell. The woman who opened the door was in her midthirties, with blond hair that she wore in a ponytail. She was dressed in black yoga pants and a loose yellow T-shirt. Her feet were bare. The crimson polish on her toes matched the polish on her fingernails.

"Yes?" She gave them a wary smile. A sheen of glistening sweat lay across her forehead.

"Ms. Boyle?"

"That's right."

"I'm Sheriff Dross. This is Cork O'Connor."

The woman eyed Cork as if trying to place him.

"Your uncle hired me to locate you and your brother," Cork reminded her.

The light came into her eyes. "Oh, sure, I remember."

"Could we talk to you?" Dross said.

"What's this about?"

"This should take only a few minutes," Dross said. "May we come in?"

The woman stepped aside and let them enter.

Cork found the house in the same shape as when he'd interviewed the woman a few years earlier. It was clean, well kept, the carpeting and furniture all in white hues. It smelled of patchouli now, something he didn't remember from his first visit. A blue mat lay in the middle of the living room. Flute music that sounded to Cork as if it might be R. Carlos Nakai played quietly from an Amazon Echo on the mantel.

"I was just doing some yoga," Irene said. "It helps me relax. Won't you have a seat?" She indicated the sofa and took a matching white wing chair. "Now, what's this about? Something to do with my uncle? He's long dead."

"Not exactly," Dross said. "We found a body buried on the land that used to belong to your uncle."

"Oh." The woman, who'd been leaning casually forward, sat back. She looked pained. "Well, that's . . . that's . . . upsetting."

"The body was in your uncle's blueberry patch."

"Oh, Jesus." Now she looked truly stricken.

"Did you know about the blueberry patch?"

"Sure. The way was guarded by gnomes my uncle had carved and painted. Before my mother and he had a falling-out, we used to visit and pick blueberries in the summer. But I haven't been there in twenty years."

"A falling-out?"

"Uncle Erno was an unusual man. *Eccentric* would be a kind characterization. He insisted on living like a throwback to another century. No electricity or running water. An outhouse for doing his business. He had all kinds of odd ideas about the world, pretty Old Testament views about God. Thought the world was going to come to an end soon and we should be prepared. Mom finally said enough and just cut off all contact with him. I hadn't really thought much about him until Mr. O'Connor knocked on my door a while back."

"Did you get in touch with your uncle then?"

"No. But when he died, I received notice that I'd inherited his property. Well, my brother and I had inherited his property jointly."

"What did you do?"

Irene Boyle lifted her shoulders in a little shrug. "Nothing. At some point, I thought we'd see if we could sell the land, but I haven't been in any hurry. It's not particularly valuable. No lakeshore, no paved access. There's really nothing attractive about it. Taxes are next to nothing."

"You didn't go to view the property?"

"I didn't see any reason to. I was given a thorough description, and things didn't seem to have changed much in twenty years. Still no improvements on the property."

"What about your brother?"

"If he's checked it out, he hasn't said anything to me."

"Where is your brother?"

"Matt's a welder, works construction. For the past couple of years, he's been working on the Stockbridge pipeline."

"Do you have any idea who else might have known about the blueberry patch?"

She thought for a brief moment, then shook her head. "There's no one else in our family. And like I said, we lost touch with Uncle Erno a couple of decades ago."

"I'd like to talk to your brother. How can I reach him?"

"He's renting a room in Dahlbert while he's working the current section of the pipeline. I can give you his address."

"Does he have a cell phone?"

"Of course. I'll give you his number."

She left the room. While she was gone, flute music continued to play softly, and Dross gave Cork a look he couldn't quite interpret. Irene returned with a small piece of paper on which she'd written an address and cell phone number. She handed it to Dross and sat again in the white wing chair.

"I'm sorry about whoever is buried up there," she said. "Do you have a name?"

"Not yet."

"Could it be that missing girl all over the news? What's her name?"

"Olivia Hamilton," Dross said. "You're a social worker, is that correct?"

"I was. Mostly I worked at placing children in foster care. So, I know what it is to worry when a child goes missing."

"Do they go missing often?"

"I wouldn't say often, but more than any of us would like. Placements don't always work out and some kids simply run away. Almost always they show up somewhere else, and we take them back into the system and try again to place them. So many kids in foster care come from traumatic environments. They can be difficult."

Cork thought about Olivia Hamilton, who, as far as he knew, hadn't come from a traumatic environment but had, it seemed, been a difficult child. And he thought about Crystal Two Knives, who'd been difficult but had been working at changing her life, and then she'd disappeared. Was there some commonality he was missing?

"You said you *were* a social worker," Dross noted. "You're not anymore?"

"I'm director of a school for troubled youth. I have been for a couple of years now."

Dross drew the interview to an end, and Irene Boyle saw them to the door.

"Good luck with your investigation," she told them. "And if there's anything more you need from me, you know where to find me."

Dross sat at the wheel and looked at the piece of paper Irene had given her.

"Dahlbert," she said to Cork. "Not exactly on the way back, but I'd like to talk to Mathias Paavola. You game?"

"Leave no stone unturned," he said.

She smiled. "You should've been a cop."

CHAPTER 11

Rainy drove her two stepdaughters and Maria in her old Bronco. On the way to the encampment, Jenny explained about the Stockbridge oil pipeline. It had been controversial from the beginning, designed to carry crude tar sands oil from Alberta more than a thousand miles to a refinery on the shore of Lake Superior in Wisconsin. The pipeline was scheduled to run through critical wetlands and cross the Jiibay River at a place called Spirit Crossing, an area sacred to the Anishinaabeg of Minnesota. Despite the fact that other pipelines built by the company had a history of catastrophic spills and that an enormous hue and cry had arisen against the proposal, approval for the project had been granted at all governmental levels. And then it had been up to the people to do what they could to try to stop the inevitable.

From the moment work began in Minnesota, pipeline protests had accompanied the construction. At Spirit Crossing, a stand was being made, both legally and physically. A suit had been filed by a Native organization called Mother Earth League alleging the pipeline posed a threat to a number of burial sites, to several wild rice areas that were important culturally and economically to the

Ojibwe, and to the primary source of water for at least one reservation community. Until the lawsuit was settled, construction of the pipeline at Spirit Crossing had been put on hold. But that hadn't blunted the ongoing protests. Arrests were common, violence occasional. The protesters alleged that it was usually local law enforcement, whose salaries were being augmented by the pipeline company, who instigated the violence. Law enforcement countered that most of the violence was instigated by the protesters. For months the situation had been a powder keg waiting to explode. From the get-go, Anton Morriseau, Belle's brother, had been among those organizing the protest, and Belle had been helping with the legal defense of the protesters. Since Stephen had finished his undergraduate degree and had come home for the summer and the wedding, he was often there to assist.

"In Guatemala City, we have marched in protest," Maria said.

"Protesting what?" Rainy asked.

"Corruption, the high cost of living, the lack of basic needs for the poor, violence against Indigenous people—there are so many reasons."

"Have you been a part of the protests, Annie?"

"Where Maria goes, I go," Annie said.

Rainy drove them past the encampment, a small village of tents and teepees, which Annie estimated to number about two dozen. It had been laid out in a clearing less than a mile from the site of Spirit Crossing. It looked fairly deserted at the moment.

As they crossed the bridge that spanned the Jiibay River, Maria asked, "What does it mean, Jiibay?"

"In the language of our people, it means ghost or spirit," Rainy replied.

"How much farther?" Annie asked.

"Spirit Crossing is up the river just a bit."

Rainy turned off the main road onto a dirt track that ran

alongside the river. It was lined on both sides with birch trees that shaded the track. Wildflowers and wild grasses grew in abundance, and between the pale white trunks of the birch trees, the reflection of sunlight off the river came through in brilliant flashes of silver. It was a lovely river, the Jiibay, Annie thought.

They'd gone only a hundred yards when their way was blocked by a barricade around which a half dozen men stood smoking cigarettes and talking. Rainy stopped short of the barricade, and two of the men approached, one on either side of her Bronco. Rainy rolled down her window. Annie rolled down hers.

One of the men leaned down to Rainy. "Road's closed."

"Really? Why?"

"Cuz we said so," the man on Annie's side replied.

"That's hardly a reason," Rainy said.

"Washout," the man at her window said.

"It hasn't rained in days."

"Road construction, then. Take your pick. You're not coming through."

"We'll just park here and walk."

"Wouldn't do that, if I were you," the man on Annie's side said.

"Why not?" Annie asked.

"Can't guarantee the safety of your vehicle."

"What exactly might happen to it?" Rainy said.

"Never can tell. Lots of questionable types around here these days. Vandalism, theft, you name it," the man on Rainy's side said.

"I think we'll just go around the barricade and take our chances with the washout and the road construction," Rainy said.

"We don't need more Indians screwing up our jobs," the man at Annie's window said.

"And we don't need more oil spilling on our land and screwing up our water," Annie replied without heat.

The man at her window squinted. "You ain't even Indian. What do you care?"

"Every sentient person cares about Mother Earth."

"*Sentient?* What the hell does that mean?"

"It means a thinking, feeling person. But let me ask you a question. When you were a child, what would you have done if somebody dumped a thousand gallons of oil on your backyard?"

"Nobody did."

"But that's what might happen to my backyard here."

"It already has happened," Rainy said. "Twice. A million gallons in 1973, and nearly two million gallons in 1991. So you understand our concern."

"All I know, lady, is while you do your shit here, I'm not getting paid. I got a family to support."

"Seven generations," Rainy said.

"What?"

"Try to think ahead seven generations. What you're doing here will have an effect long after you're gone."

"You've got ten seconds to turn around," the man at Rainy's window said.

"Then what?" Rainy asked, her voice full of iron.

"I think we report that some vandals beat the hell out of your car and maybe you three along with it."

The man at Annie's window gave a sharp whistle and beckoned to the others at the barricade. The half dozen men made a semicircle around the front of the car. Two of the men carried iron pipes. One of them swung his pipe, and Annie heard the shattering of headlight glass.

"That's your last warning, lady," the man at Rainy's window said.

Several of the men were grinning, as if this were a game and they were ready for more fun.

Then the man who'd bent to Annie's window suddenly straightened up. "Cops," he said.

Annie heard the chirp of a siren from behind, not a full blast, just enough to announce an approach. She heard a car door slam, and a moment later, a uniformed deputy stepped up to Rainy's window. The man from the barricade backed away to give the deputy room.

"Boys," the deputy said. "Just go on back to your station."

The men cleared away from the car.

The deputy leaned toward Rainy. "Everybody okay in there?"

"They shattered my headlight," Rainy said.

The deputy nodded and thought for a moment.

"Ma'am," he said. "If I write this up, it'll mean you have to come back and go through a lot of legal hoops, and I'm pretty sure that these men are going to stick to some story that contradicts everything you say. It'll be a long and drawn-out process, and in the end, it'll be more trouble than it's worth. How about I just make sure you get beyond this barricade?"

"What about when we come out?"

"I guarantee they won't stop anyone leaving Spirit Crossing. Okay?"

"Okay," Rainy said.

The deputy stood upright and called, "Move the barricade, boys."

"Like hell we will!" one of them shouted.

"Move the barricade or I'll haul you in."

There was grumbling, but two of the men lifted the barricade and moved it to the side of the road.

"And leave it there," the deputy said. "Anybody else comes along here, you don't give them a hard time, understand?"

"They're the ones causing trouble!" the man who'd stood at Rainy's window hollered. "We just want to get back to work."

"And you will, when the judge says you can. Until then, you do what I say." He glanced down at Rainy. "Go on, ma'am."

Rainy inched ahead and the men parted to let the car pass.

"Lucky that deputy came along," Annie said.

"And lucky it wasn't one of the other deputies," Rainy said. "A lot of them are less understanding."

Rainy drove slowly now as the road curved to follow a bend in the river.

"Tell me about Spirit Crossing," Maria said.

"To the south is ground that has been considered sacred since The People first arrived here generations ago," Rainy replied. "Ceremonies have been held there for hundreds of years. The crossing is a gentle, shallow place where our ancestors north of the river crossed to reach that sacred ground."

"Why is it sacred?" Maria asked.

"Everything is sacred," Rainy said. "But there are places where the spirit of the Creator is powerful. You can feel it. A healing spirit."

"*Bizaan*," Maria said.

Rainy glanced in the rearview mirror. "Yes. At peace. Where did you learn that word?"

"Annie taught it to me. There is an island in Iron Lake with the name."

They began to pass people scattered on either side of the road, some still carrying placards. To Annie, they looked weary, like soldiers who'd been in combat a long time.

When they reached Spirit Crossing, Annie saw the desecration of that beautiful river. A broad line of bulldozed ground led up to the riverbank, where the birch trees and wildflowers and grasses and every other living thing had been cut and cleared away for the passage of the pipeline. The torn earth was red, a great raw wound where the soil bled into the clear river, turning the water murky. Amid the devastation sat huge earthmoving machines powerful as sleeping dinosaurs. There were still protesters, a loose line that stood between the machines and the river, but there was no evidence of conflict. As Rainy approached, a uniformed officer stepped in front of her Bronco. He held up a hand, then came to her window.

"Lady, this is a restricted area. Go on back the way you came."

"I'm a nurse. I was told there are injured people."

"A few of these nutcases chained themselves to bulldozers. They've been taken to the courthouse for processing. Nobody here now that needs tending to. So you just turn around and go on back to where it is you came from."

"Rainy!" Stephen came hurrying toward the car. He avoided the officer and approached Annie's side. "Belle's in town, working with the legal team. Anton's up at the medical tent. We've got a few injured people who could use some looking at. Nothing serious, thank God."

"Step away from the vehicle," the officer ordered Stephen. "We don't need any more arrests."

"I'm not causing any trouble," Stephen said. "These people are nurses. They're just here to help."

"And I've already told them to clear out."

Stephen took a pad of paper from this shirt pocket and a pen. "What's your name, Officer?"

The cop came around the car, walking fast toward Stephen. "My name is I'm just about to kick your ass."

Annie stepped from the car and stood between the cop and her brother. "His badge says Lewis."

"All right, that's it," the officer said. "Everyone out of the car."

"What's your badge number?" Stephen asked.

"I said out of the car. Now!"

"No badge number," Annie said. "It just says Private Security."

Officer Lewis glared at her. "One more word from you . . ." But he didn't finish because a number of people who'd been in the protest line had started drifting toward the scene. The officer turned and watched them approach. "Stay there," he warned. "This doesn't involve any of you."

"Document this!" Stephen called to them.

Several lifted cell phones as if beginning to record the exchange.

"Tread carefully, Officer Lewis," Stephen said.

"God damn, you people," Lewis said. "I've had it with you. You!" He pointed at Stephen. "And you." He pointed to Annie. "You're both under arrest!"

"On what charge?" Stephen replied.

"Obstruction."

"Of what?" Stephen said. "You really think that'll hold up in court?"

The officer pushed Annie to the side and grabbed at Stephen, who held up his hands. "I'm not resisting."

"Gimme that notepad."

Stephen slipped the pad into the pocket of his jeans before the cop had a chance to snatch it from him. The cop swung him around, slammed him against the car, and pulled out a plastic restraint. "Hands behind your back, Indian."

"He's done nothing," Annie protested.

"Shut up, lady. You're next."

The crowd of protesters had grown thicker, with lots of shouts of "Police brutality!" Annie was so near the officer she could see that his face had gone red with rage. She understood that his actions now weren't being dictated by his pledge to uphold the law but by some inner fire.

"You don't have to be afraid," she said.

"Back off!" the officer screamed at her.

"We're not going to harm you. No one's going to harm you," Annie said. "This is a place of peace."

He bent to her, his reddened face so near she could see the veins that webbed the whites of his eyes. Whatever fear was driving this man, she understood it was so powerful that it encased his heart.

The blast of a police siren made all heads turn. Annie saw the deputy who'd cleared the barricade for them pull his cruiser to a stop. He got quickly out and came to where his fellow officer had Stephen pinned against Rainy's car.

"What's going on, Lewis?"

"Lawful arrest," the red-faced officer said.

"We have video!" one of the protesters called out.

"Arrest on what charge?" the deputy asked.

Officer Lewis hesitated a moment, then said as if it were a confession forced from him by torture, "Obstruction."

"We've done nothing," Annie said.

"Obstruction of what, Lewis? I let these ladies through five minutes ago."

"Thanks for giving me a heads-up," Lewis shot back.

"Step back, Lewis, and return to your post," the deputy said.

Lewis started away, but after half a dozen steps, he turned back and eyed Annie as if somehow she were the guilty party in all this mess. He mouthed something she couldn't make out, but from the mask of anger that was his face, she could pretty well guess the timbre of the words.

After Lewis had gone, Stephen said, "Thank you—"

"Deputy Carlson," the officer said.

"I'm happy to see that all police aren't like him," Stephen said.

"He's not police. Or not anymore anyway. He's private security. And maybe not even that much longer," Carlson said, clearly irritated. "Obstruction." He shook his head, then gave Stephen a stern look. "See to it that we don't have to arrest you on other charges, am I clear?"

"Perfectly," Stephen said.

The deputy returned to his vehicle. He drove around the crowd and disappeared beyond the idle bulldozers.

Stephen looked at Annie and Maria and smiled. "Welcome to Spirit Crossing." Then he waved a hand vigorously in front of his face and added, "Where the mosquitoes are just as bad as the assholes we're fighting."

CHAPTER 12

The address Irene Boyle had given Cork and Marsha Dross for her brother turned out to be an old white one-story building at the edge of the small town of Dahlbert, a dozen miles from Spirit Crossing. Like many small towns in the area of the pipeline construction, Dahlbert's population had swelled with pipeline workers, men for the most part, seeking temporary housing. The yard was in need of mowing, the house in need of a new coat of paint. Two graveled ruts led to a garage in back, where a Jeep Wrangler was parked. Behind that was a grove of birch trees.

Dross parked in the graveled ruts, and she and Cork got out. Dross rang the front doorbell, but nothing happened. Through the screens on the front windows came the voice of an announcer giving a play-by-play account of a baseball game. Cork heard the Twins mentioned. Dross knocked, then knocked harder. Finally, an old woman in a faded pink housecoat and wearing fuzzy pink slippers opened up and stared at them with a hostile expression. The odor of cigarette smoke came off her in a foul wave.

"What?" she said, a challenge, not a question.

"We'd like to speak to Mathias Paavola."

"He don't live here."

"We were told he does."

"Lives in back."

"The garage?" Dross said.

"Converted garage," the woman said as if she'd been insulted.

"Thank you," Dross said.

The woman shut the door without replying.

"Landlady from hell," Cork said.

"Come on."

Dross led the way to the garage but got no response when she knocked at the side door. She pounded harder, with the same result.

"I'm guessing that's his Wrangler," Cork said. "Doesn't strike me as the vehicle of choice for the landlady from hell."

"So either he doesn't want to talk to us or he's out somewhere." Dross leaned near the door. "This is Sheriff Marsha Dross, Mr. Paavola. I'd like to speak with you."

When she still got no response, Cork said, "Maybe he just walked to a bar. We passed a couple in town. Why don't you give him a call?"

Dross slipped her phone from her pocket and punched in the number Irene Boyle had given her. Inside the garage, a ringtone played the first few of bars "Ramblin' Man," then stopped.

"Maybe left his phone when he went out?" Cork said.

"My ass." Once more, Dross pounded furiously on the door, then tried the knob, which didn't yield. "Come on."

She led the way back to the front door of the house, which she assaulted with her fist. The old woman responded much quicker this time. "What?" she squawked.

"Your renter. I'm concerned about his safety. Do you have a key?"

The old woman squinted at her. "Who are you?"

"Tamarack County Sheriff Marsha Dross."

"You got ID?"

Dross pulled out her wallet and flashed her badge.

"You got some sort of order says I should let you in?"

"It's called a wellness check," Dross said. "It's legal."

The woman squinted at them both. "All right. Give me a minute."

While she was gone, Cork heard the announcer go nuts over a grand slam home run. He hoped it was for the Twins. The landlady came back, still in her faded housecoat and fuzzy pink slippers. She handed Dross a key.

"Pretty quiet, that one. When he ain't working, he's usually drinking. Probably just passed out or something."

"Thank you."

Without another word, the woman shut the door.

Cork followed Dross back to the converted garage. Dross knocked once more, announced herself, then used the key.

The interior of the garage had been converted into a studio apartment. The place was a disaster. Clothes lay thrown everywhere, sheets half-torn from the bed, dishware and pizza boxes strewn about the floor. A stained easy chair was positioned in front of a thirty-two-inch flat-screen TV that sat on a squat stand. On the shelf beneath was a PlayStation console. There was a kitchenette with a small refrigerator, a sink stacked high with unwashed dishes. No stove, but there was a microwave oven and a hot plate on the minuscule counter next to the sink.

"Looks like someone tossed the place," Dross said.

"I'd guess Mathias just has no interest in housekeeping."

Thin wallboard had been used to create a tiny bathroom in one corner, with barely enough room to squeeze in a toilet, sink, and shower. Cork stepped inside. The bathroom was drastically in need of a good hard scrubbing. Or maybe, Cork thought, looking at the grunge that covered every surface, some gasoline and a match.

"Police scanner," Dross said from the main room.

Cork returned and saw the unit sitting on a night table next to the bed. "What's he need a police scanner for?"

"And where's his phone?" Dross asked.

"Give him another call," Cork suggested.

Dross punched in the number, but this time there was no ringtone in the converted garage.

"His phone just happened to die?" Dross said.

Cork stepped to the stained easy chair and picked up a beer can that sat on the floor beside it. "Still cold and only half empty. He must have bolted when we went back to get the key. In any case, he's not here. What do you want to do?"

"A stakeout," she said. "Collar him when he comes back. I want to know why he ran."

"Now?"

"I'll take you to Aurora, then I'm coming back."

"I'd just as soon stick around. I'm as curious as you are."

Dross looked about the place and shook her head. "Who lives like this?"

"Bachelors," Cork said.

It was a brief stakeout. Dross drove a hundred yards farther into the tiny community and pulled off on a side street. She and Cork walked back to a ragged lilac hedge that separated the house of the landlady from hell and the next nearest dwelling. Through gaps in the hedge, they had a clear view of the garage apartment. In less than ten minutes, a man emerged from the grove of birch trees that backed the property, walked to the garage, unlocked the door, and went inside. Dross led the way across the yard and pounded on the door.

"I know you're in there, Mathias. This is the police. If you don't open the door, I swear to God we'll break it down."

She still had the key the landlady had given her, but Cork liked the bravado of her threat. If he'd been inside that garage, he'd have believed every word she spoke.

The knob rattled and, in the next instant, the door swung open.

The man who stood before them appeared to be about thirty. His narrow face was framed in hair that fell limp and oily nearly to his shoulders. His cheeks were deeply shadowed with stubble, his eyes bloodshot. Drops of mustard spotted his black T-shirt like a yellow rash. A smell came off him as if from a dirty laundry hamper.

"What?" he said angrily.

"I'm Tamarack County Sheriff Marsha Dross. This is my associate Cork O'Connor. We just want to talk."

"About what?"

"The property you inherited from your uncle."

"What about it?"

"Mind if we step in?"

He didn't look happy, but he moved aside. The television was on, a video game paused on the screen. While Dross and the man talked, Cork studied the mess of the apartment more carefully than he had the first time they were inside.

"When was the last time you visited the property?" Dross asked.

"I don't know." He made a show of thinking, then shrugged. "Maybe two, three years ago. Was trying to figure if it was worth selling."

"Did you ever pick blueberries in that special patch of his?"

"Sure, when I was a kid."

"We found a woman buried in your uncle's blueberry patch. Now your blueberry patch."

"Like I said, I haven't been back there in years."

"That blueberry patch isn't easy to find. Do you know anyone else who might be aware of it?"

"No."

"Think about it a moment."

He gave it brief consideration, then said again, "No."

"You work the pipeline," Cork said, lifting his eyes from the mess and focusing on the man who'd created it. "What do you do exactly?"

"A welder."

"Worked on the pipeline long?"

"Since it crossed the border."

"You're not working now."

"Not my choosing. Damn Indians."

"What do you do when you're not working?"

"Drink, play video games, wait for the all clear to get back to work."

"Where do you do your drinking?"

"Here, mostly."

"Ever go to bars?"

"Sometimes."

"Ever been to the Howling Wolf bar?"

"Don't know that one."

"Why do you have a police scanner?"

"No law against it. Look, I'm kinda busy here."

"One more question," Dross said. "Why did you run?"

"I don't know what you're talking about."

"You were here when we first knocked, then you took off. Why?"

"Didn't take off, just . . ." He seemed to cast about for what to say next. "Are we done?"

"For now," Dross said.

As they left, he shut the door hard behind them, and Cork heard the lock click.

They returned to Dross's cruiser and sat for a moment.

"You didn't give the landlady her key," Cork said.

"If I come back with a warrant, I won't have to kick the door in. I'm not sure one word of truth came out of his mouth."

"I can tell you there was one thing he was definitely lying about. In all that clutter on the floor there was a T-shirt with a familiar logo."

"Yeah? What?"

"A howling wolf."

CHAPTER 13

Cork rolled up to the house on Gooseberry Lane just as Stephen and Belle arrived in Stephen's Jeep. Cork hadn't seen Belle in a while, and he gave her a bear hug.

"How'd it go at Spirit Crossing?" he asked.

Belle looked tired but, as always, determined. "Since the helicopter incident and the negative publicity for the police, they haven't been so heavy-handed."

Cork liked Belle Morriseau enormously. He thought his son couldn't have found a better life partner. Belle was an attorney, working for Justice North, an organization that offered significant legal assistance to the Native people of Minnesota's Arrowhead region. She was Leech Lake Anishinaabe, twenty-five years old, a great softball player, and whenever Daniel could be persuaded to haul out his accordion, Belle provided accompaniment on her fiddle. She was also responsible in many ways for Stephen's decision to apply to law school.

"Rainy and Annie were there," Stephen said. "And Maria. They were a big help. Where have you been, Dad?"

"Come inside and I'll fill everyone in," Cork said.

Rainy had reheated a big pot of leftover lentil soup for dinner. She called upstairs, and Jenny and Waaboo came down. They all sat around the big dining room table. Rainy offered a blessing and began ladling soup for everyone.

"Aren't we going to wait for Dad?" Waaboo asked.

"He might not be home for a while," Jenny said.

"How'd it go at the blueberry patch?" Cork asked.

"We didn't stay long. Daniel and Monte Bonhomme were going to continue the search," Jenny said, explaining about Waaboo's wish not to be there.

"I didn't like that place," Waaboo said. "And I didn't like that haunted cabin."

"Haunted cabin?" Cork said.

"Paavola's old cabin," Jenny clarified.

"*Maji-manidoog,*" Waaboo said.

"Devils?" Cork gave his grandson a bewildered look.

"That place is bad."

"Well then, I'm glad you didn't stay long," Cork said and ruffled his grandson's hair.

"What about you?" Rainy said. "How did you and Marsha do?"

Cork filled them in on his day.

"Do you think this Mathias Paavola has something to do with what happened to Olivia Hamilton?" Jenny asked.

"He certainly acted like someone with a lot to hide."

"Will you interview him again?" Belle asked.

"I'm sure that's on Marsha's agenda."

They heard the door to the mudroom open, and a minute later, Daniel stepped in from the kitchen. He didn't look happy.

"Sit down," Rainy said. "I'll dish you up some soup."

"Thanks, Aunt Rainy."

"Did you find the other lady?" Waaboo asked.

"No, Little Rabbit, we didn't."

"I'm sorry," Waaboo said.

"Not your fault, Son."

Waaboo was quiet, all the features of his little face squinched up as if he was deep in a difficult consideration. Then he said, "I want to go back."

"Why, Waaboo?" Jenny was surprised and, Cork could see, distressed.

"Mishomis said I needed to be strong. I wasn't strong."

"I don't think this is a good idea," Jenny said firmly.

"I want to go," Waaboo said.

The look on Jenny's face was like something chiseled from granite, and Cork was sure his daughter was never going to agree.

"What if we asked Henry to be there?" Daniel suggested. "To guide Waaboo, maybe help him understand."

Jenny frowned and looked at her son.

"Please, Momma," Waaboo said.

It took a few moments, but she finally gave a slow nod. "But you're not going without me."

Cork lay in bed that night, sorting through the puzzle pieces. Olivia Hamilton and her disappearance. Mathias Paavola, who was hiding something, but what exactly was still unknown. The possibility of another body still undiscovered in the clearing. And Waaboo's sense of evil at Paavola's cabin.

"Can't sleep?" Rainy said in the dark beside him.

"I feel like a juggler with too many balls in the air."

"How did it feel today?"

"What do you mean?"

"Working with Marsha, just like you were a cop again. Did it make you miss the badge?"

"Nothing makes me miss the badge. For Marsha, the badge ties her hands in a lot of ways. Me, I don't have to worry about that anymore."

"Meaning what?"

"Meaning that I might just have a talk with Mathias Paavola on my own and in my own way."

He felt her hand laid lightly on his chest. "Don't do anything stupid. Or dangerous."

"When have I ever?"

"Oh, please," Rainy said and kissed his cheek.

Jenny stood at the bedroom window, staring into the night. Daniel rose from the bed and joined her.

"I wish Waaboo wasn't a part of this," she said.

Daniel took her hand. "Not his choice. It's like Henry told him. He has to be strong. And he is strong. He was strong from the moment he was born. He survived under that rock until you found him."

"And all I've wanted to do since is protect him. I don't think I've done a very good job of it."

"I'm guessing all parents feel that way. We would love to shield our children from all the stones the world is sure to throw at them. Which is impossible."

"Doesn't make me feel any less guilty. I keep asking myself, Why my son? Why would the Great Mystery place this burden on his shoulders? That's something I'm going to ask Henry the next time I see him."

"It's not Henry's fault. Or yours."

"Maybe it will pass," she said hopefully. "Maybe it's just this onetime thing."

"Stephen's had visions his whole life. It seems to me the question we should be asking ourselves is how we help Waaboo accept and handle what he's been given."

"Does that include taking him back to that awful place tomorrow?"

Her words were harsh, and Daniel felt their sting.

"He asked, Jenny. It's what he understands he has to do."

"Why?"

"I don't know. But I think we need to help him figure it out. And I don't know how to do that unless we take him there."

She was quiet a long time, staring into the darkness beyond the window. "But I'll be beside him every step of the way."

"Of course you will," Daniel said. "We'll both be there."

Annie wasn't sleeping either. She lay staring up at the ceiling, thinking about what she'd left behind in Guatemala and what she'd found on her return home. What she'd left was often turmoil, the struggle of common people for something as simple as a decent life. Not wealth or riches, just a roof over their heads, enough food on the table, and days without the worry of gangs or governments shattering the fabric of their families. They wanted a life without the sting of racial prejudice, which was something Maria had known from birth. Yet, what had Annie found in Minnesota but people struggling to protect the safety of their homes and their land, struggling against money and power, struggling to end the lies and fear at the heart of racial prejudice?

Struggle—was that really the fire at the heart of all existence? Was that really what life was about no matter where you came from?

Annie felt Maria lay an arm gently across her. "Trouble sleeping?"

"Sorry. I didn't mean to wake you."

"You never sleep well anymore."

"How could anyone?"

"It is a mystery," Maria said. "Like how do they get those little papers inside fortune cookies."

Annie smiled. "I couldn't do this without you."

"I wouldn't let you," Maria said.

They kissed, and Annie felt herself yielding, felt the possibility of peace, and soon felt herself drifting off to sleep in Maria's arms.

CHAPTER 14

Early the next morning, Daniel stood with Cork, Monte Bonhomme, and LuJean Desjardins near Erno Paavola's cabin.

"I don't need ESP to tell me this place is haunted," LuJean said, eyeing the old structure. "This looks like every damn cabin I've ever seen in a horror movie. Next thing you know, some asshole with a chain saw is gonna charge out that front door."

Monte laughed. "You've got your sidearm with you."

"You ever seen one of those movies, Monte? Hell, bullets don't mean a thing to a crazy man with a chain saw."

They'd been there only a few minutes when a familiar ATV came up the overgrown lane. At the wheel was Prophet, and beside him sat Henry Meloux. The old Mide seldom left Crow Point except to walk his beloved woods. When he ventured farther, it was usually in the ATV with Prophet at the wheel.

Prophet parked next to Monte Bonhomme's tribal police Tahoe and hailed them with *"Boozhoo!"*

Meloux stepped from the vehicle, and the men greeted him respectfully.

"Thank you for coming, Henry," Cork said. *"Chi miigwech."*

Meloux eyed Paavola's cabin. "Is that the place with evil spirits?"

"*Maji-manidoog*, Waaboo told us," Daniel replied.

Meloux nodded. "Something is wrong here. There is no peace, no harmony. Where is your little rabbit?"

"Jenny's bringing him. He'll be here soon."

"Good," the old man said.

"Jenny's not happy about this, Henry," Daniel said. "Waaboo's just a child."

"In the little we really know, who among us is not? Even this old man still has much to learn. Maybe your son has something to teach us. We should listen carefully."

Jenny's Forester came up the dirt lane and parked. She got out, along with Waaboo, and they came to where the others stood.

"*Boozhoo*, Mishomis," Waaboo said.

"*Aaniish naa ezhiyaayin?*" the old man said, asking the boy how he was feeling.

Waaboo looked cautiously at the cabin, then said, "Okay, I guess."

"I've brought him," Jenny said, clearly not happy about it. "But I'm not sure why."

"To someone who listens, these woods speak." Meloux knelt and looked into Waaboo's eyes. "You listen when the woods speak."

Waaboo nodded.

"You sense it. There is something not right here."

"*Maji-manidoog*." Waaboo pointed at the cabin. "There."

Meloux said, "Are you afraid?"

Waaboo hesitated, then replied, "Yes."

"Good." The old man rose and looked toward the cabin. "There is much to fear in this darkness."

Daniel said, "The Feds and BCA went over that cabin, right, Monte?"

"They did. According to Dross, they didn't find anything useful."

"They were looking with their eyes," Meloux said. "There are other ways to see. Come with me, Little Rabbit."

Jenny, who stood behind her son, gripped him fiercely. Meloux put his hand over hers and said, "You call him Waaboo, but he has the heart of *makwa*." Which meant bear. "Come, too, if you wish."

In the end, they all followed Waaboo and the old Mide.

In the investigation conducted earlier by the FBI and BCA, the lock and hasp on the front door had been pried off. Meloux stopped there. "Little Rabbit?"

"Inside, I think," Waaboo said.

"Hold on." Monte took a pair of latex gloves from his pocket and pulled them on. "Nobody touch anything." He reached out and opened the door.

Daylight fell through the doorway, illuminating the inside of the cabin. Dull light filtered through the dirty panes of glass on the windows as well. The place smelled of mildew, and there was a chill inside, which Daniel attributed to the coolness of the night before. But Waaboo stopped and said, "It's cold. Bad things."

"What do you mean 'bad things'?" Monte asked.

"I don't know. Everything is all mixed up. Afraid. Mad." Daniel's son squeezed his eyes shut. "Sad. Really sad."

Monte looked around and said, "What did they miss?"

"Dark," Waaboo said. "All dark."

He held himself as if he were cold, and Jenny knelt and put her arms around him.

Like Meloux's cabin on Crow Point, Paavola's cabin was a single room. An ancient cast-iron stove dominated one wall. There was a bunk without a mattress, a sink with an old hand pump for water, a table in the center of the place with two chairs, and against one wall, a large, badly scratched wood cabinet. A few vestiges of Erno

Paavola's time there remained—stacked pans, a kerosene lantern on the table, a dish, fork, and knife in the sink, all crusted brown.

"Not much to see here," Monte said. "Maybe a dark place outside?"

Waaboo shook his head. "In here."

Daniel slowly walked the room. There was no pantry, no place for storage, except the big, scratched-up wood cabinet. He opened the doors. Inside, the shelving was wide and deep, and although they may once have held food, maybe canned or dry goods, the shelves were now empty. He turned and surveyed the single room. He didn't have Waaboo's extraordinary sensibility, but he felt that something wasn't right. It took him a minute to put his finger on it.

"There's no dust on the floor," he said. "Nobody's lived here for two years. There should be dust everywhere."

Monte carefully eyed the floor and nodded. "Someone swept up. Probably making sure they didn't leave any footprints or other traces."

Daniel tried to think *dark*. Dark as in night? This far from the lights of any town and on a night without moonlight, the dark would be nearly impenetrable. The cabin had no electricity, only the single kerosene lantern on the table. So, maybe dark as in no interior light?

Or, Daniel wondered, maybe a different kind of darkness altogether. He'd stumbled onto so many empty, forgotten places in the great North Woods, and the souls of these abandoned places had always struck him as sad and dark.

LuJean said, "The wood cabinet."

Daniel said, "I looked. It's empty."

"No, check the floor."

Then Daniel saw it, too. Scratches on the old floorboards. "It's been moved."

"Give me a hand," Monte said.

Although it was empty, the cabinet was heavy, and the men grunted as they slid it away from the wall. When they'd finished, they both saw it—a trapdoor with a small metal ring in the center. Daniel hooked the ring with his gloved index finger and lifted. The trapdoor came up as a piece, and Daniel set it aside.

Cold emanated from the dark space beneath and with it came an odor that Daniel recognized only too well.

"*Poowah*," LuJean said, which in the Ojibwe language meant "It smells."

Wooden steps led down. Daniel took his cell phone from his pocket, tapped the flashlight app, and shone it into the dark below, illuminating a small room whose wood walls were lined with shelves stacked with canned goods.

LuJean, who was looking over his shoulder, said, "His stockpile for the end of the world?"

"Is that a cot down there?" Monte asked.

Daniel shone the light into a corner of the room. Monte was right. There was a cot. And on it a blanket with something beneath.

"I think you have found Little Rabbit's dark," Meloux said behind them.

"We don't need to be here any longer," Jenny said. "I'm taking Waaboo out." And with that, she guided her son out of the cabin.

Daniel eyed Monte. "I'll go," he said.

There were ten stairs, the incline quite steep. Daniel descended carefully. He felt the cold in that room, which seemed to him more than just the result of being insulated because it was underground. It felt unnatural, and he thought he understood something of what Waaboo had sensed.

He stepped onto the wood planking of the floor. Here, the dust had not been swept away and there were myriad footprints. He walked in a straight line the four steps to the cot, which was shoved against a wall beneath some shelving. The foul odor that had come up when he'd lifted the trapdoor was strong there. He hesitated a moment before he pulled back the blanket.

"Well?" Monte said from above.

Daniel exhaled all the foulness of the air he'd breathed in. Then he said very quietly, "Olivia Hamilton."

CHAPTER 15

Henry Meloux and Prophet left before Sheriff Marsha Dross and the legion of agents from the FBI and BCA arrived at Paavola's cabin. Because of his past, Prophet needed law enforcement to remain ignorant of his presence in Tamarack County, and Meloux had done nothing but gently guide Waaboo. So everyone had agreed not to mention their involvement. As the Crime Scene Team from BCA went carefully over everything, all the others who'd been there when Olivia Hamilton's body was discovered had been moved away from the cabin, separated, and interviewed. While this was going on, the body of Olivia Hamilton was taken away.

Sheriff Marsha Dross stood back, observing, relegated for the moment to the level of simple bystander. Another woman stood with her, and she and Dross talked quietly until the interviews with Cork and Jenny and Waaboo had been completed. Then Dross and the woman approached them.

"This is Agent Danette Shirley," Dross said in introduction. "She's from the Bureau of Indian Affairs. She's with their Missing and Murdered Unit."

Cork knew about BIA-MMU. Jurisdictional complications, poor interagency communication, and complaints about the lack of due diligence from local law enforcement when it came to investigation of missing Indigenous people had led to the creation of this relatively new unit of the bureau. Dross explained that as soon as it was clear that the body buried in the blueberry patch was Native, she'd made a call to MMU.

Agent Shirley was different from the BCA and FBI agents. Older, for one thing, maybe around fifty, Cork speculated. But she was also Native. She had long graying hair done in a single braid that hung down her back. She wore beaded earrings and on her wrist a silver bracelet set with turquoise. And she had a comforting smile when she looked upon Waaboo.

"I have five grandkids," she told him. "One about your age. They call me Yaya."

Waaboo grinned and pointed at Cork. "I used to call him Baabaa."

Cork could see that she'd immediately put his grandson at ease.

"I understand that you saw Olivia Hamilton. Is that right?" she asked gently.

"I didn't see her. I just kind of felt things when I was in the cabin."

"What exactly did you feel?"

Waaboo thought a moment. "Scared. Mad. Sad."

"So you didn't really see her or speak to her?"

Waaboo shook his head.

"But the woman buried in the blueberry patch, you saw her, is that right?"

"Uh-huh."

"And she talked to you?"

"Not like you and me are talking. I just sort of heard it in my head."

"What did you hear?"

"That she was lost. She wanted to walk the Path of Souls."

"The Path of Souls?"

"The way to the next world," Cork clarified. "An Ojibwe belief."

"Ah," Agent Shirley said and nodded. "I'm Lakota. We say they 'walk on.' Did she mention Olivia Hamilton, Waaboo?"

"We just went over this with the other agents," Jenny said. "It was clear what they thought of Waaboo and his visions. I'd like to take my son home."

"As I said, I'm Lakota. Believe me, I understand about visions." Agent Shirley smiled again at Waaboo in that grandmotherly way. "Just a few more questions. Okay?"

He nodded.

"Did you hear the woman in the blueberry patch mention Olivia Hamilton?"

"Unh-uh. Just that there was another lost spirit."

"In the cabin?"

"She didn't say."

"So, how did you know where Olivia Hamilton was?"

"I didn't. I just felt *maji-manidoog* here."

"*Maji—*?"

"It's an Ojibwe word," Cork said. "Evil spirits. Devils. After Waaboo told us he sensed something evil, we went inside to check."

She nodded, then smiled encouragingly at Waaboo. "What did you sense in the cabin?"

"Someone was lost in the dark. And someone else was really mad. And scared. And mean."

"Another person?"

"It was kind of confusing. It was like a lot of noises everywhere."

"Would you be willing to go back into the cabin and see if you sense anything more?"

"No," Jenny said. "Absolutely not. There's no way I'm going to let my son set foot in that place again."

"I understand," Agent Shirley said with what struck Cork as sincerity. "But it might help us know who put that poor girl down in that dark place."

"You believe Waaboo, Agent Shirley?" Cork said.

"Please, call me Danette. And I've seen stranger things."

"I'll go," Waaboo said.

Agent Shirley looked at Jenny. "All right?"

Jenny's face was stone, but she said, "Not without me. And I'd like my husband there, too."

"That's fine," Agent Shirley said.

"I'll get him," Cork said.

He walked to where Daniel was still being questioned by a couple of agents, one from BCA and one from the FBI, both of whom looked to Cork as if they'd only just turned old enough to shave.

"Excuse me," he said. "Agent Shirley needs Officer English."

"Shirley?" the FBI agent said.

"She's BIA-MMU," the BCA agent told him. "We're pretty much finished here anyway. Go ahead, English."

Agent Shirley introduced herself to Daniel and explained what they were about to do. Daniel gave his okay.

"Are you ready, Waaboo?" Agent Shirley asked.

The little boy nodded.

Jenny took her son's hand and they stepped inside.

Rainy, Annie, and Maria sat under an umbrella on the deck of the Four Seasons hotel, which overlooked Iron Lake. The surface of the lake was mirror-still, reflecting a sky that was a soft cornflower blue. The day was already warm and on the humid side.

"This reminds me of a lake in Guatemala," Maria said.

"Atitlán?" Annie said. "But we need a few volcanoes."

"The water is so blue, so inviting."

"The air reminds me of Guatemala, too," Annie said. "I'll be sweating bullets pretty soon."

"Will you go back right after the wedding?" Rainy asked.

Annie caught Maria's eye and looked away quickly, studying the lake. "I'm not sure exactly what I'll do."

"We'd love to have you stay as long as you'd like," Rainy said. "Both of you."

"Thank you," Maria said. But Annie was silent.

"I would like to go back to that place," Maria said. "Where we were yesterday? What do you call it?"

"Spirit Crossing," Rainy said.

"Yes. I would like to help there, if I can."

"I'm sure any help you give would be welcome. I've been there many times with Belle and Stephen. Things have turned ugly more than once."

"Maria knows what it's like to fight the tyranny of bullies," Annie said, smiling.

Maria put a hand over Annie's. "In my experience, we stand firm against the bullies only if we link arms. The more arms, the better."

The waiter brought them the coffees and scones they'd ordered. Annie and Maria were on an outing to find a suitable gift for Stephen and Belle's upcoming wedding. They'd brought with them from Guatemala a brightly embroidered huipil blouse for Belle and a traditional shirt of handwoven corte fabric for Stephen. But they wanted to find something to give as a combined wedding present—a serving dish or piece of pottery, perhaps. Also, Cork had called and filled them in on what was going on at Paavola's cabin and they'd hoped to distract themselves from dwelling too much on that tragic situation.

Still, like a powerful magnet, the discovery of Olivia Hamilton's body at the cabin pulled their talk in that direction eventually.

"It is a terrible thing," Maria said. "I am sorry for the grief of her parents."

"I can't help thinking that although it's terrible, to know nothing forever may be worse," Annie said. "I think about all those still missing in Guatemala."

"Or the family of Crystal Two Knives here," Rainy said.

Annie felt a prickle on her neck, the sense that someone was standing behind her. She turned, but no one was there.

"What is it?" Maria said.

Annie dismissed it. "Nothing."

When they'd finished their coffee, Rainy said, "I'll let you two go on with your shopping. I want to browse the bookstore. Text me when you're ready and we'll meet back at my car."

As they rose to leave, Annie turned and saw a man sitting at a table some distance away. Despite the heat, he wore a stocking cap pulled low down over his head. He looked familiar to her, but she couldn't quite place him. He appeared to have been watching them, but when she looked at him, he turned away and seemed intent on studying the cornflower blue reflection on the surface of Iron Lake.

Inside the cabin, Cork felt cold even though the day outside was already warming so that it augured a scorcher. He wasn't sensitive in the way that Stephen and Waaboo were, but he was sure the cold wasn't a physical thing.

The agents of the FBI and BCA were about their work, mostly climbing into and out of the lower room. Agent Shirley herded her group to a corner where they wouldn't interfere with any evidence collection.

"Are you okay?" Jenny asked Waaboo. She stood with a protective arm around her son.

"Uh-huh," he said with a nod.

"Would you like us to be quiet, Waaboo?" Agent Shirley asked.

"It's okay."

"Do you feel anything?"

"Uh-huh."

"What do you feel?"

"They're worried."

"They? Do you know who they are?"

Waaboo shook his head.

"Is it Olivia?"

"I don't feel the dark anymore. I think she's gone now."

"Can you focus on them, Waaboo? These others?" Agent Shirley was eager, Cork could tell, but trying to be gentle with the little boy.

"Okay." Waaboo closed his eyes. After a moment, his little face squeezed up as if he was in pain.

Jenny dropped to her knees and hugged him to her. "It's okay, Waaboo. I'm here."

Daniel knelt, too, and spoke quietly to his son. "What is it, Waaboo?"

Cork's grandson opened his eyes. "They're really mad and afraid. And they still have murder in their hearts." He looked up at his father. In a voice filled with fear, he asked, "What if they know about me, Daddy?"

CHAPTER 16

The headache came with blinding suddenness, as it often did now.

They were outside a shop that displayed the work of local artists, pottery in particular. They'd been eyeing a large platter with a lovely pattern that Maria thought would be both attractive and useful.

Then it was like the sun had thrust itself into her head, and Annie nearly fell over.

Maria grabbed her. There was a bench nearby, in front of a Ben Franklin store, and Maria guided her there. When they were seated, Maria took ibuprofen and a plastic bottle of water from her handbag. Annie downed them. It would be a while before they had any effect, and in the meantime, Annie's head would continue to explode.

She didn't know how much time had elapsed before the pain eased and she could see and think clearly again. When she did, Maria was holding her hand and a number of people had gathered and were offering sympathy and help. A few others stood back watching, and among them, Annie saw the man who'd been on the deck of the Four Seasons.

"She will be all right," Maria told them. "It passes."

Annie tried to smile. "I'm fine," she lied. "Just a bit of a head-ache."

The people scattered, went back to their errands, and Maria and Annie sat together for a while.

"Still bad?" Maria asked.

"It's fading. I'll be fine in a little while."

Annie spotted Rainy coming down the sidewalk. She did her best to brighten and said to Maria, "Not a word."

"They should know," Maria said.

"I don't want them to know. Our visit is about Stephen and Belle, not about me."

"If that's what you want." Maria leaned and gently kissed Annie's hair.

A moment later, Rainy stood above them. "Any success?" Then she seemed to notice Annie's face. "Oh, dear. Are you all right?"

"Just a little tired," Annie said. "I didn't sleep well last night."

"Why don't we get you home so you can rest?"

Annie stood up and, with some difficulty, started to walk.

"Wait," Rainy said. "Your shoulder bag."

She lifted the brightly colored bag that Annie almost always carried with her. It had been a gift from Maria, handcrafted by a Mayan artisan, and was very dear to Annie.

"How could I forget that?" she asked, more to herself than to Rainy.

It was Maria who answered her. "Because you're tired."

The moment they entered the house on Gooseberry Lane, Annie felt the tension in the air. Everyone was sitting at the kitchen table—Daniel, Jenny, Cork. Monte Bonhomme, chief of the Iron Lake Tribal Police, was there, along with Tribal Officer LuJean Des-jardins. Annie was surprised to see Prophet as well. Henry Meloux and Waaboo were absent, however. And also Stephen and Belle, who'd gone to Spirit Crossing that morning.

"What happened at Paavola's cabin?" Rainy asked. She set the book she'd bought on the kitchen counter. "Did Waaboo pick up on anything helpful?"

"Things have become a little more complicated," Cork said, and he explained about what Waaboo seemed to have sensed.

"He said they still have murder in their hearts?" Rainy looked confused. "What exactly does that mean?"

"We're not sure. But Waaboo's pretty shook. He's afraid they might know about him, whoever it is that's responsible for Olivia Hamilton's death."

"Where is he?" Annie asked.

"Upstairs," Jenny said. "Henry wanted to speak with him alone."

"So, what are we going to do?" Rainy said.

Monte Bonhomme spoke up. "The Feds and BCA weren't particularly interested in identifying the girl buried in the blueberry patch. But now they will be. Her and Olivia Hamilton both on Paavola's property, that's no coincidence."

"How will they identify her?" Rainy asked. "Her body was badly decomposed, wasn't it?"

"They can still pull fingerprints. It's not easy and it'll take some time. But we have a lead already. Her name is Tacicala or Fawn. So she could very likely be Lakota. There are some databases we can check. NAMUS and MissingKids and Minnesota Missing and Unidentified Persons Clearinghouse. Maybe someone by either of those names has been officially reported missing."

"Will you tell the FBI and BCA about Fawn?" Annie asked.

"Maybe. But I'm sure their real concern is finding Olivia Hamilton's killer. To them, Fawn is just a link in a chain. I'm not eager to have them step all over us in their rush to get someone in cuffs for killing the Hamilton girl. Besides, they have their way of doing things and we have ours."

"What's that?" Rainy asked.

"The Indian way. I'll put out the word to every tribal law enforcement agency and every other Native contact I have in Minnesota and the Dakotas and Canada asking if anyone's reported a missing girl by that name. We'll see where that takes us."

"I'm going to have another conversation with Mathias Paavola," Cork said. "He was pretty nervous when Marsha and I questioned him before. And he is half owner of that cabin."

"Are you going tell Marsha?" Rainy asked.

"She'll want to wait for a warrant. Her hands are tied by legalities. Mine aren't. He's the best lead we've got. If he knows we've found Olivia Hamilton's body, he's liable to run. I want to get to him before he does."

"And I want Waaboo out of all of this," Jenny said. "I want him safe."

"Then you should let him stay with me."

They all turned. Henry Meloux stood in the kitchen doorway, Waaboo at his side.

"I have had a long talk with your little rabbit. We both think it would be a fine idea for him to spend some time on Crow Point. If you are worried about his safety, I can think of no better watchdog than Prophet."

Now all eyes turned to the quiet man, who stood near the mudroom door.

"I promise you, not even a fly will come near Waaboo," Prophet said.

Jenny motioned Waaboo to her. She put her arm around him. "Is that what you want?"

"Uh-huh," her son said with a nod.

"And you will come, too," Meloux told her.

"I won't let him out of my sight," she replied.

"There's something else," Annie said. Her headache had sub-sided, but she still felt queasy, not just from her illness but from something she'd realized now that she'd heard everything.

"What is it?" Cork asked.

"I saw someone today, watching us."

"Who?"

"I don't know. He looked familiar but I couldn't quite place him. I saw him twice. The first time was at the Four Seasons. I had the feeling he might have been listening to our conversation. And then I saw him again when—" She paused and considered how to phrase the next part. "I saw him again when I was feeling faint and Maria sat me down on the bench in front of the Ben Franklin store."

"What was he doing?" Cork asked.

Staring while I felt like my head was exploding, she could have said. Instead, she said, "Just sort of lurking."

"Familiar?" Monte Bonhomme said. "But you couldn't quite place him?"

"Maybe I knew him from high school or something," Annie said. "I've been gone a long time."

"Or maybe not," Cork said. "I think we all need to be careful. Like Waaboo said, they still have murder in their hearts."

"Come on, Little Rabbit," Jenny said, rising and taking Waaboo's hand. "The sooner we're on Crow Point, the safer I'll feel."

CHAPTER 17

Cork knocked on the door of the converted garage in Dahlbert. No one answered. He checked the windows, but all the curtains inside were drawn. He went to the house and knocked on the front door. A few moments later, the landlady from hell opened up. She was in her flowered housecoat. In the hand she hadn't used to turn the doorknob, she'd wedged a lit cigarette between her index and middle fingers. In that same hand was a can of PBR nestled inside a beer cozy.

"You again? Where's my key?" she snapped.

"That's about to be the least of your worries," Cork said. "Does the name Olivia Hamilton mean anything to you?"

"Yeah. Rich girl's gone missing. All over the news. What of it?"

"She's not missing anymore. We found her body."

"So?"

"Your renter back there owns the cabin where we found her. I need to search the place you're renting to him."

Cork was aware that he was choosing his words as if he were still with law enforcement. He was hoping that the fact he'd accompanied a sheriff on his first visit would lend credence to his charade.

The woman swore under her breath, then said, "I don't know nothing about him. He pays his rent, that's all that's important to me."

"Do you have another key?"

Through pursed lips, she let out air like a punctured tire, turned, and walked away. She left the door open, and Cork could hear the television, another baseball game being broadcast. It sounded like the Twins again, and when he heard the score, it was clear that they were getting shellacked.

She came back, beer cozy and cigarette in one hand, key in the other. "That's the only one I got. I need it back."

"When I'm finished, I'll make sure to return it." Then he added, for reasons not quite clear to himself, "Scout's honor."

On his arrival, he'd seen that the Jeep Wrangler was gone. When he opened the door to the converted garage, he found the place deserted, as he'd suspected it would be, but still a cluttered pigsty.

He'd brought a pair of leather gloves, which he put on. Carefully, he made his way around the studio apartment, then checked the bathroom. The only thing that jumped out at him was the fact that there was still a suitcase in the little closet. This suggested that Paavola hadn't packed before he left. Which meant to Cork one of two things: either Paavola was coming back or he'd left in such haste that he hadn't bothered to pack his things. Cork didn't think Paavola was coming back. So the question was this: Had Paavola fled because of the earlier visit Cork and Dross had made, or was he running from someone else?

When he rang the bell, Irene Boyle opened her front door almost immediately. Her face was flushed, her brow sweaty, and she seemed out of breath. "Sorry," she said. "You caught me in the middle of my workout."

She wore black spandex leggings, a pink tank top, and pink Reeboks.

"You were here before, with Sheriff Dross. You're . . ." She thought for a moment. "O'Connor."

"That's right."

"What can I do for you, Mr. O'Connor?"

"I'd like to talk to your brother, but I can't find him."

"Did you check in Dahlbert? That's the last address I had for him."

"He was there, but I don't think he is anymore. Has he been in touch?"

"I haven't heard from him in weeks. But that's not unusual."

"Is there anywhere else he might have gone? A friend or friends he might be staying with?"

She squinted a few moments, thinking, then shook her head. "I can't think of any. Matt's always been a loner."

"My guess is that you'll be getting a visit very soon from the BCA and/or the FBI, Ms. Boyle."

"About the girl buried in the blueberry patch?"

"No, about Olivia Hamilton. Her body was found in a room beneath your uncle's cabin."

"Oh, lord." Her mouth went wide, a great circle of shock. Then she said again, "Oh, lord." She looked at Cork as if a new understanding had just come to her. "You think my brother might have had something to do with that?"

"It's certainly a possibility. And the agents who come here will be considering the possibility that you might be involved as well."

"Me?" Her shock appeared to turn to horror. "But I haven't been to that cabin in years."

"You own the land and the cabin. It's a natural connection to be pursued."

"Oh, God." She looked down at the rich design of her Persian rug. "Damn you, Matt."

"You both knew about the room under the cabin?"

"Uncle Erno showed it to us years ago. He said that when the apocalypse came, we could join him there. I always thought he was a little crazy."

"Do you happen to have a photo of your brother?"

She didn't answer right away. She seemed lost in her anger and fear.

"Ms. Boyle?"

"What? Oh, a photo of Matt? Maybe. But nothing recent. Wait here."

He thought about what he knew of Irene Boyle's past, the difficulty of having a woman like Erno Paavola's sister, a bitter, vindictive drunk, for a mother, the swamp of an alcoholic marriage, and finally getting clear and creating a decent life for herself. But now, if in fact her brother had something to do with the death of Olivia Hamilton and the woman buried in the blueberry patch, that life was about to come crashing down around her like shattered glass.

She returned with her cell phone and showed Cork a photograph. Her brother was smiling and holding up a piece of cake. "That was on his birthday three years ago. I haven't taken a photo of him since. We haven't really been in communication for a while."

"This will do, thanks. Will you send it to me?" Cork waited while she texted him the photo. "If he gets in touch with you, would you let me know?" He handed her one of his business cards. "And encourage him to turn himself in. Authorities at every level are going to want to talk to him."

"I can't believe he would have anything to do with harming that girl. He's always been a little different, but not dangerous."

Cork thought about saying something comforting, like *I hope you're right*. But, in truth, he hoped it was as simple as it was beginning to seem.

It was late afternoon by the time Cork returned to Aurora. Even though the sun was low in the sky, the air was still hot and humid. He parked his Expedition in the lot of the Tamarack County Sheriff's Department. The deputy at the contact desk let him through. Marsha Dross wasn't alone in her office. Agent Danette Shirley was there, along with Theresa Lee, the forensic anthropologist.

"Theresa," he said with surprise and genuine delight. "I hope we don't have more bodies that need to be exhumed."

She got up from her chair and they shook hands. "Marsha asked me to examine the body found in the blueberry patch," Lee said.

"And?" Cork said.

"Female. Probably late teens. Probably Native."

"Which pretty much confirms what Waaboo told us," Cork said.

Dross said, "Look, Cork, I'm not going to proceed with this investigation based on the supposed vision of a seven-year-old boy."

"You don't believe in visions?" Agent Shirley asked.

"I didn't say that. Just that visions have no place in how we conduct a criminal investigation. Visions don't stand up in court."

"Maybe it's because I'm Lakota, but I wouldn't mind having Waaboo with me every time I investigate a missing Native girl," Agent Shirley said. "So often, there's nothing to go on."

"And there are so many," Theresa Lee added in a weary tone.

"And the jurisdictional issues, which are so complicated, get things all balled up," Agent Shirley said, just as wearily.

"Even when we find a body, despite all our best efforts, it often goes unidentified," Theresa Lee said, finishing in a tone that rang with defeat.

"I can give you a piece of information that might be helpful in our case," Cork said. "It came from Waaboo, something he sensed." He looked at Dross. "If you're okay with this kind of lead, Marsha."

"Let's hear it."

"Waaboo said she told him her name is Tacicala."

"Tacicala?" Agent Shirley said. "That's Fawn in the Lakota language."

"Exactly," Cork said.

"So she might not be Ojibwe." Agent Shirley took a notepad and pen from her purse and jotted something down.

"Do we have any idea how the Olivia Hamilton investigation is going?" Cork asked.

"A warrant to search Mathias Paavola's apartment is in the works," Dross told him.

"I don't think they'll find him there," Cork said.

"Why not?"

Cork explained about his visit.

"You went there without authorization and broke in?" Dross said.

"I'm not a cop. I don't need authorization. And I didn't break in. Like I said, the landlady gave me a key."

"And you think someone forced him to leave?"

"That's sure how it looked to me. But I could be wrong. I also made a visit to his sister."

Agent Shirley shook her head. "My FBI and BCA colleagues aren't going like it one bit that you jumped the gun on them."

"The early bird gets the worm, Danette."

"And what was the worm?" Dross asked.

"Irene Paavola claims she hasn't seen or heard from him."

"Cork," Theresa Lee said. "Could I talk to Waaboo?"

"The little guy's been through a lot the last couple of days. Why do you want to talk to him?"

"I'd like to do everything I can to help identify the girl in the blueberry patch. Maybe help bring some closure to her family. It would be . . ." She seemed to search for the right word, the right explanation. She finished simply, "It would be helpful to me. Do you understand?"

"I think I do," Cork said. "But I'll have to ask Jenny."

"Of course. Thank you."

It was late in the day when he headed home, the trees flaming with the last red-orange light of the setting sun. The world around him seemed on fire. And Cork thought about hell. He hoped with a deep bitterness and complete lack of forgiveness that the people, probably men, responsible for all the bodies of Native women and girls that Theresa Lee helped pull from shallow graves would burn for eternity.

CHAPTER 18

Annie sat alone on the porch swing. The sun was setting, the houses on Gooseberry Lane aglow in the warm light. In Guatemala, she'd lived in a row of single-room shacks built of cinder block and with corrugated metal roofs. She had no toilet, using instead a communal latrine behind the building and drawing her water from a communal spigot.

Although she'd been born here, had grown up here, had spent so many good years here, she felt uneasy in the comfort of this quiet town, this quiet neighborhood, this quiet house. She should have been in Guatemala, still doing her best to help. But that was behind her now.

Rainy stepped from the house. "Feeling better?"

"Much," Annie said.

"Okay if I sit?"

Annie said she didn't mind. "It's lovely here," she said, once Rainy was beside her. "Very different from the *asentamiento* Maria and I call home."

"What's it like?"

"A barrio on the edge of Guatemala City. Lovely people struggling with poverty and prejudice and violence. We do what we can to help." She fell silent for a moment, then nodded to a tire swing that hung from a branch on the elm tree in the front yard. "When we were kids, we had a tire swing just like that one. After we all became teenagers, Dad took it down. I like that it's back up again. Does Waaboo enjoy it?"

"We all do because he does. We take turns pushing him. His laugh is infectious." Rainy studied her, then said, "Your hand is trembling."

Annie quickly nestled it in her lap. "Still recovering a little from my headache today."

"Do you often have headaches?"

"Sometimes."

"How are you sleeping?"

"Not very well."

"I noticed when we were having coffee at the Four Seasons this morning that your hand trembled then, too."

Annie didn't reply.

"In the white culture, I'm known as a nurse," Rainy said gently. "In the culture of my people, I'm known as a healer, a Mide."

"I know."

"If you want to talk, I'm happy to listen."

"Thanks, but I'm fine," Annie lied.

"All right," Rainy said.

Maria stepped out onto the porch. "It is a beautiful evening."

"Yes, it is," Rainy said. "And I'll let you two enjoy it. I'm going to put some dinner together." She got up, offering her seat to Maria. Then she went inside.

Maria sat and Annie held out her trembling hand. "She suspects."

"You didn't tell her?"

"I'll wait. After the wedding will be soon enough."

"More headaches, more trembling, more stumbling, they will know."

"I'm not ready yet."

Annie tried to settle again into the quiet of the evening, but she felt tethered to a wagonload of concerns. "I should go back, Maria. I feel like a deserter."

"You haven't deserted anyone."

"I see their faces, the little ones especially. I wanted to do so much more for them."

"You gave them all that you could. Now it's time for you to take care of yourself."

Maria took her hand and held it. They sat together that way in a warm silence for a few minutes, until a van pulled up to the curb. Annie watched a man get out from behind the wheel and a woman exit the passenger side. As the woman approached, Annie pulled her hand from Maria's. The woman stopped at the bottom of the front porch steps and smiled up at them.

"I'm looking for the parents of Aaron O'Connor."

"Waaboo," Annie said.

"Waaboo? Little Rabbit?" The woman smiled. "And you are?"

Annie sensed something a great deal more troubling than the discomfort she'd been feeling since her return to Aurora. "How about you tell me who you are first?" she said.

"My name is Greta Hanover."

Annie offered no reply, making it clear that she was waiting for more.

"I'm a reporter for the *Duluth News Tribune*."

"Why do you want to see Waaboo's parents?"

"It's really Waaboo that I want to speak with. I understand he may have been helpful in locating Olivia Hamilton's body."

A blade of fear sliced through Annie's gut. The secret was out. "Where did you hear that?"

"I picked up chatter on my police scanner. It was a little vague, but I was able to confirm with an inside source that he was at the cabin where her body was found. Is that true?"

"I'd rather not say."

"I was given to understand that he may have actually led the police there. Some sort of vision he had."

"I think it's best that you leave," Annie said.

The woman gave a nod, as if she understood Annie's resistance. "Look, I'm sure other reporters have been monitoring their police scanners. If they make the connections in the same way I did, they'll descend, and let me tell you quite honestly, they can be vultures. If I could speak with Waaboo and his parents, we might be able to keep you all from being overwhelmed."

"Whatever you heard, it's not true," Annie said.

The screen door of the front porch opened and Rainy stepped out. "Can I help you?"

"A reporter," Annie said.

"Greta Hanover. *Duluth News Tribune.*" Then the woman said, "*Boozhoo.*"

Rainy's voice was not hostile, but there was stone in her words. "Why are you here?"

"She's heard that Waaboo helped the police find Olivia Hamilton," Annie said. "She wants to talk to him."

Rainy crossed her arms over her chest. "That won't be possible."

"As I told . . ." Hanover held out a hand toward Annie, waiting, Annie suspected, for her name, which she did not give. "As I said earlier, there may be a lot of media attention. Olivia Hamilton is big news. But if you let me talk to the little boy and his parents, maybe I can help blunt it."

"I'll pass your request along to them," Rainy said.

"Fair enough. Here's my card."

Annie saw the man who'd stayed beside the van snapping pictures with a camera.

"*Chi miigwech,*" the woman said but didn't turn away. "One thing. My grandmother was a Grand Portage Shinnob. I understand your concern. But if other reporters sniff this out, and I'm guessing they will, it's going to be almost impossible to keep them from beating down your door. If it's true that he played a part in locating Olivia Hamilton's body, your little Waaboo is news now. I'm sorry." She sounded sincere to Annie.

As the van pulled away, Rainy whispered under her breath, "Damn."

In a matter of only a few minutes, things had changed, and suddenly Gooseberry Lane no longer seemed so quiet to Annie.

As soon as Daniel walked into the house, Rainy gave him the hard news. Cork arrived at almost the same time and received the same update.

"How did she know about Waaboo?" Daniel asked, his voice pitched at the edge of anger.

"Apparently she picked it up on her police scanner," Cork said. "And someone involved in the investigation talked more than they should have. If she heard, it's likely that other reporters have picked up on it as well."

Annie saw Daniel's hands ball into fists. "No way am I going to let her interview my son."

"She seemed genuinely concerned about Waaboo and us," Annie offered. "And what she said is probably true. She's just the first. Now that word about Waaboo is out there, others are going to come, and, as she said, they could be vultures."

Outside, dark had descended. They sat around the kitchen table, where Annie remembered so many family councils taking place across her years in that house. On the kitchen counter sat the cookie jar shaped like Ernie from *Sesame Street,* the smile on Ernie's face so wonderfully sedate. She remembered the comfort of the chocolate chip cookies that came from the jar and that accompanied so many serious conversations.

"Daniel?" Cork asked after a long moment of consideration.

"Two days ago, we discovered the buried body of an Indian girl. I didn't see that make the headlines. But now they want to harass my son because of Olivia Hamilton."

"What are you going to do?" Cork said.

"Let me talk to Jenny," Daniel finally said. Then, as if it was a struggle to pull himself away from his anger, he said to Cork, "How'd it go today?"

Cork filled them in on his progress, or lack thereof. Mathias Paavola was missing, and Cork thought that maybe it was not by his own volition. The sister was no help. He told them about his visit to the Sheriff's Department, and of Theresa Lee's desire to help learn the identity of the girl buried in the blueberry patch.

"I think we might already know who she is," Daniel said, which clearly surprised them all. "Monte put out the word, and we got lucky. An officer from the Three Rivers Tribal Police called him. A little over six months ago, a girl named Fawn Blacksmith was released from the North Regional Juvenile Detention Center. The girl's grandmother eventually reported her missing, but because none of this occurred on the rez, it was out of the officer's jurisdiction and in the hands of the Deer County Sheriff's Department. He contacted them but didn't get much of a response. He hasn't heard anything more, but he said he would talk to the grandmother and to the Sheriff's Department again. He didn't sound too hopeful. Apparently, the relationship between the tribal police department and the local constabulary isn't exactly copacetic. Monte and I were planning to go down there ourselves, tomorrow, see what we could find out."

"Are you going to let Marsha Dross know?" Cork asked.

"Monte wants to keep a lid on this until we've spoken with the grandmother. Are you okay with that?"

"She'll be pissed when she finds out, but I'll hold off saying anything for now."

They heard the front door open, and a few moments later, Stephen and Belle walked in, both of them looking exhausted from whatever had occurred at Spirit Crossing that day.

"The pipeline's lawyers got a judge to sign an order for the encampment to be dismantled," Belle said. "We're trying to get the order stayed, but my brother, Anton, is pretty sure they're going to roust the encampment tomorrow. It could turn into a major confrontation."

"How're you doing?" Cork asked.

"Tired," Belle said.

"You should get some sleep," Cork suggested.

Rainy glanced at the clock on the wall. "It's late. We should all get some sleep. Maybe in the morning, things won't look so bad."

The words sounded wise and hopeful, but when Annie looked outside, all she saw was the gloom of a long night ahead.

She was used to sleepless nights. They went along with the headaches, the trembling, the stumbling. She rose from the bed as soundlessly as possible. Maria went on sleeping. She left the bedroom, descended to the first floor of the house, quietly opened the front door, then eased the screen door open and closed it behind her without a squeak of the spring. She sat on the porch swing.

There were streetlamps at the corners, but most of Gooseberry Lane lay in darkness. No lights shone warmly through the windows of the neighbors' houses. The moon had not yet risen, and Annie sat with the night wrapped around her like a blanket without substance.

In these sleepless nights, what haunted her wasn't the prospect of her death. It was the unanswered and unanswerable question of what would come after. She'd been raised Catholic, had wanted all her life to be a bride of Christ. She'd become a novice of the Sisters of Notre Dame de Namur. Then she'd become infatuated with another young woman and her life had become nothing but a web of doubt. She'd gone to Guatemala with the Order, intending to work through her doubts. Instead, she'd left the Sisters, still cloaked in uncertainty, and had thrown herself into the work of helping those whose lives were about how to survive one day to the next. Then she'd met Maria. And love had been her salvation.

The headaches began, followed eventually by the other signs. By the time the neuro-oncologist in Guatemala City told her that the tumor on her brain was advanced and inoperable, she had, he guessed a year, or perhaps two, left. That was thirteen months ago.

She had thrown herself even more fervently into the work of helping the poor and the ignored in the barrio on the edge of the city. Gradually, her strength left her. The headaches grew in frequency. The tremors were more evident, the stumbling more frequent. And more and more, the wonderment about death was on her mind.

Maria's middle name was Cocum, which meant listening in the language of the Mayan people. It was perfect for her. Annie didn't ask for answers, and Maria didn't offer them, content to supply a comforting shoulder for Annie's weary, confused head.

Growing up, Annie had believed in heaven. But she'd spent so much time in the hell of poverty and ignorance and the heartlessness of those who could help but did not that she no longer believed. Heaven was loving Maria and the comfort of lying in her arms. And she was afraid that when she died, what came after would be a hellish eternity without that love, without that comfort.

The pickup truck came up Gooseberry Lane with its headlights dark. It cruised past and, at the end of the block, made a U-turn and came back. It parked across the street. The engine died and the truck sat. The brief flicker of a flame and the dot of a yellow ember afterward told Annie someone had lit a cigarette. She couldn't see inside the cab. Although the truck was on the far side of the street in front of the neighbors' house, Annie knew it wasn't the people who lived there, the O'Loughlins, who were of interest.

Wrapped in her own cloak of darkness, she must have been invisible to the watcher. She thought of Waaboo. Someone besides the reporter knew about her nephew. Someone knew where he lived. She was glad that Jenny had moved Waaboo to Crow Point so quickly. What they—whoever these people were—were afraid of seemed obvious to Annie. They feared that the boy who saw things others did not would see them.

Her concern for herself left her. Now she was fiercely afraid for Waaboo. She stood, impulsively intending to stride down the sidewalk, cross the street, and confront them. But just as she took her first step, a light in the living room behind her came on, and she was exposed. The truck engine kicked over, and the pickup took off down the street.

The front door opened and Annie's father stepped outside.

"You okay?" he asked.

"There was a truck on the street, Dad. Someone was watching the house."

"Wait here." Cork started toward the porch steps.

"I'm going with you," Annie said.

They hurried to the street together. The pavement under Annie's bare feet was still warm from the afternoon sun.

"Which way?" Cork said.

"There." Annie pointed in the direction the truck had gone, but the street was empty now.

"Let's go back to the porch," Cork said. "I'm going to turn off the light inside. We'll see if they come back."

Her father killed the living room light, and they sat for a long time in the porch swing, waiting.

"Trouble sleeping, huh?" Cork said.

"A lot on my mind," Annie said.

"Things left undone in Guatemala?"

Instead of answering, Annie nodded toward the tree in the front yard. "I remember climbing that elm when I was a kid and my knee got stuck in a wedge between a couple of high branches."

"I remember, too," her father said. "You were ten. You were always climbing that tree."

"You climbed up and got my knee unstuck."

"And the next day, you were right back up there."

"Why didn't you just put your foot down and forbid me from climbing?"

"Wouldn't have done any good. You always had your own mind. And you only got stuck that once. The rest of the time, you were like a monkey. You were fun to watch. I always admired your fearlessness. Same when you left for Guatemala."

She wanted to tell him. She wanted to tell him everything. But despite what he said about her fearlessness, she was afraid. She didn't know how to tell her father all the things that needed saying.

After a while, Cork said, "Guess we scared them away for tonight. What say we turn in?"

They stood, but before Annie could go inside, her father took her in his arms and held her in a long embrace and whispered in her ear, "I love you. It's wonderful to have you back."

Annie choked up. All she could do was put her own heart against his, hoping he could feel the fullness of the love she could not speak.

CHAPTER 19

At first light the next morning, Cork descended the stairs and headed to the kitchen to make a pot of coffee. As soon as he turned on the kitchen light, the phone rang. A call that early was never a good sign. Caller ID told him it was John O'Loughlin, his longtime neighbor across the street.

"Have you looked outside?" O'Loughlin asked.

"No, why?"

"A van from one of the Duluth television stations has been parked in front of your house for an hour, probably waiting for a light to come on in your place."

Cork returned to the living room and drew aside the front window curtain just enough to peek outside. As O'Loughlin had said, a van with a news station logo was parked at the curb. In the early light, he could see two men sitting inside. They appeared to be drinking coffee from disposable cups. As he watched, a man got out of a car on the other side of the street, walked to the van, and began conversing with its occupants. They seemed to be laughing. Although he couldn't hear the discussion, he could imagine the brunt of their joking. Waaboo. Then another van drew up.

"Oh, Christ," Cork said.

"You want me to run them off with my garden hose, I'm happy to oblige," O'Loughlin offered.

"I'll take care of them, John," Cork said. "My best to Sue."

"She's right here, waiting for the fireworks to begin. Anything we can do to help, just let us know."

By then, Rainy had come downstairs. She stood next to Cork, eyeing the vans through the gap in the curtains. "What are we going to do?"

Cork pulled the curtains closed. "I'll wake Daniel, then we'll have some coffee and figure things out."

It began, however, before they could enjoy that coffee and make plans. At 6:20, the doorbell rang.

"Oscar Benson, Saint Paul *Pioneer Press*," the man who stood on the other side of the screen door said. "Sorry to disturb you so early, but I saw the kitchen light go on. I'd like to speak with you, Mr. O'Connor. You are Cork O'Connor? Aaron O'Connor's grandfather?"

"I'm talking to no one at the moment. No one in this house is talking to anyone before we've had our breakfast."

Quick as a cobra strike, the man reached out and opened the screen door so that nothing stood between him and Cork. "I understand your grandson helped locate Olivia Hamilton's body and that it was as a result of some kind of vision he had. That, in fact, he spoke to her ghost."

"Let me ask you a question," Cork said. "Do you believe in ghosts?"

"This isn't about me."

"Just answer the question."

"Not personally."

"Well, there you go. You want to report something that's complete nonsense?"

"I have a source that says it's not nonsense."

"Then your source is full of shit. There's no such thing as ghosts."

"Could I have just a few words with the boy?"

"Here's a few words for you," Cork said. "Get the hell off my porch. If you come back again, I'll have you arrested for trespassing." He yanked the man's hand off the screen door and pulled it closed. Then he slammed and locked the front door.

The whole house had been awakened by then. They gathered in the kitchen for a conference, just as they had the night before. The phone rang. Someone checked Caller ID. A local news outlet.

"That could go on all day," Cork said. "Maybe I should just unplug the phone."

While they talked, Daniel and Stephen set about making scrambled eggs and toast. Rainy poured orange juice. Annie, Maria, and Belle stayed out of the way.

Daniel had called Jenny the night before and got her permission to let Theresa Lee speak with Waaboo. "I can't take her out to Crow Point," Daniel said as he stood at the stove that morning. "Monte and I are headed over to Deer County to talk with Fawn Blacksmith's grandmother. We'd like to speak to her before the BCA or Feds get to her."

"I'd take her," Rainy said. "But I'd rather go with Stephen and Belle to Spirit Crossing. If things turn ugly, I might be able to help."

"I can take her," Cork said. He stood at the kitchen window, a mug of coffee in his hand, eyeing the vans on the street. "The Feds and BCA will be all over the Olivia Hamilton investigation. Not much more I can do there."

Maria said, "I'd like to go to Spirit Crossing with Belle and Stephen, if you'll have me. I might be able to help, too."

"If you go, I want to be with you," Annie said. "Would that be okay?"

"Of course," Belle said.

"Sounds like we all have somewhere to go. That'll leave the house empty." Cork sipped his coffee and smiled at the circus on Gooseberry Lane. "There won't be anybody here to badger."

"Maybe we can do one more thing," Rainy said.

"What's that?" Cork asked.

"Maybe we could talk to just one of them. Then maybe all the other vultures would flock to her instead of us."

"Her?"

"The woman who was here last night." Rainy pulled out the card she'd been given and read from it, "'Greta Hanover.' She wasn't pushy. And she has Ojibwe roots."

"For what it's worth, I thought she was sincere," Annie said.

"What do we think?" Cork asked.

"Wouldn't it be like letting the floodgates open?" Daniel said.

"It could be more like letting some air out of an overfilled balloon," Belle offered. "Especially if we all tell the same story but alter a few details."

"Like what, Counselor?" Stephen asked.

"Waaboo didn't talk to a ghost. Ghosts aren't real. But how about this? When he was hunting blueberries with his family on the Paavola property, he smelled something foul, something dead, which led to the discovery of the body under the cabin."

They spent a few minutes discussing and settling on the particulars and decided that Rainy and Daniel should take the lead. "Everyone else, just nod," Belle advised.

"If she's a good reporter, she may smell a rat," Daniel said.

"Let's call her and find out." Cork turned to his wife. "You spoke with her, Rainy. You still have her card. You want to do the honors?"

Fifteen minutes later, Hanover came to the mudroom door, as Rainy had instructed. Daniel let her in. She seemed surprised when she saw them all there in the kitchen, eyeing her. "*Boozhoo. Indizhinikaaz* Greta Hanover. *Migizi makwa,*" she said, offering them a greeting and telling them in Ojibwemowin that her name was Greta Hanover and she was of the Bear Clan.

"*Boozhoo. Biindigen,*" Rainy replied, welcoming her in. She introduced them all, then said, "The truth is that we're hoping if we give you an interview, it might stem the flood of reporters. What do you think?"

"Once I have the scoop, you probably won't be such a big draw," Hanover agreed. "I can't guarantee that you won't still experience some harassment. Quite honestly, some of my colleagues have the ethics of gutter rats. But I'll do my best to be both truthful and helpful. How's that?"

Cork said, "Fair enough."

Hanover spent half an hour in the kitchen, listening and taking notes. As she left, she looked knowingly at Rainy, then the others. "Stick to your story. It makes perfect sense. It may not stop the circulation of rumors, but it will probably get the gutter rats off your doorstep. And like all news stories, this will blow over soon. With the next big headline, everyone will forget about Waaboo and maybe even Olivia Hamilton. It's the way of the news world."

"From your mouth to God's ear," Belle said.

Rainy took the reporter's hand and gazed deeply into her eyes. "*Chi miigwech.*"

They left, one vehicle at a time. Cork was the last out of the driveway. He saw Greta Hanover talking with a small gathering of what he assumed were other journalists. They watched him go, then turned their attention back to Hanover. She kept shaking her head, as if dismissing something they were pressing upon her. As he pulled away, she caught his eye and nodded. Cork gave her a nod of thanks in return.

He picked up Theresa Lee at her home and drove to the double-trunk birch that marked the trail to Crow Point. He kept an eye on the rearview mirror just to be certain no nosy journalist was following. Jenny's Forester was parked off the road near the trailhead.

As they started along the path, Lee said, "I've walked this way many times over the years, but it's been quite a while since I visited Henry."

"He moves more slowly these days, but his mind hasn't slowed down a bit."

It took more than half an hour to walk the two miles through the forest. They talked little. For Cork, there was almost always a kind of sacred quality in that approach to Crow Point, as if he were preparing for something important. Some of this was because of the place itself, the way the voice of the wilderness spoke to his soul. And, of course, it was also because of Meloux and the solace the old man usually offered a visitor.

But on this visit, as they left the trees and entered the meadow, Cork heard Waaboo scream on the far side of the point. Without a word, he broke into a run.

The cry came from the other side of two rock outcroppings beyond which lay the fire ring where Cork had often sat with the old Mide, staring into the flames and receiving advice. Cork cut across the meadow directly toward the rocks. He heard Waaboo scream again, and he kicked up his speed.

Breathing hard, he hit the well-worn path that ran from Meloux's cabin and between the outcroppings nearly a hundred yards distant. The rocks rose above Cork as he cut through and another scream came. When he reached the fire ring, he stopped dead, his heart still pounding.

Meloux sat on a section of cut log. Jenny was beside him. Waaboo was nowhere to be seen.

Jenny looked at him with surprise. "Dad? What are you doing here?"

"Where's Waaboo?" Cork asked between deep breaths.

"There," his daughter said and pointed toward Iron Lake, whose sparkling blue water was clearly visible through breaks in the birch along the shoreline.

Cork spotted the little boy, splashing in the lake along with Prophet. As he watched, Prophet grabbed Waaboo, lifted him high, and threw him. Waaboo screamed as he flew—a scream of delight—then plunged into the water.

"I thought . . ." Cork said but didn't finish.

"Fear misshapes everything," Meloux said. "What we hear, what we see, what we think, what we feel. Your little rabbit is safe here, Corcoran O'Connor."

Theresa Lee came up behind Cork. She was also breathing hard.

"Is everything okay?" she gasped.

"It was quite peaceful," Meloux said. "Now, not so much. But it is good to see you. It has been a long time."

"*Boozhoo*, Henry," she said. "*Boozhoo*, Jenny."

"Sit." Meloux indicated another section of pine log that had been cut and laid for sitting near the fire ring. When they were seated, he said to Theresa Lee, "Speak."

"Cork has told me the story of how Waaboo sensed both the spirit of the young woman in the blueberry patch and the spirit of Olivia Hamilton. I've been a part of lifting many bodies from the earth, Henry, but I've never sensed their spirits."

She paused a moment, as if waiting for the old man to reply. When Henry remained silent, she went on.

"So many are put into the earth brutally, Henry. And if they're found, they're often impossible to identify. I would love to be able to hear them speak, as it seems Waaboo does. I would love to be able to help their families find peace."

The old man shrugged. "The Great Mystery gives the gifts. Who can say why? But I suspect they are given to those with a spirit strong enough to accept them."

"And that's not me?"

"It is your spirit," Meloux said. "Only you know the truth."

Jenny said, "Waaboo's spirit is strong enough, Henry?"

"You know that it is."

Waaboo screamed again and Jenny's eyes went toward where her beloved son was being an ordinary seven-year-old boy.

"The gift the Creator has given him is both a blessing and a burden," Meloux said. "I believe he is strong enough to accept this. But are you?"

She didn't answer. And Cork wasn't sure if he could give a truthful answer to this question either.

Meloux reached out and gently took her hand.

"When you first found him, he was a newborn baby hidden under a rock to keep him safe from those who wished him harm. There is a reason you found the little rabbit. He is your blessing. And," he added in a kind voice, "your burden."

CHAPTER 20

It was an almost two-hour drive west to the Three Rivers Reservation. On the way, Agent Danette Shirley shared her story with Daniel and Monte Bonhomme.

"I grew up on Pine Ridge. Lowest life expectancy in the country. Little town called Rockyford. There weren't many ways to leave the rez life, at least on Pine Ridge. One of them was in a pine coffin. That's how my father went when I was seven. He was killed in Rapid City, shot by a white man drunk out of his mind. My mother raised me. I was lucky because she was a teacher, believed if her daughter was going to rise above all the challenges of being Native and living on a reservation, education was the way. So I graduated from Oglala Lakota College in social work." She shook her head and gave a sardonic little laugh. "As if that might make some kind of difference in the long run. But I gave it a shot."

"How'd you get into law enforcement?" Monte asked.

"I had a friend I'd met in college. She came from Rosebud. She became a cop because she firmly believed we needed an Indian presence inside law enforcement. Did her training at the Indian Police Academy in New Mexico and went to work for the BIA. It was hard, sure, but she felt she was making a difference, giving a voice to our people in that way. I got so frustrated with the system I'd become a part of—hands always tied, resources always abysmally short—that I thought maybe my friend was right. So I became a cop, too. BIA like her. I've worked lots of cases involving missing and murdered Indigenous people over the years. When they created the Missing and Murdered Unit, I applied right away. There are so many issues that need addressing in Indian Country. I can't help with all of them. So this is where I've settled. This is what I do."

"I believe we make a difference," Monte said.

"If I didn't," Daniel said, "I'd have become a professional accordion player."

"Oh? You play the accordion, too?" Agent Shirley said, looking pleasantly surprised.

"Yeah. And you?"

"My grandchildren beg me to play."

"That'll change when they become teenagers," Monte said. "Mark my words."

With a sweep of his hand, Chief of Police Chris Hayner indicated the three straight-back chairs where Daniel, Monte, and Agent Shirley should sit.

"So, Fawn Blacksmith," he said, resuming his place behind his desk. "You believe the body you found there in Tamarack County is her?"

Hayner was not quite six feet tall, but he seemed larger in stature. Daniel thought this might have been the result of his general robustness. Although his shock of hair and bushy mustache were both going gray, he still had the look of an avid outdoorsman. Monte had done a good deal of hunting and fishing with the man.

He'd also told Daniel that Hayner once built a boat and sailed it across the Atlantic. Like so many law enforcement officers in Indian Country, Hayner had no Native heritage in his blood. But Monte had assured Daniel that Hayner had a good heart and ran a good department.

"Like I explained over the phone," Monte said, "we have a boy who has a spiritual connection. He says it's what the girl's spirit told him."

"Spiritual connection." Hayner used his index finger to scratch his mustache. "That's your evidence?"

"When it appears you've hit a dead end, Chris, you've got to look for other ways to proceed. And what harm can it do?"

"It can break Daisy Blacksmith's heart again."

"The girl's grandmother?" Agent Shirley asked.

"Yep. That old girl hasn't got a lot of life left in her. If it is Fawn you found, I expect it'll just about kill her. Right now, she's got some hope, holding on to the idea that her granddaughter just ran off again and will turn up someday somewhere."

"She was the one who reported the girl missing?" Daniel asked.

"Like I told Monte on the phone yesterday, she called me six months ago saying Fawn had disappeared. The girl had turned eighteen and been released from the North Regional Juvenile Detention Center and was supposed to come back up here and live with Daisy, but she bolted again. Daisy finally called me. I advised her to talk to Buck Sondergaard—he's our county sheriff—report Fawn as missing. It was the only thing I could do. Daisy lives off the rez, and neither her or Fawn are enrolled tribal members here. So, out of my jurisdiction. Near as I can tell, Sondergaard didn't do much, if anything. The guy's about as Indian friendly as General Custer. When nothing happened, I went ahead and entered Fawn into NCIC as missing and advised Daisy to talk to Alicia Fineday, an advocate here on the rez. As I understand it, Alicia called MMIR. You know, the Missing and Murdered Indigenous Relatives office down in the Cities."

"I know it," Monte said.

"They're good people, but they've got no teeth when it comes to compelling law enforcement to do anything. So they probably did their best to light a fire under Sondergaard, cited Brandon's Law, et cetera. But as near as I can tell, nothing much has been done. You got a case file on her?" Hayner asked Agent Shirley.

"I checked. We were never informed."

"See, that's a big part of the problem. Communication between all the agencies involved."

"Can you give us the address of the girl's grandmother?" Monte asked.

Hayner spent a minute on his computer, then wrote something on a Post-it and handed it over. "I've included her phone number, but I'll call her now, make sure she's expecting you."

"She'll be home?" Daniel asked.

"Doesn't go out much these days. When you talk to her, you'll understand."

The address was in a gathering of run-down trailer homes a few miles from where summer houses the size of the Taj Mahal fronted a series of beautiful lakes, along with resorts where well-off folks spent a carefree week or two away from the sweltering heat of the Twin Cities. Daniel suspected that the people who serviced the resorts and the restaurants and the gas stations and the grocery stores and the fun little amusement parks lived in that collection of flimsy trailers lining the grid of dirt lanes.

Monte parked his Tahoe in front of the address Hayner had given him, and he, Daniel, and Agent Shirley got out. A dog tied to

the mailbox of the trailer next door went crazy barking, but someone inside hollered "Shut up, Lester!" and the dog fell silent. As
they approached Daisy Blacksmith's trailer, the door was opened
by a young woman, who gave them a hard look.

"You the police?" she said.

She was thin, wore a black T-shirt with an image of Prince on it
and *Purple Rain* printed in purple letters above. Her hair was done
in a single long braid that hung over her shoulder. The braid was a
shade of purple that didn't quite match the T-shirt's letters. Daniel
put her in her midteens.

"'Raspberry Beret' is my favorite," he said.

"What?" She looked at him as if he were an idiot.

"Prince. It's my favorite song of his."

She looked down at the image. "Got this at Goodwill."

"We're looking for Daisy Blacksmith," Monte said.

"Took you long enough," the girl said.

"We came straight here from Three Rivers," Monte said.

"I mean to get around to looking for Fawn."

"Who are you exactly?" Daniel said.

"Nyla. I help out Granny."

"Daisy is your grandmother?"

The girl shook her head. "Just call her that cuz she's been like
a granny to me and my mom. We live over there." She pointed to
a trailer on the other side of the dirt lane.

"Is she here?" Agent Shirley asked.

The girl nodded. "She gets tired, so go easy, okay?" She turned
and directed her words inside the trailer. "They're here, Granny.
Letting them in."

She stepped aside and gave her head a small jerk, indicating
they should go inside, which they did—Monte first, then Agent
Shirley, and Daniel last.

"You should give him a try," Daniel told the girl as he passed. "He was pretty awesome."

"Who?"

"Prince."

"Yeah, whatever."

The trailer was cluttered but not trashed, more the look of careless upkeep rather than constant neglect. Magazines—*People, Reader's Digest, Women's Health*—were scattered on the sofa and the coffee table, where an empty cereal bowl also sat, still cradling a spoon. A flowered robe had been carelessly draped over a threadbare armchair. A single slipper lay beneath the chair, on its side like a dead fish. The place smelled of cigarette smoke. And also of gingerbread.

Daisy Blacksmith stood at the counter of her small kitchen. She was short and heavy, much of her black hair gone deep gray. Her right leg ended just below the knee, and a crutch was nested under each of her armpits. She turned from the cutting board on the counter, a bread knife in her hand, and smiled.

"The gingerbread is still warm. Would you like some?"

"*Miigwech*," Monte said.

"Shinnob, eh?" Daisy said. "Me, Lakota."

"I'd like some," Agent Shirley said. "Smells delicious."

Daniel said he'd also have some.

"Sit." Daisy lifted her chin, using it to point toward the sofa and chair in the little living room area. "Just move the crap. Nyla, would you take this?" She handed the girl a plate on which sat several slices of gingerbread, and Nyla set the plate on the coffee table. "Something to drink?" Daisy offered.

When they'd all said no thank you, Daisy Blacksmith crutched her way from the kitchen and settled herself in the threadbare armchair. Nyla took the crutches and leaned them against the wall, then leaned there herself.

"Got me an artificial leg a couple of years ago, but it broke a few months back," Daisy explained. "Can't afford to get it taken care of. But I get around okay. So." She fixed each of them with her dark eyes for a moment, then said, "I understand you're tribal folks and you might have news about my granddaughter."

They introduced themselves and Monte said, "We might have news about Fawn, but first I need to know a little more about you and her, if you don't mind talking about it."

"I learned a long way back that the truth of things don't get hid for long. What do you want to know?"

"You were at one time Fawn's legal guardian, is that right?" Monte said.

"Yep. Long story."

"We're in no hurry," Agent Shirley said.

"All right, then. When I was a kid, I was in one of them boarding schools, over in North Dakota," Daisy began. "I still get nightmares. Used to drink trying to make 'em go away, and the drinking got me in a lot of trouble. I had me a daughter, Celia Marie, with a Lakota man over in North Dakota, but he ain't really a part of this story. He skipped out before my Celia Marie was born. Like I said, the drinking got me into all kinds of trouble. When Celia was ten, I got into some real trouble and they sent me to jail. Well, they called it a correctional rehab center, but it was a jail. Lost my daughter. While I was there, I met some folks from White Bison. They got a wellbriety program. Uses the Medicine Wheel and Twelve Steps. They helped me get sober, and eventually I got my Celia Marie back. But by then it was too late. She was a teenager, into all kinds of craziness, drugs and the like. She already had a child, my granddaughter. Named her Fawn. Tacicala in the Lakota language cuz the father was Lakota. Only like Celia Marie's father, he ain't a part of this story at all. She and Fawn, they ended up here in Minnesota, and I came after 'em, trying to stay connected, trying to do what I could to help. When Fawn was twelve, the child protection people finally stepped in and took her away from Celia Marie in the same way they took Celia Marie from me. It took me a while, but I was able to get custody of Fawn. She was a sweet child, really. Helpful, you know. She was born with FAS."

"Fetal alcohol syndrome," Agent Shirley said.

"Yeah, but you couldn't tell. She looked normal. Real pretty. She had some trouble tying her shoes and things, but nothing that was a big deal. Like I said, a sweet child. I hoped my daughter might get clean, like I did, and get Fawn back. But it's hard. In our blood maybe. I heard it called blood memory, anyway. All the trauma our people have gone through somehow still in our bodies. Celia Marie, she finally ended up going missing. Just disappeared. At first, I thought she was off again, you know, doing God only knows what kind of damage to herself. She always come back, real sorry and mostly wanting to see Fawn. Only this time she didn't come back. I think something bad musta happened to her. I don't expect I'll ever see her again."

Daisy stopped for a few moments, and Nyla asked, "You okay, Granny?"

"Yeah." Daisy took a deep breath and went on. "So, I have this diabetes. Had it a long time. Eventually, they took my leg. I had me a job. Waitress at the Blue Moose there in town. But I couldn't work no more, so they took Fawn. Claimed I couldn't look after her good enough. Put her in foster care. Foster hell, you ask me. She run away. Come back here, cried to me, told me they treated her real bad in that place. Sounded like the things they done to us in that boarding school. But they come and took her away again. She run and they took her and she run. You get the picture. She got picked up while she was shacking up in some rat hole of a house with a bunch of druggies in Duluth. They put her in a school for problem kids. She run away from there. This time she got picked up for prostitution, ended up in that juvenile jail."

"North Regional Juvenile Detention."

"Call it what you like, it's still a jail. I think about that sweet thing having to sell her body, just kills me inside." Daisy had been dry-eyed through her recounting of her history, but now a little glistening trail of tears ran down each of her ample cheeks. "When she got out, she was eighteen, not a juvenile no more. They had this plan for her. She was supposed to come back here, live with me, get herself a job, put together a better life for herself, you know? I got no car, so Nyla and her mom drove over to get her. I gave them a bracelet I'd beaded myself, a gift to give to Fawn."

"She liked it, Granny. She put it on right away."

Daisy smiled at that, then looked sad again. "They didn't even get her back here before she ran again."

Daniel looked at Nyla. "What happened?"

"She said she needed to use the bathroom. We stopped at a gas station. She went in, didn't come out. I went in to look for her." Nyla shook her head. "Gone."

"Is that when you reported her missing?"

"Not right away," Daisy Blacksmith said. "I mean, she run away so many times, I didn't know what to think. So, maybe a month went by. Finally I decided I had to do something. Like I said, I'm not Shinnob, but I am Indian, so Nyla's mom drove me up to the rez, and I talked to Chris Hayner there. You know, heads up the tribal police. He told me he couldn't really do nothing but said I should file a missing person report with the county sheriff. Hell, that was like spitting in the ocean and thinking it'll make a difference."

"The sheriff's people weren't helpful," Monte said.

"Took my information, said they'd get back to me. Never did. I called 'em a bunch of times, always got the same runaround. That Chris Hayner, he told me to talk to an advocate on the rez. She was helpful, called some folks in the Twin Cities—"

"Missing and Murdered Indigenous Relatives," Agent Shirley said.

"Yeah, them. But . . ." Daisy gave a shrug. "Still nothing. Till you folks show up." She took another deep breath and seemed to steel herself. "So, tell me about Fawn."

Monte carefully approached telling her about the body that had been found in the blueberry patch and Waaboo's vision of a girl named Tacicala. "We don't have confirmation yet of her true identity," he cautioned. "So it might not be your granddaughter."

Daisy's face was something carved of wood. She didn't blink, didn't move a muscle.

Nyla finally said, "Granny?"

"I knew." Daisy's words were hardly audible. "I knew. I just didn't want to open my heart to it."

Nyla put her arms around the woman. "I'm here for you, Granny. Me and Mom, we're here for you."

"Like I said, we don't have confirmation of identity yet," Monte offered.

"Don't matter. I know it's her." Daisy patted Nyla's hand and said, "Will you get the picture from my bedroom? You know the one."

"Sure, Granny." The girl disappeared into the back room and returned a moment later with a framed drawing. She handed it to Daisy, who looked at it a long time as tears began to gather in her eyes. She held it up for them to see. It was a pastel rendering of Daisy Blacksmith that made her look quite lovely.

"Fawn did this. She said she wanted to capture the true me. She said I was beautiful."

Now the tears began to flow down her cheeks. There were several long moments of silence while Daisy wept.

"I wonder if you have a photograph of Fawn that we could take," Monte said gently.

Daisy nodded. "On my dresser, Nyla."

The girl came back with a framed photo of a smiling young woman proudly holding up a wooden plaque.

"She got that for a picture she drew at the school she was at for a while, the one for problem kids. Contest they had. She got first place," Daisy said. "Can I have it back?"

"Of course, we'll return it," Monte assured her. He stood and took the photograph. "We'll stay in touch," he promised.

Daisy gave a nod.

"Thanks, Nyla," Agent Shirley said. "Take care of her."

"Like she's took care of me," Nyla promised.

Outside, the dog next door started barking again, and again the disembodied voice hollered, "Shut up, Lester."

They stood at Monte Bonhomme's Tahoe. From the trailer they'd just left came a long wail of sorrow.

Agent Shirley said, "I wish I could have given her more hope. It might not be Fawn. We really don't know for sure yet."

"The beaded bracelet," Daniel said, as if that settled the matter.

"Doesn't matter if she wasn't Daisy's granddaughter," Monte said. "She's still the granddaughter and daughter of someone else who'll be awash in grief in the end."

Daniel said, "To be Indian is to walk with loss. It goes before us and it follows us. It is our shadow self." When he saw Monte and Agent Shirley staring at him, he said, "From a poem I wrote a while back."

"You're a poet?" Agent Shirley said.

"Used to be," Daniel said.

"Won himself a slew of awards," Monte said.

"But you're not a poet anymore?" Agent Shirley asked.

"I got tired of writing only sad poems." Daniel said. Then to the tribal police chief he said, "So what now, Monte?"

"Whoever buried Fawn knew about Paavola's blueberry patch.

And whoever killed Olivia Hamilton knew about Paavola's cabin. That old Finn's property is the connection. What do you know about Erno Paavola, Daniel?"

"Not much. I didn't know the man. But Cork did."

"All right, then. Let's go talk to your father-in-law."

CHAPTER 21

The main highway to Spirit Crossing had been blocked by a police barricade a quarter mile from the bridge over the Jiibay River. For nearly a quarter mile in advance of the barricade, the shoulders of the highway were lined with parked vehicles. Stephen and Belle were ahead in Stephen's Jeep. Rainy, Annie, and Maria followed in the Bronco. Stephen pulled over and parked and Rainy drew up behind him. They got out and joined the stream of people heading toward Spirit Crossing. A couple of hundred yards beyond the barricade was the encampment, from which the sound of drumming came like distant thunder.

"Plenty of folks rallied up for this," Rainy said.

"There are going to be two groups," Belle said. "One will protest at the encampment, the other at the Crossing."

"Where should we be?" Annie asked.

"Take your pick," Stephen said. "Belle's going to stay at the encampment. I think the bulk of the confrontation will be there. Rainy, there could be injuries, so you might be needed. Belle's brother Anton is with the group at the Crossing to keep the focus on the reason we're all here. That's where I'll be."

"Do you need someone with medical training there?" Maria asked.

"It might be helpful. It's hard to know how things will play out. Would you be willing to come with me?"

"Of course."

"Then that's where I'll be, too," Annie said.

A solid line of protesters had already linked arms, standing between two bulldozers and the dozens of tents and shelters that made up the encampment. A cadre of law enforcement officers stood ready to ensure compliance with the order to evacuate the site, which had been issued by a judge in the state's Ninth Judicial District, a man Belle claimed was in the pocket of the pipeline company.

"The order came late yesterday. They knew we'd file to stay it," Belle said. "So these bastards were ready and they've hurried things along to get it done before our request can be ruled on."

"What's with the bulldozers?" Annie asked.

"Those blades'll knock down any shelters left standing," Belle replied. "Then they'll bring in front loaders to scoop up everything, put it in dump trucks, and haul it away."

"Looks like nobody's taking their tents down," Annie pointed out.

"Or planning to get out of the way of the bulldozers," Rainy added.

"Like I said," Stephen told her, "things could get really heated today."

They split up, and Stephen, Annie, and Maria continued toward the river and Spirit Crossing. In a meadow midway to the river, a fleet of law enforcement vehicles had parked. It was clear from the insignia on the doors that they represented a number of agencies—local law enforcement, state troopers, and oddly, Annie thought, Customs and Border Protection. There were ambulances standing by as well. Annie could feel the grip of dread in her gut.

"This could get really bad," she said.

"Water cannons, tear gas, LRAD, which are sound cannons. They've all been used before," Stephen said. "At a place called Standing Rock in North Dakota. I was in school so couldn't be there, but I heard about it."

The day was hot already, and Annie felt sweat wetting the back of the T-shirt she'd chosen to wear, maroon with an image of a colorful parrot, a Mayan ruin, and, in bold letters, GUATEMALA. She was already feeling a little weak and was praying silently that she would get through whatever was ahead without stumbling or trembling or being felled by a headache. She wanted to contribute and not be one of those in need of help.

They turned up the dirt lane that two days earlier Annie and Maria had taken with Rainy when they'd been stopped by the bullies at the barricade and then harassed by a security cop. Because the main highway had already been blocked to traffic, there was no barricade today, and protesters streamed toward Spirit Crossing.

It was inspiring to Annie to see so many people willing to put themselves in harm's way in protest of what seemed to be an unstoppable monster. There were billions of dollars behind the pipeline, governmental approvals at so many levels, the possibility of jail time for those who stood in the way, and yet here they were, regular folks, young and old, of many ethnic backgrounds, standing together in the face of huge odds. The vehicles parked along the shoulder of the road had license plates not just from Minnesota but from as far away as New Jersey and California. She was, Annie realized, part of a small, dedicated ragtag army from far and wide. In her heart, she believed that in the end they would fail. But it moved her deeply to see that they would not go down without a fight, and she was proud to be among them.

The big machines still sat idle, with a phalanx of protesters several deep standing symbolically between them and the place on the river that the Anishinaabeg called Spirit Crossing. Annie estimated the protesters numbered more than a hundred. At the encampment, she'd guessed there were twice as many, and they'd still been arriving.

"Stay near me," Stephen said. "If things get wild, keep track of each other. If somehow we get separated, plan to rendezvous back at the bridge, okay?"

Annie and Maria followed Stephen and became part of the phalanx near the river. A large gathering of law enforcement officers stood on the far side of the big machines, just observing at the moment but dressed in riot gear. Among them, Annie saw Deputy Carlson, who, the last time she had been there, had let them pass through the barricade the bullies had established and then admonished the security guard named Lewis, who'd been intent on arresting Stephen.

"Lewis!" Annie said suddenly.

Stephen and Maria both gave her quizzical looks.

"The man at the Four Seasons and then when I had my episode in town. It was Lewis."

"Who's Lewis?" Stephen asked.

"The security cop who tried to arrest us."

Stephen frowned. "You're sure?

"I couldn't place him in Aurora. He was out of uniform. But yes, I'm sure."

"He followed you?"

"He must have."

"Why?" Maria asked.

"I don't know. I just know it was him."

"Is he here?" Stephen began scanning the small army of law enforcement.

Annie looked, too. "I don't see him."

Drumming began and a woman with a bullhorn chanted, "Mother Earth Not Dirty Dollars!" The crowd joined in, and Annie felt the energy in the air start to change, crackling as if electric.

Suddenly, the woman with the bullhorn rushed forward and a man from the crowd ran with her. She moved with catlike quickness as she mounted the nearest machine, a great earthmover with its huge bucket poised just above the ground. The bucket's teeth pointed toward the earth so that its back formed a slightly curved but sturdy platform. And that's where the woman and her companion took up their position. Annie saw that her agility belied her age. She wasn't young. Her hair was fully grayed, her face deeply lined. She wore a tie-dyed T-shirt and feather earrings, and around her neck hung an intricately beaded medallion.

As she and her companion scrambled onto the earthmover, a kind of ripple went through the line of law enforcement officers, as if a great beast were testing its muscles, but no one in uniform moved yet to intervene.

Once the two protesters were perched atop the bucket, the woman held the bullhorn to her mouth and the drumming ceased.

"My name is Lorna Wigmore. I am Mikisew Cree First Nation from Canada. I'm here with you to stop the relentless destruction of Mother Earth. The oil this pipeline will carry begins with a great wounding of the land of my people. The forests where as a child I walked freely are gone, torn out by their roots. In their place is black mud as far as the eye can see, laced with killing chemicals. We are dying from the cancers caused by the heavy metals and hydrocarbons and acids that have leached into the water we drink. It is in our food, in the fish we eat, in the animals we hunt and trap. As the mining and the drilling expand, we have been forced to leave the villages that have been our homes for centuries. I weep for my people. I weep for Mother Earth. And I will fight with my last breath against the greed at the heart of this killing. Are you with me?"

In response, she received an enthusiastic cry of "Yes!" from the deep line of protesters that surrounded Annie.

The Cree woman handed the bullhorn to the man who'd mounted the bucket with her. Stephen leaned to Annie and said, "That's Anton, Belle's brother."

He was a commanding figure, powerful looking as he stood erect on the great machine. His hair was long and ebony and hung draped over both shoulders. He wore a black T-shirt with PEOPLE BEFORE PROFITS printed in bold white letters across the chest. He put the bullhorn to his lips.

"My name is Anton Morriseau. I am Leech Lake Anishinaabe. I am here because this pipeline, if it continues to be built, will cross land sacred to the Anishinaabeg. It will cross wetlands that not only are home to so many wild and beautiful creatures but also provide the wild rice that our people have harvested since our ancestors first came here centuries ago. The streams and rivers give us the water we drink and cook with and bathe in.

"The oil people tell us that the pipeline is safe. That's bullshit. To the west, the Keystone Pipeline, which that company claimed would be the safest ever built, has leaked millions of gallons of crude oil in at least twenty-two separate spills in the last dozen years. These people lie. They lie for money. They lie to protect their profits. They lie to feed the insatiable hunger for oil in a world where our climate is collapsing. And they expect us to swallow those lies. A mile away, they're preparing to destroy the village we built to shelter us in our battle here. With their bulldozers, they hope to wipe us out. They want us to stand aside and meekly let this happen. I, for one, refuse to do that. Are you with me?"

The cry in response was a resounding "Yes!"

"Then will we stand together to protect Mother Earth?"

The response was another "Yes!"

Anton Morriseau raised the bullhorn to his mouth once more, but before he spoke another word the melee began.

What happened would always be a confusion in Annie's memory. Whether it was the protesters who poured forward or the police, she couldn't recall. All she remembered was that very quickly the protest had turned into a riot. The crowd broke and uniforms seemed to be among them everywhere. Screams arose and bodies flew past her. She lost track of Maria and Stephen and found herself pushed along with a group of protesters who were surging toward the machines.

Her head exploded, all pain and blinding lights. She stumbled and the crowd swarmed past her. She went to her knees and dropped the shoulder bag she'd brought with her, the one gifted to her by Maria. She tried to reach for it, but the pain was like a black curtain and she squeezed her eyes shut against it.

When she opened them, she saw him. He stood above her, glaring down from a face framed by a riot helmet. She looked up into his eyes and all she saw before she blacked out was pure hatred.

Annie woke in a groggy haze. She lay in the shade of a birch tree. Sunlight, broken into bright shards by leaves and branches, littered the ground around her. She was not alone.

"She will be all right," she heard Maria say.

"You're sure? This has happened before?" A man's voice.

"Yes."

"I'm all right," Annie managed to say.

"Can you sit up?" Maria asked.

"Help me."

Maria and a man in a police uniform gently lifted Annie and helped her scoot backward so that she sat against the trunk of the birch. She realized that she was in a small grove of trees that stood along the bank of the Jiibay River. She couldn't see any of the big machines or the crowd of protesters, though she could still hear angry shouts from somewhere distant. Stephen was gone.

"Where am I?" Annie asked.

"We carried you here," Maria said.

"We?" She looked at the officer, who was very near to her, down on one knee.

"Deputy Chet Carlson," he said. "We met a couple of days ago."

"I remember. You stopped Stephen from getting arrested." Annie looked around in a sudden panic. "Where's the other one?"

"Other one?"

"The one who tried to arrest me and my brother."

"Lewis? He was fired."

"Why?"

"I reported him. He'd already been a pain the ass, but that screwup with you and your brother was the last straw."

"He was here."

Carlson scowled. "You saw him?"

"Just before I . . . just before everything . . ."

"Was he in his uniform?"

"Yes."

"Did he hurt you?"

"I thought he was going to. Then I blacked out." Annie closed her eyes a moment. Her head no longer hurt, but she felt exhausted, drained. It was like that after an episode. "Where's Stephen?"

"I don't know," Maria said. "We got separated."

"I need to be going." Deputy Carlson peered with real concern into Annie's eyes. "You're sure you're all right?"

"Yes," Annie said. "And thank you."

The deputy hesitated a moment before leaving. "Look," he

said to them. "Not everyone wearing a badge thinks what's going on here is right. I'm concerned about our environment too. It's just . . . well, I've got a job and a duty."

"Thank you for your kindness," Maria said.

Deputy Carlson tipped the brim of his hat, then left the birch trees.

Now Annie could hear more clearly the sound of voices, distant, still raised in shouts of protest.

"It's not over?" she asked.

"For you it is. We'll find the others and get you home."

"My shoulder bag," Annie said, suddenly remembering.

"It's here." Maria gave it to her, then took her hand to help her up.

But Annie didn't move. "I was a star athlete in high school. Did you know that, Maria? I wanted to be the first female pitcher for the Minnesota Twins. Now look at me. I can't do anything without stumbling or blacking out."

Maria kissed the top of her head. "You are strong. And you are beautiful."

"I don't feel that way."

"It is how I see you. It is how I will always see you. Come."

But before Annie could rise, she had a sudden realization that made her grip Maria's hand fiercely. "Lewis," she said.

"What about him?"

"Maybe he was the one in the truck outside our house last night." She looked up into Maria's dark eyes and felt herself go rigid with a combination of rising anger and deep concern. "There's nothing but hatred in that man. If it was him, he knows who we are and he knows where we live."

CHAPTER 22

It was early afternoon when Cork headed back to Aurora. Jenny wanted to stay with her son, so Cork left Crow Point the way he'd come, in the company of Theresa Lee.

"Did you get what you needed?" he asked as they walked the long path to the double-trunk birch.

"There's something unique about that place. It comforts the soul."

"Henry says it's always been that way, the reason it called to his spirit in the first place."

"Your grandson seems happy there. Which is good. He has a lot he'll have to deal with in his life. I hope Henry stays alive long enough to help guide him."

Cork smiled. "We all hope Henry will live forever."

They were quiet for a long while, letting the feel of the woods, the calling of the birds, the sunlit darting of insects fill their senses. The walk to and from Crow Point had always been a time of contemplation for Cork.

"Your little Waaboo told me that Fawn is still trying to find her way to cross to the other side," Theresa said.

"Still looking for the Path of Souls."

"Even though I'm Ojibwe, I admit that I've always thought the idea of actually crossing to the other side, walking some spiritual path, was just a metaphor. Now I wonder. And I think about Fawn, whoever she is, or was, and it saddens me to think of her as lost."

"I've been to a lot of burial ceremonies, traditional Anishinaabe, Catholic, Protestant. They all have one thing in common, it seems to me. They help us say goodbye. Part of it, I'm sure, is just support in our grieving and a way to move on. But I've always thought that there is this *something* that connects us to the spirit of the dead, this *something* that assures us of a life beyond this world, a better existence. If my grandson is somehow more in touch with that *something*, maybe he can help lost souls like Fawn." Cork took a deep breath. "It is, as Henry said, a heavy burden for the little guy."

Theresa reached out and placed her hand gently on his arm. "And for those who love him."

They arrived at the double-trunk birch, and as Cork climbed into his Expedition, he got a call on his cell phone.

"Monte and I would like to have a talk with you as soon as possible," Daniel said without preamble.

"Fine. I'm on my way back to Aurora now. Let's meet somewhere. Not Gooseberry Lane. The news vultures could still be hovering."

"How about the sheriff's office?" Daniel suggested. "Marsha Dross might like to be in on this, too."

"Where are you?"

"Driving back from the Three Rivers rez. We should be in Aurora in about an hour."

"I'll call Marsha and meet you there."

He dropped Theresa Lee at her home, then just to satisfy his curiosity, he headed to Gooseberry Lane and paused at the intersection up the block from his house. There were no media vans in evidence, but that didn't mean someone wasn't still staked out somewhere waiting to pounce. He drove on.

"The body in the cabin has been officially identified as that of Olivia Hamilton. Now that she's been found, the FBI is withdrawing their agents. From now on, BCA is in charge," Dross told them after they'd gathered in her office. "Although they're focused on the Hamilton girl, they're willing to give us any help they can regarding the body in the blueberry patch. There's still no confirmation that it's Fawn Blacksmith. I've requested BCA obtain dental records, if possible, for comparison."

"The beaded bracelet the buried girl was wearing nails it for me," Daniel said. "Daisy Blacksmith told us she gave her granddaughter a bracelet that she'd beaded herself."

"Of course, we'll need to show Daisy a photo of the bracelet to confirm they're the same," Agent Shirley said.

"BCA should check with the North Regional Juvenile Detention Center," Daniel said. "Fawn spent time there."

"Also, there's a school for problem kids where Fawn spent some time," Monte Bonhomme threw in. "I can check with Chris Hayner, see if he knows the name of the place."

"From everything we learned in Deer County, I think we can operate on the pretty solid assumption that it's Fawn," Agent Shirley said. "Except for the location of the bodies, I just can't see a connection with the murder of Olivia Hamilton. But there's got to be one."

"Erno Paavola didn't operate much with money," Cork said. "He did a lot of bartering. If he paid me in blueberries, chances are he paid someone else in the same way."

"So," Dross said, looking glum, "there could be a lot of folks in Tamarack County who know about that blueberry patch."

"But not a lot who'd know about that bunker under Paavola's cabin," Daniel said.

"Which brings us back to Mathias Paavola, who's dropped off the radar," Cork said.

Bonhomme said, "Tell me about your investigation of the night Olivia Hamilton went missing. Any indication at all that Paavola was at the Howling Wolf?"

"We got the call at eleven twenty-three P.M.," Dross began. "Altercation at the bar. By the time my guys responded, the worst of it was over. Cy Cedarholm, who owns the bar, didn't want to press any charges. But that was when Harvey Green, the kid who brought Olivia Hamilton there, claims to have lost track of her. Claims he looked high and low before going back to the camp."

"But he didn't report her missing?"

"Not until the folks at the camp became aware that Olivia was gone. The kid might not have fessed up except another counselor ratted on him. We leaned on Green hard. It was clear the kid probably didn't have anything to do with her disappearance aside from helping her sneak off to the Howling Wolf. He told us she seemed pretty comfortable with the rough crowd there.

"The problem is that we don't really have a good idea who all was at the bar that night. We got a list of sorts from the bartender and the barmaids. Some of them were regulars or semis at least. And we can't be certain we got every name in that biker gang from Fargo. Pretty uncooperative bunch. So . . ." Dross shook her head. "We could well have missed someone. But that's as far as we got before the Feds and the BCA came in and took over the investigation."

"I've got the photo Paavola's sister gave me," Cork said. "Why don't I have Cedarholm and whoever was working there that night take a look, see if they recognize Paavola and if they saw him at the bar when Olivia Hamilton was there."

"If he was there that night, it might explain Olivia Hamilton, but what about Fawn Blacksmith?" Agent Shirley said.

Cork shrugged. "Pull one thread, maybe it's attached to another."

"I'm going with you," Dross said.

"I've been thinking about Fawn Blacksmith," Bonhomme put in. "Her grandmother told us that before she went to that school for problem kids, she'd been living in a house with a bunch of druggies in Duluth. I'm wondering if she might have gone back after her release from the detention center. I'd like to know about that house and who was in it. I've got a friend in Duluth PD. I'll give him a call, see if he can track down an address for me."

"I can't help thinking maybe there's more that Waaboo might sense at the blueberry patch," Daniel said. "Something that might help us understand what happened to Fawn."

"He was just out there yesterday," Cork said. "You can't be serious about taking him back."

"He was at the cabin yesterday. That was about Olivia Hamilton. This is about Fawn. The blueberry patch is where Waaboo touched her spirit."

"Jenny'll kill you."

"I think I have to try."

"What do you want written on your headstone?"

"Maybe I can enlist Uncle Henry's help."

"Now I'm thinking two headstones," Cork said.

"Let us know if you're still alive and if you've got anything," Bonhomme said.

As they dispersed it felt to Cork as if they were dandelion seeds catching the wind, and God alone knew where they might end up.

Cork knew Yellow Lake and the Howling Wolf well. The bar had been a thorn in his side when he was sheriff of Tamarack County, a frequent source of incident reports.

"If I could, I'd put a fence around the joint with barbed wire on top," Dross said as they drove to the tiny community.

"When my dad was sheriff, he tried to close the place down," Cork said. "Back then it was mostly loggers who drank there. The county commissioner was part owner of the place, and Dad got nowhere. When I was sheriff, I tried to get an ordinance passed about the number of calls we would respond to before we began to charge the bar for our time. Trouble was that whenever an altercation occurred, even if things started inside the bar, Cedarholm made certain that it took place outside, usually in the street. Broke up some big to-dos in my time."

"It hasn't changed," Dross said.

"Figured as much."

The town of Yellow Lake was a smattering of run-down abodes and trailer houses set among pines next to a small body of water that was more mire than lake, more likely to attract mosquitoes than investment. It was on no main highway, so unlikely to get unwary visitors. You had to want to get lost to go to Yellow Lake, and the Howling Wolf provided the alcohol to do just that. It was an old log construction, with a dirt parking area. When Dross pulled her cruiser to a stop, there were a half dozen other parked vehicles, all of them pickups covered in a patina of road dust and dried mud.

It was midafternoon, and when Cork stepped inside the bar, it was so dark that it took a few moments for his eyes to adjust. When they did, he saw the faces of the drinking men turned his way, all of them stone. They weren't so much eyeing him as they were Dross in her sheriff's uniform. Two of the men got up from their chairs and walked out. The others, after a few moments, simply turned back to their drinks. No one said a word.

Cy Cedarholm stood behind the bar. His head was as bald and smooth as a river boulder, and just as big. His arms were like sections cut from the trunk of an oak tree and fitted to either side of his massive chest. His eyes were as black as beetles that had dug into the skin below his jutting brow. He looked like a man who could handle trouble as easily as most people could swat a fly.

"Jesus Christ, ain't I been harassed enough?" Cedarholm said.

"Not by me, Cy," Dross replied, walking up to the bar.

"Ain't seen you in a month of Sundays, O'Connor. Which is just fine with me. You ain't a cop anymore, so what the hell are you doing here?"

"Just along for the ride, Cy."

Dross had printed a photo of Mathias Paavola from the birthday picture his sister had texted to Cork. She put the photo on the bar and slid it toward Cedarholm. "Familiar?"

Cedarholm said, "No."

"You didn't even look at it, Cy," Cork said.

Cedarholm lowered his black beetle eyes for a nanosecond. "No."

"Take a good look," Dross said.

Cedarholm picked up the photo, studied it, put it back down on the bar, and said, "Like I said, never seen him before."

"Who was working here the night Olivia Hamilton went missing?"

"I'm always here."

"Behind the bar. What about your barmaids?"

"They been talked to by cops till they're silly. Don't bother them no more, okay?"

"Their names, Cy."

"Look, they're about to quit on me. This whole Hamilton girl thing. You go harassing them, and I swear if they do quit—"

"Names, Cy," Dross said.

He offered them reluctantly, and Dross wrote them down.

"Got addresses?"

"Use a phone book."

The bar brightened for a moment, and Cork turned back to where the door had just been opened. He saw one of the customers walking out.

"Jesus, see that?" Cedarholm said. "You're killing my business."

Cork eyed a gnome carved of wood perched above the liquor shelves behind the bar. The craftmanship looked familiar. "Tell me about Erno Paavola."

"What about him?"

"Regular customer?"

"He came in sometimes. Heard he died a while back."

"Did he pay for his drinks or did he barter?"

"I don't remember."

"I'm pretty sure that's his handiwork up there."

Cedarholm glanced to where Cork was pointing at the gnome. "Yeah, maybe."

"Did he happen to barter anything else? Blueberries maybe?"

"I don't remember. Look, are we done here? I got a bar to run."

"Don't be taking any vacations for a while," Dross said. "We may want to talk to you some more."

They left. As they headed toward the sheriff's cruiser, someone hollered, "Hey!"

The man stood at the side of the Howling Wolf, in the shadow the building cast. With a flick of his hand, he motioned them to him. Cork realized he was the customer who'd just left the bar. He was maybe in his late forties, with a brown beard that reached nearly to his chest. He wore a stained green ball cap and, although it was hot, a flannel shirt with its sleeves rolled up to his biceps, which were like bowling balls. Cork figured him to be a logger.

"Mind if I have a look at that photo?" the man asked.

"Why?" Dross said.

"Might know him."

She pulled the photo from the pocket of her uniform blouse and handed it over. The man studied it, then said, "Seen him a few times. Usually comes in with another guy. Work buddies, I gather. That pipeline, as I understand it."

"Got a name for this other guy?" Cork asked.

The man shook his head.

"Can you describe him?"

"Maybe six feet. Good build on him."

"Hair color?"

"Always wears a stocking cap, no matter how hot it is. Pretty sure it's because he's got this funny-looking ear, kind of misshaped. You only notice it if the stocking cap rides up a bit and you look at him from the side. Right side, I think."

"Anything else?" Dross said.

"That guy with the bad ear, he never talks about women without calling them sluts."

"Were they here the night Olivia Hamilton went missing?"

"Don't know. Wasn't here that night."

"Mind giving me your name?"

He spelled it for her, and Dross wrote it down, along with a cell phone number.

Cork said, "Why are you helping us?"

"I got a daughter," the man said. "And I hate the word *slut*."

CHAPTER 23

Waaboo wasn't on Crow Point. Jenny explained to Daniel that he'd gone into the woods with Meloux and Prophet, who were teaching him how to track.

"Deer?" Daniel asked.

"People," Jenny said. "Prophet is leaving a trail, and Henry is showing Waaboo how to read the signs."

"I could have shown him that."

"You've been busy. How's it going?"

Daniel filled her in.

"That poor woman," she said when she'd heard about Daisy Blacksmith. "To lose your child and your grandchild, my God." She looked across the meadow toward the deep woods where, Daniel assumed, Waaboo had gone. "It would kill me to lose our son."

"Native people lose family all the time. To alcohol or drugs or gangs or jail or they just go missing."

"Like Crystal Two Knives?"

"Like Crystal."

"Still bothers you," she said.

"The numbers bother me. So many. But I knew Crystal. I should have been able to do more."

"Do you think she's . . . like Fawn Blacksmith?"

"She's been gone a long time. Not much hope left. I keep thinking of her lying buried in a shallow grave somewhere."

"Do you think you have a chance of arresting whoever is responsible for Fawn Blacksmith's murder?"

"We're pulling threads, as your dad put it. We'll see what unravels."

"Here they come," Jenny said.

Daniel saw them, too. The old man, a little bent and using his staff. The strong, erect figure of Prophet. And between them, the young boy who, along with his mother, took up almost all the room in Daniel's heart.

When Waaboo saw his father, he ran ahead.

"Guess what I've been doing!"

"I heard. Tracking."

"Come on, Daddy. Let's go into the woods and I'll track you."

Meloux had reached them and he said, "I think you have had enough practice for one day, Little Rabbit." Meloux eyed Daniel and said, "And I think your father has had a full day of tracking, too."

"Will you stay for supper?" Prophet asked. "We've got plenty."

"*Miigwech*," Daniel said.

"Can I go swimming again?" Waaboo asked.

"It will take me a while to put the meal together," Prophet said. "I'll call you."

"I'll go with you," Jenny told her son. "Coming, Daniel?"

"I'd like to talk to Henry."

Waaboo hurried off toward the lake with Jenny trying to keep up.

They sat on the bench in front of Meloux's cabin with the

late afternoon sun resting on the treetops to the west, casting all of Crow Point in a saffron light. To Daniel, this had always been a place of peace, but at the moment, he didn't feel that peace inside him.

"You spent the day tracking in your own way," Meloux said. "What did you find?"

"A woman whose heart has been broken too many times."

"That is the blessing of the heart. It can be broken again and again and still it heals."

"But so much pain, Uncle Henry. So much loss. Our people carry it like a great stone."

"And yet we walk strong."

"Not all of us."

"You cannot lift up every person who stumbles and falls, Daniel English."

"Not every person, maybe. But I ought to be able to help those I know about."

"And so?"

"Uncle Henry, I'd like to take Waaboo back to the blueberry patch."

"To what end?"

"If the spirit of Fawn Blacksmith hasn't begun to walk the Path of Souls yet, maybe there's more to learn that might help us understand what happened to her."

"I have never seen anything more fierce than a mother bear protecting her cub."

"I don't understand."

"You will when you suggest this to your wife."

"I'm asking for your help."

"I am afraid of mother bears, too."

"Like you said, Uncle Henry, I can't help everyone, but I can help some. Maybe help this girl's spirit find rest. Maybe help her grandmother find closure. Maybe keep some other lost girl from being grabbed by predators."

"Your ambition is noble. But Mother Bear will be ferocious."

"That's why I'd like your help. Jenny may not listen to me, but she might listen to you."

The old man thought this over, then gave a nod. He sat back against the side of his cabin and closed his eyes. In the late golden light of the day, his face was like a warm fire. "I will talk to her with you."

"That will help, I'm sure, Uncle Henry. *Chi miigwech.*"

"I am old. I am ready for death. If it is at the hands of an angry she-bear, so be it."

"No," Jenny said. "Absolutely not."

"It might help."

"You saw what happened the last time you took him there. He was scared to death."

Waaboo had gone to bed, sleeping in the cabin where Prophet had slept before Jenny and Daniel's son had come seeking shelter on Crow Point. Prophet now slept in a tent among the birches on the shoreline of the lake. At the moment, he stood inside Meloux's cabin, with his back against the wall, listening to Daniel plead his case with Jenny, who sat with Meloux at the little birchwood table Meloux had made himself decades before. The sun had finally set and the twilight sky outside the cabin was sapphire. Meloux had not yet put a flame in one of his kerosene lanterns, and the cabin was lit only with a dismal ghost of light that slipped through the old man's windows.

"Uncle Henry will be there with him," Daniel argued.

"You're a part of this, Henry?" Jenny shot the old man a killing look.

"I am here to offer what I can, only that."

"I don't care what you say. I'm not letting Waaboo go back to that cursed place."

"Jenny, there were two young women murdered by someone who's still out there. Maybe right now he's planning to prey on some other young woman. Don't you want me to stop him if I can?"

"That's your job, not Waaboo's."

"But he might be able to help me."

"At what cost? Do you want him traumatized?"

"Waaboo has a gift. We can't protect him forever."

"I'll protect him as long as I can."

"So will I. I won't let anything happen to our son, I swear to you. And if he can help stop others from being hurt, from being killed, shouldn't we do all we can to guide him in that way?"

Jenny lowered her head, and her body seemed to lose spirit, as if she were a balloon emptying of air. "I'm just afraid, Daniel."

"To be afraid is to be human," Meloux said gently.

Jenny lifted her head. "Are you ever afraid, Henry?"

The old man smiled. "There is not much that stands between me and the Path of Souls now, not much that I fear for myself. But I am sometimes afraid for those who still have a long journey ahead of them."

"Like Waaboo."

"And many others. They will need courage, which is something I cannot give them because courage comes from within. The best I can do is help them find it in themselves."

"Courage? In a boy of seven?"

"He has already shown that he has a brave heart. Did he not return to the place of the *maji-manidoog*?"

"If you remember, he refused to set foot in that blueberry patch again."

"He may make a different choice this time. And is that choice not his to make?"

"I won't force him, Jenny, I promise," Daniel said. "But can I at least ask him?"

"Don't you remember how afraid he was that someone might know about him, what he sees?"

"I love him. He's my son, too. I would die before I'd let anyone hurt him."

Jenny stared at Daniel, and her eyes were knives. "I may hate you for this."

Daniel felt a crack go all the way across his heart. "I know," he said.

CHAPTER 24

There were injuries at the Spirit Crossing protest, and Maria stayed with Rainy to help. Stephen took Annie back to Aurora, a drive of just over an hour. The whole way, Annie struggled to understand what had happened at Spirit Crossing. Had she really seen the man named Lewis or had she imagined him? Hallucinations had sometimes been a part of the episodes of her blinding headaches. If the encounter was real, what was the source of the hatred she'd seen in him? Was it directed at her, or was it just a part of some larger pool of violent emotion stirred up by the protests?

"You're awfully quiet," Stephen said. "You okay?"

"Yeah," Annie said, a little too quickly. "Sorry you had to take me home. I know you'd rather be at Spirit Crossing, helping there."

"Family first," Stephen said. "I'll drop you off, then go back to see what I can do. So, what's going on, Annie? What is it with these episodes, as you call them?"

"Nothing. A reaction to some medication I'm taking," she said, lying.

"What medication?"

"It wouldn't mean anything to you."

"What's it for?"

"Something I picked up in Guatemala."

"Is it serious?"

"Let's talk about something else. What do you think he's up to?"

"Who?"

"Lewis."

"He's pissed. We got him fired. Well, we didn't. That was his own stupid doing. Guys like that, they screw up, then blame everyone but themselves."

"He looked more than just pissed, Stephen. He looked ready to kill."

"If that's true, it's a good thing we're getting you away from there."

"But if he was the one in the truck outside our house last night, we might not be safe there. If murder is in his heart, we might not be safe anywhere."

She saw how he looked at her, as if her fear was overblown, a paranoid speculation.

"When I was in Guatemala," she explained, "there wasn't any safety at home. Gangs, soldiers, you name it could burst through your door at any moment."

"Did they break down *your* door?"

"No, but I saw it happen to others."

"And it made you afraid." He said this as if he'd diagnosed her current fear.

"Actually I wasn't afraid. At least not for me. I was afraid for all the vulnerable people. We marched, Stephen. Once we walked right up to a line of soldiers with their rifles pointed at us."

"You never mentioned that in any of your emails."

"I didn't want you to worry about me. So . . ." She put a hand on his arm. "Don't worry about me now."

"Are you saying I shouldn't worry about whatever this medication that you won't talk about is for?"

"You worry about your wedding. I'll worry about my health."

It was late afternoon when they turned down Gooseberry Lane, the trees casting long shadows over the lawns. The street was empty of media vans.

"Looks like the vultures finally gave up waiting for one of us to come home," Stephen said. "That or they got a lead on some other lurid story and flew off to harass someone else."

Stephen saw Annie inside the house. "Lock the doors after I'm gone. And you might want to keep the phone unplugged in case the vultures keep calling."

She said she would.

"Get some rest," he advised. "Honestly, you look like death warmed over."

When he'd gone, she checked all the doors to be sure they were locked, made certain the the landline was still unplugged, then lay down on the sofa to rest. The house was silent around her, something that should have made resting easier. But she found instead that she was listening intently, poised to leap into action at the smallest of sounds. She realized that she was, indeed, afraid. She recalled seeing a baseball bat, her old Louisville Slugger, in the back of the hallway closet. She got up, went and grabbed it, and was amazed at how familiar that stick of wood felt in her grip. Her father had given her the bat when she'd first started playing softball. He would toss the ball to her in the backyard, and she'd swing the bat. Eventually, she swung with great power and precision. When she hit a ball that shattered an attic window, they'd moved their practice to the park.

Bat in hand, she walked to the front window and drew the curtain aside just enough to look outside.

She hadn't told Stephen the truth of her condition, but what she'd told him about walking arm and arm with Maria and others right up to the phalanx of soldiers was absolutely true. She'd felt some apprehension that day in Guatemala, of course, but mostly she'd felt exhilaration in the boldness of the challenge.

It was easy to have courage when you walked arm and arm with others, she thought now. Alone, it wasn't so easy to be brave.

She stood at the front window, staring at the empty street, very glad that the media vans had moved somewhere else. She hadn't come home to be a part of some circus. She'd come home to . . . to do what? Simply die? She could have done that in Guatemala, with Maria at her side. Was it solely for Stephen's wedding? She was happy for him, of course, but it wasn't just that. She'd come, she knew, in the hope of doing battle with death.

In Guatemala, the doctors had given her no hope. Death was all that was left to her there. She and Maria had flown to Mexico City to get a second opinion, which only confirmed what the doctors in Guatemala had told her. Everything in Annie had bridled at the prognosis because she had no intention of going gently into that good night. She'd always been the rebellious O'Connor. She'd been an athlete, involved in the game, not a sideline cheerleader. She'd been a voice, never an echo. Although as far back as she could remember she'd wanted to be a nun, when the time had come to yield her will to the Church, she had opted not to take the vows. And so death, as it approached, was a prospect that angered her, made her ready for battle. Even as the doctors had told her there was no cure, no hope, she'd thought that somewhere, somehow there must be a way. For Annie O'Connor, it was a choice either to go meekly like a lamb to the slaughter or to fight it with all the strength of will she could muster.

Home, she'd thought, would give her strength. But it hadn't. Every day, she felt weaker. Every day, she felt the erosion of her will to fight. And these damn headaches, the blackouts that sometimes followed, they were like knives slicing off pieces of her will-power, pieces of her very soul.

She felt exhausted and lay back down on the sofa. She put her Louisville Slugger within easy reach. She wished Maria were there. She closed her eyes, thinking that, when the time came, what she would hate most was losing Maria forever.

She hadn't realized that she'd drifted into sleep until the little cry of the springs on the mudroom door woke her. She was instantly alert. She sat up too quickly and, for a moment, felt dizzy. She let that pass, then hurried to the window. It was twilight, the street bathed in pale blue. There was no vehicle parked in the drive or on the street. No one from the O'Connor household had come home.

She tried to remember, had she really made sure all the doors were locked?

She heard the back door of the kitchen, which led onto the mudroom, open, then close.

She stood in the semidarkness of the evening, terribly aware that she was no longer alone in the house.

She grabbed the Louisville Slugger. It still felt familiar in her grip, like an old friend. She crept to the kitchen doorway and stood off to the side, with her back to the dining room wall.

The man stepped from the kitchen. Annie let him pass, then brought the bat up to strike. He must have sensed her presence and turned. When he saw the bat, he quickly lifted his hands in surrender.

"Hold on there, Annie! You remember me? John O'Loughlin, from across the street."

"Of course." She lowered the bat, letting herself breathe again. "Of course. I'm sorry. You just startled me. How did you get in?"

"I have a key. Whenever everyone here is gone, I check on

things, water the plants, et cetera. It's what neighbors do. Cork has a key to my house."

"What are you doing here now?"

"Your dad tried to call you but didn't get an answer. With everything that's been going on, he was worried, asked me to check." He studied her. "Are you okay?"

"I'm fine. Really, I'm fine."

He nodded toward the Louisville Slugger. "I appreciate that you didn't use my head for ball practice."

"Yeah. Sorry about that."

"So . . . Guess I'm done here. Good to see you."

Annie walked him to the front door. Before he left he asked, "Is it true about Waaboo?"

"Is what true?"

"That he talked to the ghost of Olivia Hamilton?"

"Is that what people are saying?"

"Small town. Word gets around. And then"—he swung his hand toward the street out front—"all those reporters."

"Talked to a ghost? Does that really sound plausible?"

He gave a small laugh. "You're right. Crazy rumor."

"Will you do us a favor? Don't help spread the rumor."

"Of course."

She watched him descend the porch steps and cross the street. She closed and locked the door. She plugged the landline back in, just in case one of her family called.

Then she looked at the baseball bat still in her hand.

She'd almost become a nun. She'd ministered to the poor and the desperate. She'd marched in the name of peace. Had she really been prepared to knock the brains out of someone?

Who am I? Annie wondered. *Who have I become? What is death doing to me?*

For this, she had no answer.

CHAPTER 25

Cork and Marsha Dross interviewed the two barmaids who were serving customers the night Olivia Hamilton went missing. The women recognized the photo of Mathias Paavola, but neither of them could confirm that he was in the bar that night. When Dross asked about the man with the misshapen ear, they both reacted negatively.

"Real bad vibes off him," one of them said.

But because of tension in the bar that night caused by the two biker gangs, neither of them could say for sure whether he'd been there.

It was twilight when Cork and Dross headed back toward Aurora. Cork used his cell phone to call Agent Shirley. He put her on speakerphone and filled her in on their interviews with Cedarholm, the bearded customer, and the two barmaids.

"So, Mathias Paavola was regular enough at the bar to be recognized," Shirley said. "But no confirmation that he was there the night the Hamilton girl went missing."

"That's the size of it," Cork said. "Apparently he didn't usually come alone. But no ID on his drinking buddy."

"And you say there's an Erno Paavola gnome in the bar?" Shirley said. "Bartered?"

"Pretty sure."

"Is it possible, you think, that Paavola bartered blueberries as well?"

"It's possible."

"So this Cedarholm might have known about the blueberry patch. I think we need to sweat him a little more. It's also possible Mathias Paavola told his drinking buddy about the blueberry patch. We need to ID him."

"Not much to go on there. Six feet tall, good build. Brown hair. His most telling features seem to be an odd ear and a habit of harassing women."

"Maybe Paavola's sister can help out," Agent Shirley suggested.

"We'll give that a shot and let you know."

Cork tried calling the number Irene Boyle had given him. When he got no answer, he left a voice message.

"We're less than an hour away," Cork said to Dross. "What do you think? Worth the drive?"

She said, "I don't punch a time clock. You need to get back?"

"I'd rather get a few answers first, if we can."

There was still a faint glow of daylight in the west when they pulled into the driveway of the small rambler in Cloquet. The house was dark. They got no answer when they rang the doorbell, and the same result when they knocked.

"Must've gone out," Dross said.

"Let me check for a car." Cork walked around to the side of the attached garage, where there was a window. He used the flashlight app on his cell phone to illuminate the inside. It was a one-car garage, and the car was there. He returned and reported what he'd found.

"Gone for a walk?" Dross said.

"No lights on inside, so if she's gone for a walk, she left before dark. Long walk."

"Maybe at a neighbor's?"

"Or maybe on her deck and she just can't hear the doorbell?"

"Let's check."

They circled the house to the backyard, which sloped down toward the Saint Louis River. In that last, late light of day, the river's surface was the dark blue of an old bruise. They climbed the half dozen stairs to the redwood deck. There was a round glass-top table with four chairs. A small vase of flowers had been set in the middle of the table.

"Check it out." Cork nodded toward a shattering of glass on the boards of the deck.

The sliding door that led into the dining room had been left open. Dross led the way. "Irene!" she called out. "It's Sheriff Dross! We need to talk!"

The house was sunk in the dimness of twilight, the white walls and carpet and furniture bathed in a dismal blue-gray hue.

"Irene?" Dross said in a loud, commanding voice. When she got no response, she said to Cork, "Check the bedrooms."

There were two, both of them empty. But in the master bedroom, Cork saw that the bedding had been carefully turned back, as if prepared for someone to slip under the covers. He could also smell the faint hint of perfume.

He rejoined Dross, who was in the kitchen, eyeing a counter where a plate sat, arrayed with cheese and crackers. There was also an unopened fifth of Johnnie Walker Black, a whiskey glass, and an empty Perrier bottle.

"She said she's been sober for years," Dross said. "I'm guessing the Perrier was hers."

"The seal on the Johnnie Walker hasn't been broken. So

whoever that was for either didn't show or maybe had a different agenda in mind when he got here."

"That broken glass on the deck is disturbing," Dross said. "Let me try calling her." She tapped in the number on her cell phone. She waited, eyed Cork, shook her head, then said into the phone, "Ms. Boyle, this is Sheriff Marsha Dross. I need to speak with you. It's urgent. Please call me back."

"What do you want to do?" Cork asked.

Dross scanned the empty house. "I think we should give Cloquet PD a call."

Two officers responded, one male, the other female. Dross flashed her badge and explained their presence.

"We have reason to believe this may have something to do with Olivia Hamilton's murder," she concluded.

The surprise of the two CPD officers was obvious. "How so?" the female cop, who'd given her name simply as Officer Wardell, said.

"The girl's body was found in a cabin that Irene Boyle and her brother own."

"How come nobody told us about that?" the other cop, an Officer Grayden, said.

"Talk to BCA," Dross told him. She led them out to the deck and showed them the shattered glass.

Wardell said, "But there's no indication of foul play, really. Just broken glass."

"She's gone and her car's still in the garage," Dross pointed out. "Judging from what she's left in the kitchen, it appears that she was expecting someone. I think it might be worth checking with the neighbors. Maybe somebody saw something."

"We know how to do our job, Sheriff. We'll take it from here," Grayden said. To his partner, he said, "I'm going to call this in."

He headed through the house and out to the cruiser they'd parked in front.

"Do you know her?" Dross asked Wardell.

The officer nodded. "I ran into her occasionally at the courthouse. She used to be a social worker. Foster care placements, I believe. Last I heard, she was working at Sizemore."

"Sizemore?"

"Sizemore School. A private facility for troubled youth. The campus is in Bixby, about ten miles west of here. Excuse me. I need to check the rest of the house."

She left them, and Cork looked at Dross. "Didn't Daniel and Bonhomme say that Fawn Blacksmith was at a school for problem kids for a while?"

"That's right," Dross said. "Same school?"

"How many schools for troubled kids are there? Let me give Agent Shirley a call." He tapped in her number on his cell phone. When she answered, he put her on speakerphone and briefly explained the situation.

"I spoke with BCA after your last call," Agent Shirley told them. "The guy I talked to said they intended to interview Irene Boyle tomorrow."

"Looks to us like someone was afraid of what she might tell them," Cork replied. "This afternoon, didn't you say that Fawn Blacksmith was in a school for troubled kids? Do you know the name of the school?"

"I don't."

"Well, get this. Irene works at a school called Sizemore, for troubled youth."

"Same school?"

"A good bet. We definitely need to check it out. Has there been any lead on her brother yet?"

"Nothing as far as I know," Agent Shirley said. "When will you check out this school?"

Cork looked at Dross, who gave a nod.

"No time like the present," he said.

They left the situation at Irene Boyle's house to the Cloquet police. On the way to Sizemore, Cork used his cell phone to look up the school online. It had been in operation for over a decade. Its central building housed the administrative offices and the educational rooms. There was also a dormitory and a gymnasium. The curriculum was designed to educate and rehabilitate. Residents came from both the private sector and the court system. As far as he could tell, there were no complaints or issues regarding the school's oversight of its charges.

It was full dark by the time they reached the campus. The large administrative building was unlit, but there were lots of lights on in the dormitory building. Dross pulled into the empty parking lot, and they walked to the dormitory. As they neared the entrance, a security light came on. The door was locked, but a sign on the wall advised that they should ring the bell for admittance, which they did.

"Yes?" a voice said through a wall-mounted speaker.

There was security camera high in a corner of the entrance alcove, and Dross lifted her badge toward it. "Sheriff Marsha Dross. I'd like to come in and speak with someone in charge."

At the sound of the buzzer, they opened the door and entered. To the right of the entrance was a reception desk, behind which sat a young man whom Cork figured to be in his late twenties, with a scruffy beard and a ponytail. He wore a blue T-shirt that bore an image of a bicycle and under it the word CYCOLOGIST. He stood up when Dross and Cork approached the desk.

"I'm Tim Foley," he said. "One of the resident counselors. What can I do for you?"

"We're trying to locate Irene Boyle."

"She's not on the campus at the moment. What's this about? One of our kids?"

"We need to speak to Ms. Boyle on another matter."

"You might try her home. She lives in Cloquet."

"We've just come from her home. She's not there."

"I'm not sure I can help you then."

"How well do you know Irene?" Dross asked.

"We're kind of a close-knit family here."

From somewhere out of sight arose the swell of bombastic music. Foley smiled. "Movie night in our lounge. It was girls' choice this time. They're watching *The Hunger Games*."

"How long have you been here?"

"You mean today?"

"Employed as a counselor?"

"A little less than a year."

"Familiar with a former resident named Fawn Blacksmith?"

"Doesn't ring a bell."

"You say you're like a close-knit family," Cork said. "Any idea if Irene was seeing anybody?"

"Seeing?"

"In a relationship," Cork clarified.

"I couldn't say. Guess we're not that close-knit. But . . ."

"But what?" Cork said.

"We had a staff meeting scheduled late today. She got a phone call in the middle of it. Took the call out in the hallway. When she returned, she said she had to leave, no explanation."

"Did she seem worried?"

He thought a moment. "I'd say eager. Look, there are others on staff who've been here longer and probably know her better. Maybe Candyce Osterkamp. She and Irene are good friends. She'll be back in the morning. You could check with her then."

"Do you have her phone number?"

"I don't. I'm sorry."

Dross asked him to spell the name, wrote it down, then handed him her business card. "If you think of anything that might be helpful, give me a call."

Before heading to Aurora, they swung back by Irene Boyle's house. The Cloquet PD cruiser was gone. Dross called the department.

"Apparently, they canvassed the neighbors and came up with nothing," she told Cork when she'd ended the call. "They said there's no reason to suspect foul play at the moment. They'll check the residence again in the morning to see if she's returned. If not, they'll make a decision about how to proceed."

"Try her cell phone again?" Cork suggested.

Dross did and again got no answer.

"Tim Foley said she got a call that made her leave the meeting this afternoon," Cork said. "Maybe we can get her phone records, find out who that was."

"We won't be able to get anything until Cloquet PD decides to investigate tomorrow. But I'm thinking tomorrow might be too late."

Cork eyed the woman's darkened house and shook his head. "I'm thinking it might be too late already."

CHAPTER 26

Annie woke to the ringing of the phone. She hadn't meant to sleep. She'd just intended to lie down on the sofa for a little while. She was always tired, it seemed, and the strain of the day at Spirit Crossing, her headache episode, and the scare from the neighbor across the street had all contributed to an overwhelming exhaustion.

Night had descended and the house was dark. Annie had no idea how long she'd slept. She sat up slowly, a little disoriented, and stumbled her way to the phone on the stand near the stairs. It was only as she lifted the receiver that she thought about the deluge of calls from reporters earlier in the day, but it was too late. She mumbled, "O'Connor residence," which was how she'd always answered the phone when she was growing up, when she lived under the roof of the house on Gooseberry Lane, when her life was still an unknown road stretching ahead of her, full of possibility.

There was no response from the other end of line. Then whoever it was simply hung up.

Annie set the receiver back in its cradle. Her first thought was that it must have been a wrong number, but as the fog of her sleep cleared away completely, her next thought was *It's him.*

She was alone in the house. She tried to recall if she'd locked all the doors. The front door, after John O'Loughlin had left and gone back across the street? She rushed over and checked the lock. It was set. Then she thought about the back door, the one their neighbor had unlocked to come in and check on her. Had he reset it?

She hurried to the kitchen and checked the door to the mud-room. It was secure, thank God. Annie leaned back against the door and felt how tense she was, how fast and shallow she was breathing. *That's what fear does,* she thought. In her time in Guatemala, she and fear had become well acquainted. The screams in the night or the gunshots that could come at any hour as the gangs took what they wanted from those who already had next to nothing, or fought with one another, or the soldiers swept through the barrio yet again.

She left the kitchen and went to a front window in the living room, where she drew aside a curtain to look out. The streetlamps were on, and the intersections on Gooseberry Lane were illuminated with fluorescent pools. All the houses she could see were dark. There were no vehicles parked on the street.

Maybe it was just a wrong number, she told herself.

But in the next instant, she heard it. The sound came from the dining room, a jiggling of the handle on the door that opened onto the backyard patio.

Earlier, when she lay down to rest, she'd set the Louisville Slugger on the floor beside the sofa. Now, she moved from the window and once again took the bat in her hands. Although the house lay in darkness, she still held to the cover of the wall as she crept toward the dining room. She peered around the corner and saw the figure at the patio door, solid dark against the backyard, which was dimly lit by a gibbous moon low in the sky. She couldn't see who it was, but she could see, rising like a straight stick from his right shoulder, the silhouette of the barrel of a rifle that must have hung from a strap.

Annie didn't waste any time. She reached around the corner of the wall to the light switch and flipped it. The room exploded with brilliant illumination from the chandelier above the dining table. Which was good and not good. The good was that it made the figure stumble back immediately. The bad was that the glare off the patio door panes made it impossible for Annie to see the intruder clearly.

At almost the same moment, she heard the mudroom door in the kitchen rattle.

Two of them? she thought, glancing that way. Her grip on the bat tightened.

When she swung her eyes back to the patio door, the figure was gone. She turned her attention to the intruder at the mudroom door, moving swiftly in that direction. As soon as she entered the kitchen, she hit the light switch and drew the bat back, ready to swing. But it wasn't a menacing stranger who came in.

"Whoa," her father said, holding up his hands in surrender. "It's just me."

"Someone tried to break in," Annie said quickly.

"Where?"

"The patio door."

"When?"

"Just now."

"Wait here."

Her father rushed past her, but she didn't remain behind. She followed him, the bat still gripped in her hands. Cork opened the patio door and ran out. He stood in the rectangle of light cast by the dining room chandelier, looking left and right. He glanced back at Annie.

"Close and lock the door. Lock the kitchen door, too. Don't open up unless it's me knocking." He vanished into the darkness where the light didn't reach.

Annie did as he'd said, locked both doors, then went to the living room and waited. The knock at the front door came a couple of minutes later. She turned on the porch light but didn't look out.

"Dad?"

"It's me."

She unlocked and opened the door. "Did you see him?"

Her father shook his head. "Nothing. And nothing parked on the street. I heard an engine fire up next block over, so he might have parked there. Whoever he was, he's gone now."

Annie's jaw went tight. "Lewis."

"Lewis?"

"I need a cookie and milk," Annie said.

In the kitchen, she took two chocolate chip cookies, one for each of them, from the Ernie cookie jar while Cork poured milk into a couple of small tumblers. They sat at the table, and Annie related everything that had transpired regarding the security guard named Lewis.

"But you can't say for sure that he was at Spirit Crossing today?" Cork said.

"When the headaches are really bad, I sometimes see things that aren't there."

"And you can't say for sure that he was the one at the patio door?"

"No."

"If he's been a cop, he probably had no trouble finding out exactly who you are and where you live and our telephone number here. I'll get our phone records tomorrow and see who called tonight. That may nail him." Then he furrowed his brow and said, "What's going on, Annie? These headaches, what're they about?"

Maybe it was the physical and emotional strain of the day. Maybe it was simply that a human being couldn't hide a painful truth forever. Whatever the reason, all that she'd held back for so long behind a dam of fear and a desire to spare herself the pity of others and a deep sense of the hurt that the truth would bring to those she loved came pouring forth. She began to weep, and her father took her into his arms and listened as she pressed her face to his heart and told him everything.

Cork lay in bed, unable to sleep. Annie was dying. His beloved daughter was dying and there was nothing he could do about it, nothing anyone could do. Another medical opinion, he'd suggested. Mayo Clinic in Rochester. But she told him the doctor who headed the medical team in Mexico City, the best, she'd been assured, had trained at Mayo. She was finished seeing doctors. He'd made a promise to Annie to let her tell the others in her own time and in her own way. After the wedding, she'd said, so that nothing would interfere with the celebration. He'd sworn he wouldn't even tell Rainy. Now this awful truth was an iceberg floating inside him, its sharp, icy edges cutting into his heart.

Glioblastoma. Brain cancer. This alien thing in her body, slowly killing her. A year, maybe, Annie had told him.

She'd been gone forever, it seemed, living her life in a place he could barely imagine, a crumbling barrio on the edge of a Central American city he'd seen only in the photographs she sometimes attached to her emails. He'd looked forward to her return for Stephen's wedding with such great joy, the chance after too long to reconnect with this child who'd strayed so far from home.

No, not strayed. She'd chosen very definitely the course of her life. She'd always known her own mind, been a strong woman, a fighter in every way. When he'd come home that night, she'd held a baseball bat in her hands, ready to clobber an intruder. Then she'd put her face to his chest and wept as she told him the truth of this thing she could not fight.

He slipped from bed. Rainy lay sleeping soundly. She'd come home in the early morning hours with Stephen and Belle and Maria, all of them dead tired from the work they'd done helping at Spirit Crossing. There'd been injuries and arrests, at both the encampment and the crossing itself. Things were spinning out of control. She and Belle and Stephen feared there would be more trouble the next day, and they would be heading off early to do what they could to help. He looked down at his wife, this good human being, with whom he shared so much. But he could not share with her this awful truth in his heart. This awful sadness. Because he'd promised Annie, and he was a man true to his word.

He left the bedroom and went downstairs, opened the front door and slipped outside. He sat on the porch swing. The night had cooled a bit and a soft breeze brushed against his face. A lopsided gibbous moon hung in the black sky, showering faint silver across the lawn. Where the moon didn't eat their light, the stars were a glittering sea of diamonds. It should have been a lovely night. Except that two young women were dead, another woman was missing, someone was menacing the O'Connors. And Annie was dying.

In that moment, it was too much. Cork bent his head and began to weep. Deep sobs broke from him, the only sound in the night. Everything was beyond his control. He wanted to rail at God, at the Great Mystery, at whoever or whatever was responsible for all the horror in the world. He lifted his tear-streaked face to the heavens and asked that eternal and unanswerable question: "Why?"

Except for the sound of one man's grieving, the night was silent.

CHAPTER 27

Cork was up early the next morning, making breakfast. It had been three days since Waaboo had discovered the body that was almost certainly that of Fawn Blacksmith buried in Erno Paavola's blueberry patch, and Cork was still struggling to understand what exactly had happened to her and to Olivia Hamilton and what, if anything, might tie the two murders together.

The night before, as he and Dross had returned from Cloquet, Cork had called Daniel's cell phone and filled him in on what they'd found. Daniel had told Cork that Waaboo had agreed to return to the blueberry patch to see if he could once again touch the spirit of Fawn Blacksmith. Cork said he wanted to be there and to let him know when they left Crow Point.

As he was making oatmeal, he heard the *thunk* of something hitting the front door. He peeked through the living room window and saw that the street was empty, no media vans. On the porch, he found the morning paper. The front-page story in the *Duluth News Tribune* was the discovery of Olivia Hamilton's body in the room beneath Erno Paavola's cabin. The byline was Greta Hanover. She did give Waaboo credit for his sense of smell, which led to the discovery of the body beneath the cabin, but she made no mention of talking to a ghost.

Cork went back to making breakfast for everyone. They all had agendas. Stephen, Belle, and Rainy planned to head back to Spirit Crossing. Annie, when Cork told her about Waaboo returning to the blueberry patch, asked if she could be there, too. And wherever Annie went, Maria was sure to follow.

They ate together at the dining room table, discussing the intruder the night before. Breakfast was oatmeal with blueberries, sweetened with maple syrup.

"It had to be Lewis," Stephen said. "Looking for some kind of revenge."

Cork thought this over. "He was involved in security with a lot of cops. Suspended or not, it wouldn't have been hard for him to get our address and phone number, I suppose. I'll call Marsha and ask her to follow up on it."

Belle added a few more blueberries to her oatmeal. "He'd have to be pretty stupid to try something like that."

"He didn't strike me as the sharpest tool in the shed," Stephen said.

"Is it possible that whoever is responsible for Olivia Hamilton and Fawn Blacksmith knows about us?" Rainy said. "About Waaboo, I mean? And they're afraid of what he might find out if he connects with the Blacksmith girl's spirit?"

"Hard to believe someone coldhearted enough to kill two girls would be open to the idea of visions," Stephen said.

Annie hadn't eaten much. She never did anymore. "And Waaboo was barely mentioned in the news story," she pointed out. "And nothing about the vision he had."

"Maybe it was someone monitoring the chatter on a police scanner," Rainy suggested. "That's how Greta Hanover knew."

"It's possible," Cork said. "That's why Waaboo is with Henry and Prophet. I think that from now on, we never leave anyone here alone. Until all this is settled, we run in packs. We are, after all, Wolf Clan."

Rainy, Stephen, and Belle left first for Spirit Crossing. Cork got the call from Daniel shortly after that, and he and Annie and Maria headed to Paavola's cabin.

They arrived before the others. Cork got out of his Expedition and smelled the fresh scent of the pine in the morning air. If he didn't know the truth of Paavola's land and all that it had hidden, he would have thought it was just another part of the Northwoods, of the beautiful place he called home. He didn't have Waaboo's gift. He couldn't sense the *maji-manidoog*, the devils. He had to rely on his all-too-human brain to sort out evil.

Annie and Maria left the Expedition and stood with him.

"Except for the yellow police tape, it just looks like any old cabin," Annie said.

"It's more than just any old cabin. It was going to be Paavola's sanctuary come the apocalypse," Cork said.

"He died alone here?" Maria asked. "This Paavola?"

"He did," Cork told her. "It was weeks before his body was discovered. He kept a post office box in town. When he hadn't picked up his mail for a while, our postmaster let the sheriff's office know, and a deputy came out to check."

"To die alone," Maria said. "That is so sad."

Which rang a dark bell in Cork, and he glanced at Annie.

She saw his look and she took Maria's hand. "I won't die alone, Dad."

The ATV with Meloux and Prophet came up the overgrown dirt lane, followed by Daniel in his crew cab pickup with Jenny and Waaboo. Last to arrive was Monte Bonhomme. They all gathered and eyed the cabin.

"Has this always been a bad place, Mishomis?" Waaboo asked.

"Everything is born in innocence and beauty, Little Rabbit. But the spirit of a place, just like the spirit of a human being, can be poisoned."

"Are you ready?" Daniel asked his son.

Waaboo gave a brave nod.

They walked in silence along the path to the blueberry patch. Cork noted that they all surrounded Waaboo as if to protect him. When they came to the clearing, Waaboo paused, and the others did as well.

"Are you okay?" Jenny asked, resting her hand on her little boy's shoulder. "We don't have to do this."

"I'm okay," Waaboo said and began to walk slowly ahead.

They followed him to the place where Fawn Blacksmith's body had been buried, then Waaboo paused. The others stayed a few feet back, as if to give him room to reach out with his unusual sensibility.

"Do you feel anything?" Daniel asked.

Waaboo closed his eyes for a long moment, and slowly turned, then his face scrunched up as if in pain. "Something bad is here. But it's not her. Bad . . . and . . . alive," he said.

"Alive?" Daniel said.

Waaboo's eyes were still closed, his face twisted. "Mad . . . angry . . . kill . . ."

"Stop, Waaboo!" Jenny said.

She crossed the few feet that separated her from her beloved son, reached out, and drew him against her. In that same instant, the shot came. The bullet kicked up dirt where Waaboo had just been standing, and the report of the firearm followed almost immediately.

Daniel knocked Jenny and Waaboo to the ground and covered them with his body. Annie and Maria dropped to the ground, too. Cork, Bonhomme, and Prophet all spun toward the tree line from which the sound of the gunshot had come. Prophet leapt in that direction, sprinting through the sparse undergrowth of the clearing. Cork and Bonhomme followed, but Prophet was faster and reached the trees long before they did, vanishing among the pines.

When Cork and Bonhomme arrived at the place where Prophet had disappeared, they stopped, looking for signs of where he'd gone. "There," Cork said, pointing at a vague deer path that led through the trees and up the slope. They ran along the deer path a quarter mile, until it came out on the main road a couple of hundred yards from the lane to Paavola's cabin. Prophet knelt there, looking at the imprint of tires in the dirt shoulder of the road.

"I heard his vehicle leave, but he was gone before I got here," Prophet said.

"Did you see him at all?" Cork asked.

Prophet shook his head, then held out his hand, in which he gripped a ball cap, pale green and with an image in black that Cork recognized immediately. Under it was printed a single word: AN-IMIKII.

"Found it over there." Prophet pointed toward where the deer trail broke from the trees. "Looks pretty new. I figure the lowest branch of that birch sapling must've caught the bill and flipped it off his head. He was in too big a hurry to stop and pick it up."

"*Animikii*," Cork said. "Anishinaabe for Thunderbird." He looked at Bonhomme, then at Prophet, feeling bewildered and betrayed in the common ancestry they all shared. "Jesus, Monte, is this guy Shinnob?"

"Let's give it to BCA," Bonhomme said. "If they can pull DNA from it, maybe we'll know for sure."

Cork called Daniel on his cell phone and they arranged to rendezvous back at Paavola's cabin. Everyone except Prophet, who told them he wanted to check the deer path to see if he could find anything more the shooter might have left behind or abandoned.

Waaboo looked shaken when he arrived, but less so than his mother. Jenny gripped Waaboo's hand, and Cork could feel the anger coming off her like bolts of lightning.

"I didn't want him here," she told them all. "I knew something bad would happen."

Meloux said quietly, "You also have the gift of second sight?"

"Don't joke with me, Henry."

"It is not a joke. I mean only that no one, not even our little rabbit, could see this coming. We cannot hide him on Crow Point forever. If he touched the spirit of this young woman again, and in this, helped to find the evil at the heart of all that has happened, would that not have been a good thing?"

"But he didn't touch her spirit," Jenny said. Then she looked at her son. "Did you?"

Waaboo furrowed his little brow, thinking. "For a moment. Then all I felt was the devil. He kind of blocked out everything else."

"And in that moment?" Meloux asked.

"She seemed . . ." He thought a moment more, then smiled at Meloux. "Not so sad."

"Because we're trying to help her?" Daniel offered.

"Don't put words in his mouth," Jenny snapped. "This is exactly what I was afraid of. They know about him."

Which, Cork figured, was hard to argue with.

"How did they know we were here?" Annie asked.

"Maybe someone's been watching Paavola's cabin, just in case?" Daniel suggested.

"A long vigil," Bonhomme said. "I think they must've had a more efficient way of keeping tabs on one of us."

"How?" Jenny said, a sharp edge to that word.

"A tracker would be my first guess," Bonhomme replied. "We need to check our vehicles."

They spent a good deal of time going carefully over each vehicle. They found it on Cork's Expedition, a little white disk hidden behind his back license plate, an AirTag.

"How long has it been there?" Daniel said.

"My guess?" Cork said. "Only a couple of days. Probably since we began poking into the two girls' deaths."

"Since Waaboo touched their spirits," Daniel said. He looked to where Jenny and Meloux, and Annie and Maria huddled around the little boy as if to shield him from harm. "They want to make sure he doesn't help us any further."

"A desperate move," Bonhomme said. "They must be afraid of how close we're getting."

"Which is maybe why Waaboo sensed that the spirit of Fawn Blacksmith was not so sad," Daniel said, sounding hopeful.

Cork spotted Prophet coming from the trail that led past the gnomes to the blueberry patch. When Prophet reached the men, he said, "I found this where he hid and fired the shot." He held out his hand. In his gloved palm, he cradled a shell casing.

Cork put on gloves, took the casing, and checked the headstamp. "Remington thirty-aught-six. Annie said the guy who tried to break into our house last night had a rifle slung over his shoulder."

"She thought it was this Lewis guy, right? The security cop from the protest?" Daniel said. "But he was white, not Shinnob. If it was him, what was he doing wearing a cap with the Thunderbird on it?"

Cork said, "We need to find Lewis and ask him."

CHAPTER 28

Daniel returned to Crow Point with Jenny and Waaboo. They didn't say much on the drive or on the long walk in from the double-trunk birch. Waaboo, normally talkative, seemed deep in thought. And as for Jenny, Daniel could feel the wall she had erected, built with the bricks of her anger at him for putting Waaboo in danger.

Prophet had driven Meloux to Crow Point in the ATV, and the two men sat on the bench in front of Meloux's cabin, waiting. When the others arrived, Meloux rose and said, "Walk with me, Little Rabbit."

Daniel watched the old man and the boy cross the meadow. His heart was heavy because he knew Jenny was right. He'd put their son in harm's way, and for what? Fawn Blacksmith and Olivia Hamilton were dead. Sacrificing his son in an attempt to discover who was responsible for the crimes wouldn't bring them back.

"Waaboo has a lot to learn," Prophet said, breaking the long, tense silence Daniel and Jenny had brought with them. "Henry is doing what he can to help. He asked me to speak to you."

"I hope that you're going to tell me my son is no longer in danger," Jenny said.

"Will you sit?" Prophet held his hand toward Meloux's bench. When they seated themselves, he said, "Henry already told you that the gift Waaboo has been given is one that may often put him in danger. The why of it, only the Great Mystery knows. My own guess is that it's because Waaboo has a spirit strong enough to shoulder this responsibility. And my guess as well is that the Great Mystery had a reason for choosing you to find that child under the rock where he'd been hidden."

"If you're going to tell me it's because I'm strong, too, I don't want to hear it," Jenny said.

"Then maybe I can tell you something else. I never knew my parents. I grew up in a residential school in Canada. Most of my life, I had no idea who I was. You already know that when I met Henry, it was because I was hunting him, leading men who wanted him dead. Everything in my life changed when I found him waiting for me in the Boundary Waters. It took me decades of struggle to reach the place the Great Mystery had always meant me to come to. I had no one guiding me, loving me, reassuring me. Waaboo is different. He's been given you. You can't protect him forever, but you can be his comfort on the difficult path ahead. If I'd had that, I still might not have come to this place of peace, this place of harmony, this place of my own destiny any sooner, but I'm sure the journey wouldn't have been so hard, so full of regret."

"If that's supposed to make me feel better about someone shooting at my son, it doesn't," Jenny said.

"I love our son, too." Daniel took Jenny's hand. "I would never knowingly put him in danger. We can never be sure what will or won't put him in harm's way. But one thing is for sure. He can't stay on Crow Point forever."

Jenny looked away from him, stared across the meadow at

where her son and the old Mide had become two small figures in the tall grass. "He can stay here until we've found these devils."

"There will be others," Prophet said.

"I will fight them like a she-bear," Jenny vowed.

"And I'll be right there beside you," Daniel promised her.

"He's just a child," Jenny said. Tears began to roll down her cheeks.

Daniel took her in his arms. "I would die before I'd let anyone hurt Waaboo. Or you."

Prophet said, "He has one other gift, your little rabbit, just as important as the one that's put him in danger now."

Jenny wiped her eyes and looked up at him, expectantly.

"He walks surrounded in the beauty and strength of those who love him. And there are so many."

Daniel kissed Jenny's cheek and echoed, "So many."

He left his wife and child on Crow Point and headed to the office of the Iron Lake Tribal Police. LuJean Desjardins greeted him with "Monte told me about the shooter this morning. When we catch that coward, and we will, I say we string him up by his balls."

"Where's Monte?"

"A meeting with Sheriff Dross in Aurora. Your father-in-law is there, too. As I understand it, they're coming up with a strategy. I'd love to be in on that, but our chief says someone needs to see to law enforcement on the rez. And because you seem to have your hands full, he dropped that job in my lap."

"Anything happening here?"

"Wanda LeFevre called in a complaint about a wolf giving that new goat of hers a scare. Zippy took a run out there. Turned out to be Simon Chevalier's dog Junker. Big old hound, but gentle as a kitten, really. Just curious about the goat. Simon assured Zippy that Junker's curiosity was satisfied and he wouldn't be giving that goat or Wanda any more worry. Other than that, I got Monte's paperwork. A boatload related to the powwow next month. Care to give me a hand?"

"Did Monte say anything about me?"

"Not specifically. He didn't know how long you'd be out on Crow Point."

"Then I think I'll head to Aurora, see what I can contribute to this strategy session. Zippy can give you a hand with the paperwork when he comes back in."

"That'll thrill him no end."

When Daniel walked into the sheriff's office, he found that Agent Shirley had joined the others. They brought him up to speed.

"I've let the BCA know about the shot this morning at the blueberry patch," the sheriff said. "I've also let them know about the connection between Fawn Blacksmith and Irene Boyle, who, according to Cloquet PD, is still missing. They said they'll take that under advisement."

"Advisement," Agent Shirley said with a note of disdain. "I talked to them as well and got an update on their investigation. They believe they have a good lead on one of the bikers who was at the Howling Wolf the night Olivia Hamilton went missing. Seems he was picked up in Fargo last night for assaulting an undercover cop posing as a prostitute. He managed to get away from the arresting officers. Now a lot of their manpower has been diverted to helping locate this biker. Apparently, that's where all the media attention has gone."

"Which may go a long way in explaining why Gooseberry Lane is quiet again. The vultures are circling somewhere else. Any connection between this guy and Paavola?"

"They didn't have a chance to interview him. But he's their

main focus at the moment." She shook her head. "Still barking up the wrong tree, if you ask me."

"What about the call last night to our place?" Daniel said.

"Marsha's people checked," Cork said. "Burner phone. No way to trace it. But we've got a lead on Lewis."

"Before he went to work on security for the pipeline, Lewis was employed as an officer on the Hibbing police force," Dross explained. "I spoke with the chief of police there. He told me that a year ago Lewis—first name Adrian—was fired following a number of complaints from both citizens and his fellow officers. I've got an address for him. Cork and I are going there today."

Monte Bonhomme said, "I spoke with my friend in Duluth PD, got the address for the house where Fawn Blacksmith was picked up before she went to that school in Bixby. It's a place a lot of Indian kids know about. Apparently, they clear it out periodically, after the neighborhood complains enough, but squatters keep coming back. I'm wondering if she might have headed back there when she got out of juvenile detention. Agent Shirley and I thought we'd check it out. Care to come with us, Daniel?"

"You betcha."

Dross said, "Then let's roll."

Monte drove Agent Shirley and Daniel to Duluth in his Tahoe, stopping at a smoke shop on the way so that Daniel could buy a few packs of Newport Menthol 100s. "Street currency," he explained. He also bought that day's issue of the *Duluth News Tribune*. The headline read: SUSPECT IN HAMILTON KILLING FLEES POLICE.

Agent Shirley shook her head and said again, "Barking up the wrong tree."

"Fawn Blacksmith got no headlines when she went missing,"

Daniel said with an acid note. "Crystal Two Knives didn't either. They weren't white."

"They also weren't the daughter of a state senator," Monte pointed out.

"Wouldn't have made a difference. A white girl would still have made the headlines and you know it."

"Not arguing with that," Monte said.

The address was in Lincoln Park, a dilapidated two-story on a dead-end street, a structure just barely held together by a few rusty nails. The yard was all dead weeds. The sidewalk looked like an earthquake had shattered it. The porch was furnished with a pale green sofa that vomited gray stuffing. There was no screen, just a wood door, leprous in the way it was peeling white paint.

Agent Shirley said, "Your uniforms are going to scare them. I'll knock."

Daniel and Monte stepped to either side of the front door, out of sight. Agent Shirley knocked, got no response. She knocked again, this time persistently.

The door opened, and Daniel heard a raspy voice say angrily, "What?"

"I'm looking for someone who might have known a girl named Fawn Blacksmith."

"Never heard of her."

"Ojibwe girl. Pretty. Here's her picture."

She held it out, but no hand reached to take it.

"Look, lady, get lost."

Daniel stepped into view next to Agent Shirley. "What about me? Want me to get lost?"

"Or me?" Monte said and flanked the BIA agent on the other side.

"What the f—"

It was a kid, maybe twenty at most, thin, unwashed, his long black hair stringy. He was Native.

"Just look at the photo," Daniel said. The kid threw an expletive at him. Daniel calmly reached into the pocket of his uniform blouse and pulled out a pack of Newports. "Smoke?"

The kid hesitated, then took the offering.

"We're not here to bust you or anyone else," Daniel said. "We're just trying to find information about Fawn Blacksmith. She used to crash here. Take a good look at the photo."

The kid studied it, then shook his head.

"How long have you lived here?"

"Month."

"Anybody around who's lived here longer?"

"Blue. He's lived here the longest."

"Is Blue here now?"

The kid swiped a long strand of greasy hair away from his eyes. "Out signing with his dog."

"Signing?"

"You know." He lifted his hands, miming the holding of a sign. "'Need money. Anything'll help.'"

"Does he have a regular spot?"

"Lake Street, off I-35."

It was just after noon when they found Blue sitting on an overturned milk crate. An old hound, maybe part Irish setter, sat patiently at his feet. Blue was Native, older than the kid at the house, thirtyish. He wore dirty khaki shorts, sandals, a red T-shirt, holes in the armpits. A Twins ball cap shaded his face. He held a handmade sign: VETERAN. NEED HELP. ANYTHING YOU CAN SPARE. GOD BLESS YOU.

He eyed them implacably as they approached on foot. The dog looked at them the same way.

"You really a vet?" Monte asked.

"Fourth Stryker Brigade, Second Infantry Division. We were the last to leave Iraq." He stated it simply but with a note of pride.

Daniel wanted to ask about the path that took him from Iraq to signing on an interstate ramp in Duluth, but he knew being Indian meant that, even with a history of military service, there were still a thousand roadblocks to a decent life. And maybe the alcohol odor coming off Blue explained a lot.

Monte said, "I understand you crash at that house in Lincoln Park."

"What of it?"

"Been there awhile, right?"

"What's it to you?"

"Remember a girl named Fawn Blacksmith?"

From the shadow that the bill of the ball cap cast across his face, Blue eyed Monte, then a car passing on the street. "You're scaring away my daily bread."

"Smoke?" Daniel took out the pack of Newports he'd put in the pocket of his uniform blouse to replace the pack he'd given the kid at the house. That got a smile from Blue, who took it, opened it, tapped out a cigarette, pulled a lighter from the pocket of his shorts, and lit up.

"Do you remember Fawn Blacksmith?" Daniel asked.

"Yeah," Blue said blowing smoke toward the sky. "I remember Fawn. Pretty kid. Good heart. What's this about?"

"She's dead."

Blue's face barely changed, but Daniel thought he saw a flicker of the man's eyelids. "How?" Blue asked.

"Someone killed her."

"That's tough."

"When did you last see Fawn?"

Now the man's face changed, grew wary. "You think I killed her?"

"No. But we're trying to find out who did."

Blue lifted the bill of his cap, wiped at his brow, set the cap back on his head. "She was at the house when I first got there. Then they busted the place and we all split. Couple of weeks later, I went back. New people kept showing up. Maybe six months after that, Fawn shows up again. This time she's got a boyfriend."

"Name?"

"She called him Billy Bones. Don't think that was his real name. Older guy. He didn't live at the house. He just picked up Fawn. Whenever he dropped by, he didn't pay much attention to me or the guys. He was interested in the girls. My guess, he was pimping her and looking for more. Then Fawn's gone. Heard she got busted for selling it. I never saw her again."

"This Billy Bones, what did he look like?"

"Claimed to be Indian. Could have Indian blood in him, I guess. My age, maybe a little older. Flashy. Good dresser. Smooth talker, at least to the girls."

"Did he manage to sweet-talk any of them into selling it?"

"After Fawn was gone, he didn't come around anymore."

"What's your dog's name?" Daniel asked.

"I call him Mizheekay."

"Turtle," Daniel said.

Blue smiled. "Yeah, he don't move so fast anymore. But let me show you something." He reached into the dirty pack at his feet and pulled out a folded sheet of what looked like drawing paper. He unfolded it and held it up for them to see.

"That's you," Agent Shirley said. "With your dog. It's quite good."

"Fawn drew it. That girl had talent, potential. Just, well, never had the chance to go anywhere with it. Same as so many of us."

As they turned to leave, Daniel pulled a twenty-dollar bill from his wallet. "For Mizheekay."

Blue ran his hand gently over the dog's fur and said to Daniel, "*Miigwech.*"

CHAPTER 29

The address for Adrian Lewis the Hibbing chief of police had given Dross was at the end of a road called Orchard Lane a couple of miles outside town. It was easy to see where the name came from. Although pines grew on the east side of the road, the west side was lined with apple trees. As she and Cork drove toward the address, they passed a man in a straw hat standing at the edge of the orchard, a twelve-foot pruner pole in his hand. He gave them a cordial wave as they went by.

The house was a brick rambler in a sea of weeds. They parked in the driveway, got no answer to their knock. The doors were locked, the windows curtained.

"Looks like nobody's lived here in forever," Dross said.

"He's been seen around, so he's got to be living somewhere," Cork said. "What say we talk to his neighbor?"

They drove back to where the man with the pruner pole was at work. When they stopped and got out, he leaned the pole against the branch of an apple tree and turned to them, smiling. "What can I do for you folks?"

Under the shade of the broad brim of his straw hat was the face of a man Cork guessed to be in his early fifties. Deep crow's-feet fanned out from the corners of both eyes, and laugh lines arced at the edges of his mouth.

"I'm Sheriff Marsha Dross. This is my associate Cork O'Connor. We're trying to locate Adrian Lewis."

"Well, good luck with that."

"What do you mean?"

"I haven't seen that boy in over a year."

"We heard he's in the area."

"I heard that, too. Just haven't seen him."

"What can you tell us about him?"

"What's your interest, don't mind me asking? He in some kind of trouble?"

"Maybe," Dross said. "That's really what we're trying to figure out. The more we know about him, the better sense we might have."

The man looked down the road in the direction of the derelict house. "I've been a neighbor of the Lewis family all my life. Now there was a bunch of hard-luckers."

"How so?" Cork asked.

"I went to school with Adrian's old man, Davey Lewis. Good football player, running back. Went to the U of M down in the Twin Cities on a scholarship. Got blindsided his first game. Ruined his knee. Never played again. That's probably what set him to drinking. Came home, worked in the lumber mill, married a girl from Coleraine, Lizzie, real odd one. Lots of fireworks in that house, and I don't mean the kind you shoot off come Fourth of July. Alcohol usually involved. Then Davey got killed in a mill accident. Things kinda went from bad to worse. Adrian never really stood a chance. You seen that ear of his?"

"We've never seen him," Dross said.

"He's got this funny-looking right ear. Word was his ma put a hot iron to it. Melted the skin. Don't know if it's true, but Lewis always wore his hair long to cover it. Joined the army right after high school. Didn't see him in forever. Then his ma died couple of years ago. He got the house and came back, driving a truck and hauling a fifth wheel. You know, one of those big trailers. Heard he'd been living in it for a while, don't know where or doing what. A loner though. Kept pretty much to himself. Got a job as a cop in town. Now if that boy was difficult before, he became a real son of a bitch behind that badge. Maybe because he had to cut his hair and couldn't hide that ear of his, I don't know. Anyway, lots of complaints about him. Got let go, as I understand it, about a year ago. Then him and that fifth wheel disappeared. Like you, I heard that he's been back, working on that pipeline, I guess. But I haven't seen him at the house. Must still be living out of that big trailer of his. So, this trouble he might be in, is it bad?"

"Yes," Dross said.

The man gave a nod, as if it didn't surprise him. "Like I said, good luck finding him."

Dross handed the man a business card. "If you happen to see him return home, Mr. —?"

"Gavins. Luke Gavins."

"Could you give me a call?"

"Happy to."

He watched them return to Dross's cruiser, then he took up his pruner pole and went back to his work.

As they drove away, Dross said, "Misshapen right ear. Sound familiar?"

"Mathias Paavola's drinking buddy at the Howling Wolf."

It was shortly after 1:00 P.M. as they headed back to Hibbing. Cork got a call from Daniel. He put him on speakerphone so Dross could hear and filled Daniel in on what they'd learned about Lewis.

"Still no lead on his location?" Daniel asked.

"No. We'll talk to the people in charge of pipeline personnel, see what they can tell us. Did you find out anything in Duluth?"

Daniel related what Blue had told them.

"So, after Fawn runs from Sizemore School, this Billy Bones shows up?" Cork said. "Anything more on him?"

"No. But we've been talking. A girl is usually groomed to be pimped. Billy Bones, whoever he is, had to have time to do that. We've put the timing together and there's just not enough of it between her running from the school and showing up at the crash pad again in Duluth."

"So how did this Bones get his hooks into her?"

"Could well have been at Sizemore," Dross chimed in. "Cork and I were going to head back there today. We've got a name for someone who's been at the school for a while and might be able to give us more information about Irene Boyle and whoever it is she was seeing before she went missing. Maybe she can tell us about Fawn Blacksmith's time at the school as well."

"We're closer," Daniel said. "Want us to take that while you check with the pipeline security people?"

"That would be good. The woman's name is Candyce Oster-kamp. She'll probably be at the school. If not, I'm sure they can tell you where she lives. Stay in touch and let us know what you find out."

"Will do," Daniel said and ended the call.

"Not much I can tell you about Adrian Lewis," Hank Robbins said. "He was hired to work security when we moved the pipeline con-struction into the States. We did a lot of hiring back then."

They sat in the personnel office, which was housed in one of several operations trailers temporarily situated a few miles west of

Spirit Crossing, well away from the protests. Robbins was somewhere in his fifties, solid, white hair in a buzz-cut bristle. He was
accommodating.

"Normally, I probably wouldn't even be aware of him, we have
so many men working on the line. But he's been a bit of an issue
from the get-go."

"How so?" Dross asked.

"Complaints. We've had the benefit of a very good relationship
with local law enforcement all along the route. Which we appreciate," he said, smiling at Dross. "But a number of officers who've
worked with Lewis have made allegations about his behavior."

"Such as?"

"Harassing locals for one thing, particularly women. Not in-
teracting well with official law enforcement. You can read that as
insubordinate. Reports of drinking on the job. He'd been warned.
This last incident at Spirit Crossing, which was reported by a
county deputy, was the final straw. We gave him his walking papers."

"How did he react?"

"I didn't do the actual firing. That fell to his supervisor. The
report I got, however, was that he went ballistic. Which only re-
inforced for me the wisdom in cutting him loose. The last thing
we need is one of our security people losing it during the kind of
confrontation we've been experiencing lately."

"Do you have an address for him and a phone number?" Dross
asked.

Robbins opened the folder he'd pulled from a file cabinet as
soon as Dross and Cork told him about their interest in Adrian
Lewis. "For an address, only a P.O. box number in a place called
Dahlbert." He gave that to them, then gave them the phone number from Lewis's file.

Cork said, "We have reason to believe he was at Spirit Crossing in his security uniform the day after he'd been fired. Is that possible?"

"No idea whether he turned in his badge or uniform, so I suppose anything is possible. Especially with a loose cannon like Adrian Lewis."

They thanked Robbins and left. They sat a moment in Dross's cruiser while she tried the cell phone number they'd been given.

"Out of service," she said.

"P.O. box in Dahlbert," Cork said. "Same town where Mathias Paavola was renting that garage apartment."

"Paavola's landlady didn't say anything about a roommate. So, if he wasn't living with Paavola, he must be living out of his trailer."

"Where do you park a big fifth wheel in Dahlbert?" Cork said.

Dross started the engine of her cruiser. "The town's only half an hour away. What do you say we find out?"

CHAPTER 30

By midafternoon, the July day had turned hot, but inside the O'Connor house, it was much cooler. The curtains were drawn against the heat but also to block the prying eyes of any reporters who might return. The doors were all locked. Annie lay on the living room sofa staring up at the ceiling, where a solitary fly moved in fits and starts across the textured plaster. She wondered why it didn't simply use its wings. If she had wings, she'd do nothing but fly.

Maria came from the kitchen. "I've made sandwiches."

"Not hungry," Annie said, still watching the insect on the ceiling.

"You have to eat."

"What's the point?"

"It will be a very long time before this thing in your brain kills you. In the meantime, you should do all you can for your body. And your spirit."

"What if it's not this tumor that kills me?"

Maria knelt on the carpet next to the sofa. "What else then?"

"Whoever tried to get into the house last night. Maybe whoever fired that shot this morning."

"That was meant for Waaboo."

"If you say so."

"Everybody says so." Maria reached out and stroked Annie's arm gently.

"I've been thinking about anger," Annie said.

"Yours?"

"Anyone's. If I could strike out at God for giving me this cancer, I would. Viciously."

"I don't think that's true."

"Oh, but it is. This anger inside me is sometimes worse than the pain of the headaches. So maybe if I were Adrian Lewis, I'd be sorely tempted to take revenge on whoever it was that got me fired."

"That wasn't just you."

"No, but he sure seemed focused on me. Before I blacked out yesterday, I saw nothing but hate in his eyes."

"If you really saw him."

Annie smiled, but without humor. "Like everyone else, you think I just hallucinated."

"I am only saying it's a possibility. You've seen things before. And remember, the deputy told us that man had been fired. He should not have been there."

"That doesn't mean he wasn't. And someone was sure eager to get into the house last night when I was alone here."

"You are not alone now."

Annie peered deeply into Maria's dark eyes. "What would you do if someone tried to kill me?"

"That is not a thing I think about."

"Think about it now. What if whoever fired that shot broke into the house right now, what would you do?"

"I would cover you with my body to protect you." Maria leaned down and kissed her.

Now Annie's smile was real. "I'm sure you would." She slowly sat up. "I want to talk to Henry."

"We shouldn't leave."

"It's broad daylight. I'm not going to let Adrian Lewis or anyone else keep me caged up here. I'm going to Crow Point."

"To what end?"

"Maybe an exorcism."

"What?"

"This anger. This hopelessness. This fear. This hell that's inside me now."

"You think your friend can remove all that?" Maria shook her head. "You expect too much of him, I think. And of yourself."

"Doing anything is better than doing nothing. Are you coming?"

"As your father said, we should travel as a pack. You go nowhere without me."

There was a plaque hanging on the kitchen wall that Cork had made from a slice of sanded and varnished black walnut. It had several hooks on which all the O'Connors hung their vehicle keys. When he took off with Marsha Dross that day, Annie's father had left his Expedition parked in the driveway and the key hanging from the plaque. Annie took the key and left a note of explanation.

In the heat of the day, the street was empty. The Expedition was like an oven, and Annie drove at first with the windows down. After the intruder in the night and the shooter that morning, she was hypervigilant, keeping an eye to her rearview mirror for anyone who might be following. She saw no one. After a while, she raised the windows and let the air conditioner do its work.

"It is not so humid here as home," Maria said. "But it is just as hot."

"Feeling homesick?" Annie asked.

"We have many problems, but it is still my home. You have never felt homesick in Guatemala?"

"Sometimes. But I've had you for comfort."

"And here, I have you," Maria said. She gazed out her window as they headed away from Aurora and north up the shore of Iron Lake, which was dotted with summer homes and resort cabins. "What is winter like?"

"Cold. Snowy. Quiet. Most of the places you see are empty in winter."

"I would like to see the snow someday."

"You can if you stay."

Maria said, "We have not talked about going back. What will you do after your brother's wedding?"

"I don't know." Annie took her eyes off the road and looked at Maria. "If I stay, will you?"

Maria's gaze swung away from the lake, which showed itself in blue flashes through the trees. She smiled lovingly at Annie. "*Donde tú vayas, yo iré.*"

"Whither thou goest, I will go," Annie translated. "I feel the same way."

"Then we still have much to talk about," Maria said. "But first, let's see about this exorcism of yours."

The moment they broke from the trees and stepped into the meadow on Crow Point, Annie saw Waaboo running toward them through the tall grass and wildflowers. He wore shorts but no shoes or shirt, and his skin was the tan of deer hide.

"He said you were coming," Waaboo told them breathlessly.

"Who?" Annie asked.

"Mishomis."

Annie smiled. The old Mide was well known for this bit of

what seemed like second sight. He'd explained it to Annie once, saying simply, "The woods speak of visitors. I listen."

They followed Waaboo back to the old man's cabin. Jenny was with him, inside the simple one-room structure. It had been a long time since Annie had actually been in Meloux's cabin, but she wasn't surprised to see that it hadn't changed. A deer-prong pipe still hung on a wall, along with a pair of ancient snowshoes and a page from an old Skelly calendar with an illustration of a pretty young woman in short shorts showing a lot of bare skin as she bent under the hood of a sedan to check the oil. Annie had never asked Meloux why he hung on to that calendar page, but she knew there had to be a reason. There was also a gun rack that cradled a rifle as old as Meloux.

"Just like you said," Waaboo blurted when they entered.

"*Boozhoo*," the old man said in greeting.

"*Boozhoo*, Henry," Annie said.

"Will you sit?" The old man held his hand toward the two empty chairs at his table.

"Where's Prophet?" Annie asked.

"Making cornbread," Jenny said.

"He makes the best cornbread," Waaboo said eagerly.

"Prophet is many things, including a good baker. What is it you need from me?" Henry asked, his eyes on Annie.

Annie looked at Jenny. "Would you and Waaboo go with Maria to pick some wildflowers for us? They would look lovely on the table back home."

Jenny rose and reached out her hand to her son. "Come on, Waaboo. Let's educate Maria."

When she was alone with Meloux, Annie said, "I'm dying, Henry."

"I know, and I cannot change that."

"I'm dying and I'm full of rage because of it."

"Sometimes it is not an easy thing to die."

"Sometimes?"

"To die is to yield completely to what is unknown. Some approach death with fear, some with anger."

"Does anyone ever approach with an open heart?" she said bitterly.

"Yes."

"How?"

He reached out and took her young hand in his ancient one. She felt the warmth of his palm, the calming effect of its press. "There is a single thread that runs through us all and connects us to the Creator. In birth, that thread draws our life spirit from the heart of the Creator. In death, the thread draws our spirit back into the Creator's heart. It is the same for every living thing."

"The heart of the Creator." She shook her head. "I'm not sure I believe in God anymore."

"Maria," he said simply.

She looked at him without understanding.

"Is she not proof of the love of the Creator?"

It was true. Annie had lost everything, including her belief in God. But she had not lost Maria. Her love was still there.

"I don't want to leave her, Henry. That's the hardest thing."

"When you begin your journey on the Path of Souls, she will be there. And you will be there waiting when it is time for her to take the same journey."

"How do you know, Henry? What makes you so sure?"

"Belief, like love, is a choice. It makes all the difference between approaching death with fear and anger or approaching death with the peaceful heart." Henry still held her hand. With his other, he made a wide, sweeping gesture that included the glistening blue of Iron Lake and the wildflowers of the meadow on Crow Point and the vast, deep woods beyond. "All that Kitchimanidoo has created is connected. In life and in death. And for the heart that believes, there is only beauty, here and in what comes after."

"How do I believe, Henry?"

"You choose."

"It's that easy?"

"I did not say it was easy. But I promise that it will make all the difference."

A shadow darkened the doorway. Annie looked up and saw Prophet standing there, huge and implacable. The air that came in around him carried the good aroma of baked cornbread.

"*Boozhoo*, Annie," he said.

He entered, bent to Meloux, and whispered something in the old man's ear. Meloux nodded, and Prophet stepped to the gun rack on the wall. He took down Meloux's old firearm, then opened a tin can on a shelf and took out several bullets.

"What's going on?" Annie asked.

Meloux said, "You and Maria are not my only visitors."

CHAPTER 31

Dross rang the bell on the front door of the landlady from hell. When the woman answered, she was wearing the same pink housedress and pink slippers she'd worn when they last came calling. The beer in her hand was probably a fresh one.

"If you cops don't leave me alone, I'm going to start screaming harassment."

"Cops?"

"You and them state cops and the FBI. I got nothing more to tell you."

"So you haven't seen Mathias lately?"

"No, I haven't seen Mathias lately," she mimicked as if she were a parrot.

"Did you ever see him with a man named Lewis, who was maybe wearing a security uniform?"

"He's just my renter. I don't keep track."

"Did anyone ever park a big trailer here?"

"You can bet I'd have kicked their ass if they had."

"Mind if we have another look at that apartment you rent?"

"Why would I care? A whole river of cops have already been through there. Is that it? We done here?"

They felt the door slam at their backs. Although Dross still had a key to the apartment, they found the place unlocked. Inside, it looked torn apart, which was not much different from how it had looked the last time Cork had been there.

Dross said, "Probably nothing here's going to be much help."

Cork walked slowly through the mess of the apartment, then stepped into the tiny kitchen area. He spotted a mouse as it scurried along a baseboard and slipped through a door in the counter next to the sink. He opened the door, exposing the sink drainpipe and a small plastic wastebasket. He lifted out the basket. Inside was a blackened banana peel and a mess of coffee grounds. Beneath the coffee grounds, he spotted a small, flattened green cardboard box. He reached in and pulled it out.

"What is it?" Dross asked.

"An ammo box. Remington thirty-aught-six. Same caliber as the bullet that was fired at Waaboo this morning."

"Doesn't necessarily prove anything," Dross said. "Pretty common brand and caliber."

"Still, might be evidence. What do you want to do?"

"We can't take it without a warrant."

Cork thought a moment. "If maybe you could convince the landlady that she should put the contents of the wastebasket in the trash bin at the curb in order to keep mice out of this place, you wouldn't need a warrant."

Dross gave him a little smile. "Put the box back in the wastebasket. I'll go talk to the landlady."

After she left, Cork spent a little more time looking over the messy apartment. Something felt just a bit off. By the time Dross returned, he had it.

"She's getting some clothes on," Dross said. "She'll be right out to take care of that wastebasket."

"Paavola's been back here," Cork told her.

"What makes you think so?"

"The police scanner's gone."

"The BCA or FBI could have taken it."

"Maybe. But what about the PlayStation? First time we visited him, he was playing a video game." Cork pointed toward the big-screen television. "The system's gone now."

"BCA or FBI might have taken that, too."

"Can you think of a reason why? It's not like a computer that might have information on it. But someone looking to entertain himself while he hides out might risk coming back for it. And as for the scanner, if you were worried about the police coming for you, that might prove handy." Cork looked around again. "I'm pretty sure Mathias Paavola has gone to ground somewhere else."

"Where?"

"Maybe if we can find Lewis's trailer, we'll have our answer."

At Sizemore School, Daniel and the others were told that Candyce Osterkamp had left the campus earlier that morning and wasn't expected back until the next day. They asked if there was anyone at the school who might be familiar with a former resident named Fawn Blacksmith and were directed to the art teacher, one Malcolm Crowe. They found him in the art room, which smelled of oil paint and was brightly adorned with the work of young hands. He was a small, wiry man of about forty, a pencil-thin mustache above his lip, his red hair neatly parted. They introduced themselves, showed ID.

"We were told you might know something about a former resident, Fawn Blacksmith," Agent Shirley said.

"I can understand why they sent you to me. I'm not sure there's anyone else still here who was around when Fawn came to us. We have a lot of turnover. These kids can be difficult. I arrived a few months before Fawn."

"What can you tell us about her?" Agent Shirley said.

"She had problems. All the kids come here with problems. But generally speaking, they're not bad kids. They've just had it rough. Fawn could be hostile, but I believe that was because she was so desperately in need."

"Of what?" Daniel asked.

"Love. Or probably simply to know that she was worthy of being loved. If you looked at her file, you'd see that she'd been in and out of foster care, and I'm sure her treatment was often lacking in the warmth a kid needs. Here, we try to give them a sense of their worth."

"Did she have a special relationship with anyone at Sizemore?" Monte asked.

"She had a hard shell, wouldn't let anyone get too close. But let me show you something."

Crowe went to a file cabinet in the corner, opened a drawer, and took something from a folder. He brought it to his desk and set it down for the others to see. It was a detailed pencil drawing of a woman Daniel recognized. Daisy Blacksmith.

"She was quite talented," Crowe said. "Just look at this drawing. There's love in every line. She had it inside her. She was just afraid to let it out. Or to let anyone inside."

"We think she might have been willing to let someone inside. Does the name Billy Bones ring a bell for you?"

"Can't say that it does. Another student?"

"Older. Maybe early thirties. Maybe a teacher?"

"No teacher by that name since I've been here. Maybe you should talk to Candyce Osterkamp. She's been at Sizemore longer than anyone."

"We were told she's not here today."

"Oh, that's right. She found a blueberry patch somewhere north of town. Guess she wanted to pick some of the berries before anyone else discovered it. She's quite a good baker. Her blueberry muffins are legendary."

"Did she tell you where the patch is?" Daniel asked.

"She was quite secretive."

"Is there anything else you can tell us about Fawn Blacksmith?" Monte asked.

"Why are you so interested now? Nobody came looking for her when she ran away."

Agent Shirley took a deep breath. "Three days ago, the body of a young woman was found buried in a shallow grave. We believe it might be Fawn Blacksmith."

"Oh, dear God. That poor child." He gathered himself and shook his head. "I think I've told you everything I can."

"Do you mind if I take this?" Daniel tapped Fawn's drawing. "I'd like to give it to the one person she knew that loved her."

They stood on the grounds of Sizemore School, in the shade of a cottonwood.

"If Billy Bones doesn't ring a bell for Crowe, do you think it would do any good to talk to this Osterkamp woman?" Agent Shirley said. "They were both here during the time Fawn Blacksmith was a student."

"Blueberries," Daniel said. "Coincidence?"

"There are such things," Monte said. His cell phone rang and he answered. "LuJean, what's up?" As Monte listened, Daniel saw his brow furrow and his eyes go hard. "Head out there right away. And take Zuppardo with you. We're on our way."

"What is it?" Daniel asked when Monte had ended the call.

"Trouble on Crow Point," Monte said. "Let's go."

CHAPTER 32

"Are we in danger, Henry?" Annie asked.

"Prophet will see to our protection. But it would be best to bring the others back to my cabin," Henry replied calmly.

Annie stood and hurried outside. Although she could see Waaboo, Jenny, and Maria in a far corner of the meadow, Prophet had disappeared. She ran to the edge of the tall grass and wildflowers and called out. Maria turned to her and waved.

"Come back!" Annie cried, gesturing for them to return.

They didn't come immediately. Waaboo was kneeling and appeared to be intently studying something hidden in the grass. His mother was bent over him. Annie gestured more frantically. Maria said something to her companions, and Waaboo and Jenny finally looked toward Meloux's cabin. They waved, rose, and began to amble in her direction.

That's when Annie saw the glint of sunlight reflecting among the pines at the edge of the clearing, a brilliant flash that lasted only a moment before it vanished. She knew there was nothing natural in those woods that would reflect sunlight in that way. She hoped it might be Prophet, but all her sensibilities told her different. She'd been using one arm to gesture. Now she used both arms, stretching them toward the others and drawing them back as if scooping air. She shouted, "Hurry!"

She saw the man step from the trees, a rifle gripped in his hands. He wore a ball cap whose bill shaded his face. Jenny and the others had their backs to him and could not see. He lifted the rifle to his shoulder and took aim. Annie screamed, a desperate single drawn-out word, "No-o-o!"

But the man didn't sight his weapon at Waaboo or the others. The barrel was trained on Annie.

At the same moment the crack of the rifle shot came, she felt herself grabbed from behind and thrown down into the wild grass.

"Lie still," Meloux said. "He cannot see you if you stay down."

"But Waaboo," she said.

"This one did not come for the little rabbit."

Meloux's arm lay across her, pinning her to the ground, but Annie rolled from its protection and lifted herself so she could see.

Jenny, Waaboo, and Maria were running for the cabins. Behind them, Annie saw only one figure now, and it was not the man with the ball cap. Prophet stood where the man had been. In his hands was Meloux's ancient firearm. He looked down at the tall grass at his feet and spoke words Annie couldn't hear. Then he gestured with his rifle, and a moment later a man slowly rose and raised his hands. He no longer wore his ball cap.

Annie stood up, along with Meloux. The others joined them. Together, they watched as Prophet herded the intruder across the meadow. When the man was near enough that she could make out his face, Annie's anger exploded. "Lewis," she said, the word like phlegm spat from her mouth. At that moment, if she'd had a gun, she would have shot him dead.

"Into my cabin," Meloux said to Prophet, and he led the way as the others followed.

They seated Lewis across the table from the ancient Mide. Blood ran from a knot on the side of his head where, Annie assumed, Prophet had delivered the blow that felled the man, probably with the butt of Meloux's rifle. The blood dribbled over the shooter's right ear, which was scarred and misshapen. Lewis glared at the gathering, lingering on Annie with a look of seething hatred. It was she who asked the first and most obvious question: "Why?"

He answered with a single word: "Slut."

"I've done nothing to you."

"Just got me fired is all."

"And for that you'd shoot me?"

"And my son?" Jenny said.

Lewis eyed Waaboo. "You the kid sees things?"

"You know he is," Jenny said, and now she seemed ready to shoot the man.

Prophet held up the rifle he'd taken from Lewis and said to the others, "This isn't the weapon that fired the shot at Waaboo this morning. That cartridge was a thirty-aught-six. This Winchester is loaded with two-seventies."

Meloux said quietly to Lewis, "Your heart is a rage of hate. It has been this way for a long time."

"The hell with you."

"I wouldn't speak that way to this man," Prophet advised.

"What are you going to do about it, shoot me?"

"I'm guessing no one would miss you if I did."

"I don't want Waaboo here," Jenny said.

She put her hand on his shoulder, but he shrugged her off. "I want to stay."

Meloux said, "Let him see this."

"Henry . . ." Jenny began.

"He will learn something important," Meloux said.

She didn't seem happy, but she didn't leave with her son.

"How did you find me?" Annie asked.

Lewis just smiled. He reminded her of a vicious dog baring its teeth.

"Your shoulder bag, Annie," Prophet said. "May I see it?"

From the chairback where she'd hung it earlier, Annie lifted the embroidered shoulder bag she carried with her everywhere and handed it to Prophet. He spent a minute carefully inspecting it, then brought out an item that had recently become familiar to them all. An AirTag.

"He followed you," Prophet said.

Annie eyed the little device and thought for a moment. "When I blacked out at Spirit Crossing." She glared at Lewis. "You put it in my bag then, didn't you?"

His predatory grin widened.

"How many?" Meloux asked.

"How many what?" Lewis replied in a snarl.

"How many spirits have you sent on the Path of Souls?"

"I don't know what the hell you're talking about, old man."

"Your heart is ice," Meloux said.

"Windigo," Prophet said.

The Mide nodded and said to Lewis, "It is a hunger, this thing inside you."

"I know about the Windigo," Waaboo chimed in. "It's a cannibal giant with a heart of ice, Mishomis. It eats people."

"It's just a myth," Jenny said.

Annie looked into Lewis's eyes, deep wells of inhumanity. "No, Jenny," she said. "It's not just a myth." Then she echoed Meloux. "How many?"

"You'll never know." And to Annie's amazement, his grin widened even more, so that it became like a broad doorway into the hell of his soul.

Meloux beckoned Waaboo to him and put his arm around the

little boy. "There is truth in our stories of monsters. And there is truth in our stories of heroes. The Creator does not allow one without offering the other to balance. You have the heart of a hero, Little Rabbit. Never forget that."

"What do we do with him?" Prophet nodded toward the grinning monster in Meloux's cabin.

Annie's heart, hard as stone at the moment, had an answer. "Send him on the path to hell."

Meloux had a different one. "We give him to those who see to the law."

Prophet gave a nod. "But I'd rather not have to explain this and myself to the sheriff's people. I'll call the tribal police."

LuJean Desjardins arrived in a tribal police Tahoe, accompanied by Officer Anthony "Zippy" Zuppardo. He was in his midtwenties, and although his skin was dark, it was the result of a summer tan. He had no Native blood in him at all. Still, Annie had heard from Daniel that he was a good officer and conducted himself well on the rez.

"I called Monte. Then I radioed the Tamarack sheriff's office," LuJean told them. "Deputies will meet us in Allouette and take custody of this scumbag."

"We'll need statements from everybody," Zuppardo said.

"Except you, Prophet," Desjardins said. "We'll keep you out of this."

"*Miigwech*," Prophet said. "Here's the rifle he used."

"Same one used to shoot at Waaboo this morning, you think?" Desjardins asked.

Prophet said, "No, but he could have another rifle somewhere."

"We'll get it out of him," Zuppardo said confidently.

"Oh, Zippy," Desjardins said, shaking her head. "You still have so much to learn." She cuffed Lewis, recited his rights, and said to her partner, "Put him in the back. I'll be right there."

When the young officer had gone with his prisoner, Desjardins said to Meloux, "If that man knows Waaboo is here, others may know, too."

"We have Prophet," Meloux replied.

"I'm not afraid," Waaboo said.

Jenny laid a hand on her son's shoulder and closed her eyes as if in prayer.

It was Maria who spoke a truth that made them all nod.

"The O'Connors are Wolf Clan, I am told. They stand together as a pack. In this, I am Wolf Clan, too. I think we all are, yes?"

Meloux smiled, adding wrinkles to his face, which was already webbed from a century of creasing. He looked at Annie and said, "The Creator has gifted you with a warrior."

"I've known that forever, Henry," Annie replied.

"You didn't get your exorcism," Maria said as they walked the trail back to the double-trunk birch. It was late afternoon by then, the heat of the day still oppressive. "I can feel your anger."

"There was a moment when, if I'd had Henry's rifle in my hands, I would have shot that man. He's pure evil and his hatred of women is obvious. When I asked him if there were others he's killed, he just grinned at me like a viper."

They walked for a long time in a heavy silence. Then Maria said, "Alfonso Garcia."

"What?"

"Long before you joined me in the barrio, I helped a woman give birth to her son. She named him Alfonso. He was a beautiful little baby. I watched him grow, a happy child for a while. Then his mother was killed, murdered. Alfonso was taken in by an uncle, a wretched man, cruel. He used that child in unspeakable ways, until he was himself killed in gang violence. Then Alfonso became a part of that gang. One night, a pounding at my door. There was Alfonso, covered in his own blood. He wanted me to help him, but there was nothing I could do. He died in my arms."

"What's your point?"

"No child comes into this life evil. Our world shapes us. Some of us are lucky. Others not."

"You're telling me that devil back there was once a pure spirit?"

"That is my own belief."

"Then he must have had some hell of a childhood."

"Yes."

They were almost to the double-trunk birch. Annie stopped walking. She closed her eyes and felt the cool of the forest shade. She breathed in the evergreen-scented air. She listened to the singing of the birds, so many different melodies. It took her a while, but slowly she began to relax. When she opened her eyes, she said, "Forgiveness is a hard thing to offer to a spirit so lost in darkness."

"But it is possible."

Annie finally smiled. "You should have been a nun."

"We are what we were always meant to be." She held out her hand. "And that is together."

With their fingers gently laced, they walked out of the woods and into the sunlight of that day.

CHAPTER 33

They were on their way back to Aurora from Sizemore School when a call to Monte Bonhomme's cell phone rang through the audio of his Tahoe. It was LuJean DesJardins. He, Agent Shirley, and Daniel listened as she explained what had occurred on Crow Point.

"Let the Tamarack County Sheriff's Department know," Monte said. "Then bring him into our office in Allouette, and we'll meet you there. We're about an hour out." He ended the call.

Daniel was flooded with an overwhelming sense of relief, but along with it came a significant feeling of guilt for not having been there to help. "Thank God they're all okay," he said. "And thank God for Prophet."

"Prophet?" Agent Shirley asked.

"A friend of Meloux," Monte said. "And you heard that LuJean and Zippy are on their way out to get Lewis and bring him in."

"She didn't say if they'd let Cork and Dross know," Daniel pointed out.

"Let's try to meet up with them in Allouette and sort things out," Monte suggested.

"I'll call Cork." Daniel punched in the number.

"You guys get something?" Cork asked when he picked up the call.

"Not us. Well, we did, but I'm calling about Lewis. We've got him."

"How?"

"I'm not sure of the details, but Officers Desjardins and Zuppardo are on their way to Crow Point to take him into custody. Apparently Annie was out there. Lewis took a shot at her, but Prophet stopped him before he could do any harm."

"Christ," Cork whispered on his end.

Daniel suggested that they meet up in Allouette, and Cork said he and Dross would see them at the tribal police office.

"What's Lewis got against Cork's daughter?" Agent Shirley asked.

"I don't know," Daniel replied. "But Cork says he's a buddy of Mathias Paavola, and both men drank at the Howling Wolf. So there's a thread that ties him to Paavola's cabin and blueberry patch. A man who would shoot Annie strikes me as the kind of man who could easily do harm to other women as well."

"Fawn Blacksmith," Agent Shirley said.

"Or Olivia Hamilton," Monte said.

"Or Crystal Two Knives," Daniel said. "Or maybe all three."

Monte Bonhomme cruised through Aurora at 4:00 P.M. and swung south around Iron Lake. As he turned north toward the reservation, Daniel noted a warning sign that said ROAD WORK AHEAD. They rounded a curve and came immediately to a place where a crew had been doing some repairs. The crew had finished for the day, but a backhoe sat idle off the shoulder, protected by a couple of barricades. Several orange cones directed traffic away from a torn-up section of the highway as it crossed a culvert. Monte slowed and drove around the cones, then hit the gas again and shot toward Allouette.

Fifteen minutes later they parked in front of the new tribal police office, which was a block from the community center. Two other tribal police vehicles were already parked there, along with a cruiser from the Tamarack County Sheriff's Department. Monte, Agent Shirley, and Daniel made their way inside.

Adrian Lewis was in one of the two holding cells. He sat on the bunk, back against the wall, staring into space.

"Nasty bump on his head," Monte said, standing with the others outside the bars and appraising the man. "We need to get that looked at."

"We'll stop by the hospital when I take him into Aurora," Dross said.

"I think we'd like to have a few questions answered first," Monte said.

"He hasn't spoken a word since we cuffed him on Crow Point," LuJean said.

"Not true," Zuppardo said. "He called you a slut."

"Actually, it was Indian slut," LuJean said.

"He didn't ask for a phone call?" Daniel said.

"Nope. We've got the rifle he used to shoot at your daughter, Cork. It's a Winchester. Lewis here was shooting with two-seventy Wins. So it's not the weapon that was used by whoever fired at your grandson this morning."

"That round was a Remington thirty-aught-six," Cork said. "We found an empty box of those cartridges in Mathias Paavola's apartment this afternoon."

"So, you're not only drinking buddies," Dross said through the bars to Lewis. "You're shooting buddies, too?"

Lewis's eyes slowly panned all the faces looking at him from outside the cell. Daniel thought he was about to say something vicious, judging from the way his face was twisted, but the man held to silence.

"You blame my daughter for getting you fired," Cork said. "But she's not the first woman who harmed you. We know how you got that misshaped ear, Adrian."

Lewis's eyes flashed as if lightning had struck his brain. He leaned forward in a menacing way. "They're all sluts." He looked at Dross and Desjardins and Agent Shirley. "All of you."

"Is that why you killed Fawn Blacksmith?" Cork asked.

Lewis once more set his back against the cell wall and lapsed into silence.

"Let me take him now, Monte," Dross said.

"When you interview him officially, I want to be there."

"Of course."

"I'll let BCA know we've got him," Agent Shirley said. "They'll want one of theirs present for the questioning, I'm sure. Although they're still chasing that biker who got away in Fargo."

"We'll need statements from everyone on Crow Point," Monte said. "Daniel, can you let them know and make those arrangements?"

"Will do."

"All right. He's all yours, Marsha," Monte said. "For now."

Agent Danette Shirley accompanied Marsha Dross in her cruiser, with Adrian Lewis in the backseat, maintaining a sullen silence. Daniel followed in his pickup with Cork riding shotgun. The plan was for Daniel to drive to the house on Gooseberry Lane, drop Cork off, then head out to Crow Point to be with Jenny and Waaboo. With all the focus on Lewis, Daniel hadn't had time to fill Cork in on what he'd learned in Duluth and at Sizemore School. He took care of that as he drove, explaining about a talented young woman wanting to be loved and a man named Billy Bones, who seemed to have preyed on that need.

Cork listened, then said, "So we don't really know anything about this Billy Bones."

"Might be a moot issue. My money's on Lewis for killing both girls."

"What about Waaboo?" Cork said. "You think it was Lewis who fired that shot at him this morning?"

"Paavola, I think. That box of Remington cartridges you found in his apartment is pretty damning. And the blueberry patch and the cabin are places Lewis couldn't have known about except for Paavola. I think they both got spooked when word got out about Waaboo's connection with the spirit of Fawn Blacksmith, and Paavola tried to do something about that."

"Kind of hard to believe a couple of white guys like Lewis and Paavola would worry about some Indian kid's vision. We're sure there's no Native blood in them?" Daniel asked.

"Not that we know of."

"Think Paavola's responsible for his sister's disappearance?"

"Could well be. These men we're dealing with, God only knows how their brains work."

It was late afternoon by then, the sun in their eyes as they approached the curve in the road where the pavement over a culvert had been damaged and repair was underway. The glare on the windshield was blinding when Cork hollered, "Stop!"

Daniel hit the brakes just in time to avoid slamming into the rear end of Dross's cruiser.

"Damn sun," Daniel said. "Couldn't see her. What's up?"

Cork got out of Daniel's vehicle and walked ahead just as Dross exited her cruiser. He saw then that the orange cones, which had been there when he and Dross drove to the rez, had been removed.

The two wooden barricades that had previously been next to the idle backhoe were now set across the road, effectively blocking the way.

"What's up with that?" Cork said.

"Got me. Maybe something around the curve?"

"Let's move them."

Cork took one end of the first barricade and Dross took the other.

The shot came as they walked the barricade to the side of the road, a report like the explosion of a big firecracker. Cork let go of his end and Dross dropped hers. He and the sheriff both dashed behind the protection of the parked backhoe.

"It came from over there." Cork pointed toward the west side of the road, which was edged with a mixed stand of birch and evergreen and lots of undergrowth.

Dross had drawn her sidearm and was scanning the trees. "Sun's in my eyes. I can't see anything. You?"

"Same here."

Cork glanced back at the two parked vehicles. Agent Shirley was out of the cruiser, hunkered down in its lee. Daniel was out of his truck, crouched behind its protection, his service weapon in his hand.

"Can you see anything?" Cork hollered.

"Nothing," Daniel shouted back.

"What was he shooting at?" Dross said.

"I don't know."

Cork heard it then, from beyond the sharp curve of the road, the growl of an engine starting up, followed almost immediately by the sound of tires spitting gravel as a vehicle sped away at high speed. They waited a minute longer to be sure, then Cork and Dross left the cover of the backhoe and returned to the vehicles, where Agent Shirley stood looking at the rear window of the cruiser. The inside of the glass dripped with a spray of blood and other matter. Daniel came from his truck and joined them. Dross opened the rear door. Lewis lay fallen across the seat in a shower of glass from the shattered window on the other side of the cruiser.

"Christ," Dross said.

"Head shot," Cork noted.

Daniel turned back to his vehicle. "I'll call for an ambulance."

But it was clear to Cork that nothing could be done for Lewis now, except maybe pray for his soul.

CHAPTER 34

It was dusk when Cork stood near the idle backhoe with Dross. He felt as if that day had gone on forever. Looking at the drawn face of the sheriff, he figured she probably felt the same way.

"Three shootings in one day," Dross said.

"Thank God only one death," Cork said.

They watched the deputies and Bonhomme and his officers going over the area for any evidence the shooter had left behind. Photos of the scene had been taken, the county medical examiner had certified the death, and the body of Adrian Lewis had been taken away in the back of an ambulance.

A dozen yards down the road, Agent Shirley paced back and forth, talking on her cell phone. She ended her call and joined Cork and Dross.

"Just filling in my BCA colleagues. They've apprehended their biker and are transporting him back to Fargo for questioning. They're sending a couple of agents our way to discuss what's happened here."

"They don't sound particularly interested," Cork said.

"Lewis wasn't on their radar at all. At the moment, they're not especially open to abandoning their focus on the biker. But I got something from them. The results of the Hamilton girl's autopsy are in. Cause of death was asphyxia, the result of strangulation. There was evidence of sexual activity prior to death. And the bloodwork turned up Rohypnol. Somebody fed her roofies before she died."

"Lewis? Paavola?" Dross said.

"Maybe both," Cork said.

Bonhomme and Desjardins came from the trees where they'd been canvassing the area with the others. "LuJean found where our shooter was hiding," Bonhomme said. To Desjardins, he said, "Show them what you picked up."

Desjardins held out a gloved hand. In her palm was an expended cartridge. "Remington thirty-aught-six," she said.

"Paavola," Cork said.

Agent Shirley said, "How could he have known we would be here?"

Cork said, "He had a police scanner in his apartment. Last time I was in there, it was gone. Was there any radio chatter about taking Lewis to Allouette?"

"We communicated with the sheriff's office several times," Desjardins said.

"That probably explains it."

"Why kill Lewis? What was it he was afraid Lewis might tell us?" Agent Shirley said.

They stood silent for a moment, then Cork offered an answer. "Maybe where all the others are buried."

Twilight, and Annie sat on the porch swing as Daniel's pickup pulled up to the curb. Her father got out, walked to the driver's side, and said something through the window. He stepped away and watched Daniel head down Gooseberry Lane. Then he started up the sidewalk toward Annie.

He moved, Annie thought, like an old person, bent by the weight of too many years filled with too many worries. She loved him dearly, this man who'd hovered over her across the whole of her childhood, had protected her and Jenny and Stephen so many times in so many ways. She wondered now if she'd told him enough how much she appreciated his caring.

"Nice evening," he said as he mounted the steps. He nodded toward the swing. "Mind if I join you?"

She patted the seat beside her, and he lowered himself with a heavy sigh.

"Long day," she said.

"Any more like this'll kill me." He squeezed his face up in pain. "I'm sorry. That was . . ."

"It's all right, Dad."

He reached out and took her hand. "Where's Maria?"

"Making dinner. Lots of it. Rainy and Stephen and Belle will be back sometime, and probably hungry. You too?"

"I could eat. What's she making?"

"Chicken salad."

"Sounds good." He looked west, where the last light of day was a haze of purple along the horizon. "Adrian Lewis is dead."

Annie squeezed his hand, an involuntary reaction. "How?"

"We were transporting him from Allouette to Aurora and somebody ambushed us."

"Was anyone else hurt?"

"Only Lewis."

"Thank God for that. Are you all right?"

"Just tired." His eyes were still on the horizon. "Tired of the cruelty in how we treat one another."

"Not everyone is cruel, Dad. You're not."

"Maybe I am without knowing it. Maybe everybody is."

"That's part of being human, isn't it? And that's why there's forgiveness."

He gave a little laugh. "This from my daughter who shunned the nunnery."

"I wanted to kill Lewis today," she confessed. "I didn't feel an ounce of forgiveness in my heart."

"And now?"

She shrugged. "Now I just feel guilty for hating him."

"I learned some things today about Lewis. He grew up surrounded by cruelty. Enough that maybe I can understand how he became so warped." He still held her hand, and gave it a gentle squeeze. "Maybe understanding is the beginning of forgiveness?"

"I'll still have to work on that." She shifted in the swing and the chains that held it gave a little squeal. "Do you know who killed him?"

"I think it was Mathias Paavola. And I believe Paavola was involved in killing Fawn Blacksmith and Olivia Hamilton. I think there may be others he's killed." He shook his head. "How Paavola's soul could get that evil, I have no idea."

Headlights tunneled through the gathering dark on Gooseberry Lane. Rainy pulled into the drive, and Stephen and Belle pulled in beside her. They all walked toward the front porch, looking every bit as tired and weighted as Annie's father had looked.

"Hard day at Spirit Crossing?" Cork asked as they mounted the porch steps.

"You don't know the half of it." Rainy leaned to him and gave him a kiss, then studied his face in the gloom of the evening. "You look beat, too."

"A lot to share."

Maria opened the screen door and stepped out. "I thought I heard voices. I have prepared dinner. Are you hungry?"

"Bless you," Stephen said. "I could eat a moose."

CHAPTER 35

Night came to Crow Point with the songs of crickets and tree frogs and the silent splash of stars across the sky. Meloux had asked Prophet to build a fire in the ring behind the rise of the outcrops where the old Mide often gathered those who'd come seeking his advice or his shelter. They'd smudged with sage, and now Daniel sat with Jenny and Waaboo and Prophet and Meloux, all of them aflame with the dancing light of the fire.

"It is hard, this work you do, Daniel English," the old man said.

"Sometimes it feels pointless, Uncle Henry, like I'm trying to hold back a river. Bad just keeps coming to our people. I think about Fawn Blacksmith and Crystal Two Knives and God knows how many others who may have been murdered by the likes of Lewis and Paavola. It makes me angry and sad, and I sometimes feel so helpless."

"Yet you continue to do what you can."

"What else is there?"

Jenny put her hand on his knee. "I love that you keep trying. I love that you care. About me and Waaboo and all the others who need protecting. You are *ogichidaa*."

In the language of the Ojibwe, that word meant warrior, or one who stands between evil and his people. Daniel had heard it applied to Jenny's father on several occasions. Now the word lay on him, and he felt it like a weight on his shoulders.

Prophet said, "The Creator cuts the road through the forest and we follow it. We stumble, we doubt, we sometimes curse the journey that's been laid out for us, but there's a reason for the path our reluctant feet follow."

"You sound like Henry," Jenny said.

"I take that as a compliment. Although one of the things I've learned in my time here is that I need to speak less and listen more."

Waaboo said, "I like the stories you tell me."

"What stories?" Daniel asked.

"Based on Jack London, mostly," Prophet said. "There's a storyteller for you."

"Are we safe now?" Jenny asked.

Daniel knew what she meant. Safe now that Adrian Lewis was dead. "Mathias Paavola is still out there. I'm pretty sure he was the one who shot at Waaboo."

His son looked up at him, eyes burning with light as from a fire. "I'm not afraid."

"I know you're not. But until we've got Paavola in custody, we need to be sure you're safe."

Meloux said, "The woods have been quiet. But we will listen carefully."

"Will you stay?" Jenny asked.

"Tonight," Daniel said. "Tomorrow, I need to help find Paavola."

"How will you do that?"

"I'm not sure."

Waaboo said, "He has a troubled heart."

They all looked at the boy, who was staring into the fire.

"How do you know that?" Jenny asked.

"I felt it in the cabin."

"Why didn't you say anything before this?"

"I felt a lot in the cabin. It was hard to sort out."

"Troubled how?" Daniel asked.

"Sad. Scared."

"Probably scared of being caught," Daniel said.

Waaboo shook his head. "Scared different. I don't know how exactly."

"When we catch him, we'll find out," Daniel said. "I'll grill him like meat over a fire."

"If I were you," Meloux said, "I would be like Prophet."

"How's that?" Daniel asked.

"Speak less and listen more."

"I can't believe the wedding's only six weeks away," Rainy said. "With everything that's going on, I feel like we've abandoned it. The trouble at Spirit Crossing, the dead girls, the shootings. We should be in the mood to celebrate. Instead, it feels like we're in a war."

"We'll celebrate when the time comes," Cork tried to assure her. "The Anishinaabeg have always been good at finding the seed of joy in a field of sorrow."

"Did you come up with that?"

"Actually, I read it in one of Daniel's poems."

"Which he doesn't write anymore."

"At the moment. Doesn't mean he won't write again."

They lay in bed, the window opened to the soft music of the night and a view of the stars. A breeze came through the screen, cooling after the heat of that July day.

"Jenny married her father," Rainy said.

"What?"

"Daniel's like you in a lot of ways,"

"I never wrote poetry. And God forbid that I should ever play the accordion."

"He's really good at both."

"My point exactly. Me, I have no talent whatsoever."

Rainy turned in bed and ran her hand along his chest. "I wouldn't say that," she whispered coyly. "I have a suggestion."

"What?"

"I think right now I could use a little seed of joy. And that's something you're quite talented at."

Cork smiled. For a while after that, in Rainy's arms, he let his love for her cleanse all the sullied places in his heart.

They often read to one another at night, each taking a book of poetry and sharing favorites. That night, Annie read from a collection by Ted Kooser, a Nebraska poet whose work had always affected her deeply because of its honesty and simplicity and humanity. Maria read from a collection by Billy Collins because, she said, "He is whimsical and not afraid to be silly."

Annie ended with a poem titled "This Paper Boat." It was brief and poignant, a poem about love and its remembrance. And it made Maria cry.

"I could have lost you today," she said, holding Annie's head in her hands and looking deeply into her eyes. "I promise you, I will cherish every moment we have together."

"A hard promise to keep. We still have a lot of moments ahead of us. And isn't every day filled with so much that's mundane?"

"Not lately," Maria said, and it made Annie laugh.

They prepared for bed and lay together in a long, comfortable silence. Then Maria said, "We should pray for them."

"Who?"

"The young women. And also for the man who was killed today."

"Why for him?"

"It would do our hearts good, I think, to ask God for kindness for a soul who must have suffered in this life."

"Your heart is more forgiving than mine. Don't forget that the man who helped him kill those women is still out there. Maybe he'll kill more. I'll save my prayers for those souls."

"These are not the words of the Annie O'Connor I fell in love with. She who wanted to be a bride of Christ."

"That Annie is dead."

"I do not think so. Lost maybe." She was quiet a moment. "Do you know what I pray for?"

Annie didn't answer. For some reason, she was afraid of what she might hear.

"I pray for forgiveness and understanding."

"Why? For what?"

"I am sometimes so angry with God. I pray that he will forgive me for that. And I pray that he will help me understand why he is taking you from me."

"It's not God. It's cancer."

"You once believed that God was at the heart of everything."

"I was young and naïve. And not dying."

"Dying has made you more precious to me than ever. I am thankful that bullet today did not take you from me suddenly. And maybe this is part of the grace of God. That I will be with you as you walk to the place of your crossing over."

"I like the image that Ted Kooser poem has given me. I'll just float away like a paper boat."

"And when it is my time to follow, you will be there waiting?"

"I will be there." She kissed Maria. "I promise."

CHAPTER 36

Just after sunrise the next day, Cork picked up Marsha Dross at the Tamarack County Sheriff's Department. She was waiting in the parking lot, a travel coffee mug in her hand, two Kevlar vests at her feet.

"Do you have a firearm?" she asked before getting into the Expedition.

"Got my Winchester in my lockbox in back."

"That'll do." Dross opened the rear door and threw in the vests, then joined Cork up front. "Thanks for driving. My cruiser won't be usable for a while."

"I'm glad you called. I like an early start to a hunt. So, what have you got?"

"Thirty-four RV resorts or camps in the county. I figure we hit them one by one. Lewis's fifth wheel has to be in one of them."

"Do we know what we're looking for?"

"I've got a plate number for the camper from DMV. It's a Jayco, manufactured two years ago. That's all they could give me."

"Jayco. Shitload of those up here," Cork said. "In my experience, most folks park their fifth wheel with the rear facing the back of their assigned spot. To see a plate, we'd have to get out and check every damn camper."

"Got a better idea?"

"Yeah. Why don't we start by talking to Lewis's neighbor, the guy up the road who was pruning his apple trees?"

"Luke Gavins."

"He might be able to give us a better description."

"Suits me," Dross said. "Let's go."

They headed west out of Aurora with the rising sun at their backs, drove through the landscape of the Laurentian Shield, among the oldest exposed rock on earth. Aeons ago, this had all been volcanic peaks higher than any modern mountain range. Over millions of years, they had been eroded to rugged hills covered in boreal forest and cut by fast-running streams and rivers and bejeweled with lakes of crystal-clear water. Cork never tired of the beauty of this place he called home.

"I look at all this loveliness," Dross said, "and I wonder how so many terrible things can take place here."

"Same everywhere, I imagine," Cork said. "Because people are the same everywhere. So, what did your cohorts from BCA have to say about yesterday?"

Dross and Agent Danette Shirley had met with the agents the night before and laid out for them the events leading up to the shooting of Adrian Lewis.

"They said they'd send some agents our way today to help in the investigation of Lewis's death, but they're still not convinced that he had anything to do with Olivia Hamilton. Apparently, when they caught up with the biker, he was carrying a wide range of drugs, including roofies. He continues to be their primary suspect."

"Okay by me. I'd rather we weren't all stumbling over one another," Cork said.

"Agent Shirley, Monte Bonhomme, and Daniel are planning to head down to Sizemore School today to talk to Candyce Oster-kamp about Irene Paavola and maybe Billy Bones."

"Billy Bones?"

"They're pretty well convinced he was the one responsible for grooming Fawn Blacksmith for trafficking. If they can track him down, maybe they can link him to Lewis and Paavola and to Fawn Blacksmith's murder."

"Trafficking is how you think they're all related."

"It goes along with the pipeline construction," Dross said. "Lots of men, lots of money, and particularly with this holdup at Spirit Crossing, lots of idle time."

"Christ, how many girls like Fawn Blacksmith have these men preyed on?"

"I can't answer that. But I'm going to do my damnedest to make sure these guys don't prey on any others."

It was nearing 8:00 A.M. when Cork turned off Orchard Lane and followed the drive between apple trees up to the home of Luke Gavins. It was a well-kept farmhouse, white with green trim, and a detached garage. Fifty yards away stood a big red barn. The house was surrounded by a white picket fence edged with a colorful array of flowers. As they exited Cork's Expedition, Gavins stepped from the front door and strolled down a flagstone path to greet them, a coffee mug in his hand.

"Morning," he said. "Didn't expect to see you folks again. Have you found Adrian?"

"Yes," Dross said. She could tell that Gavins was waiting for more. "He was killed yesterday."

"Oh, Jesus. How?"

"Someone shot him."

"Who?"

"That's what we're trying to figure out now. We're hoping you might be able to help us."

"How could I possibly help in something like that?"

"You told us Lewis has a fifth-wheel trailer. Could you describe it?"

"Was a Jayco Eagle, like mine."

"You have a trailer?"

"I do. Keep it parked behind the barn over there. Care to see it?"

"Sure."

He led them to where the trailer was parked. Cork judged it to be about forty feet long, maybe a dozen feet high, and about nine feet wide.

"They all look pretty much the same," Gavins said. "White, or I believe you might be able to get them in tan. They all got those swooshes along the sides, kind of like eagle wings. Got the Jayco name, of course, across the front, along with the image of an eagle. Some folks do special detailing, I suppose, but I haven't really seen that much."

"Did Lewis do any detailing?"

"Not that I recall. Of course, I haven't seen his trailer in quite some time."

"Looks like it can accommodate a lot of people."

"It'll sleep four pretty comfortably."

"Any idea where he might have parked it?"

"With all the lakes we got up here, there's a ton of RV resorts and the like."

Dross shook her head hopelessly. "Tell me about it."

"'Course, he could've parked it at his old man's fishing cabin."

Cork had been thinking that they had a long day ahead of them. He liked the sound of this. "Where is it?"

"Up on Little Trout Lake, about twenty miles north."

Cork looked at Dross. "That would put it about ten miles from Spirit Crossing."

"Any idea exactly where on Little Trout the cabin's located?"

"Can't help you there, sorry. Just know that Davey Lewis used it as a getaway from that she-wolf of a wife he had." He thought a moment. "Wait. Davey used to tell me that he liked it because it was a five-minute walk from some bar where he did his drinking. Let me think." He closed his eyes. "I believe it was called the Wild Trout or maybe Angry Trout. Place right on the lake." He gave them a puzzled look. "But if Adrian's dead, why the interest in his trailer?"

"We think a man who is also of interest to us might be hiding there."

"Got a name you're willing to share?"

"Mathias Paavola."

"Did he shoot Adrian?"

"He might have."

"Then I hope you get him."

"Thanks for your help," Dross said. "If you think of anything else, could you give me a call? You still have my card?"

"Still got it."

They found the bar. It was called the Crazy Trout. It wasn't open yet, but there was a car parked in the gravel lot. Dross pounded on the front door until a big man with an angry look on his face opened up.

"What? You can't wait for another hour to get drunk?"

Dross flashed her wallet ID. "We're looking for a man who may have been a customer here. Name's Adrian Lewis."

"Davey Lewis's kid." From the man's tone, it sounded like he didn't much care for Adrian Lewis. "He used to drink here. Not any longer. That man was certifiably nuts. I told him after the last incident that if he ever came back, I'd take great pleasure in personally stuffing his head up his ass."

"What did he do?" Cork asked.

"Made some off-color remark to one of my waitresses, then threatened her when she told him to get lost. It wasn't the first time he'd pissed me off."

"Davey Lewis, his father," Dross said. "We understand he has a fishing cabin near here."

"Yeah. Quarter mile north there's a lane runs down to the lake. Can't miss it. Big Coca-Cola billboard on the other side of the road."

They found the billboard and took the lane. It led a hundred yards through a mix of evergreen and broadleaf trees to an opening on the lake where a small cabin stood. Parked next to the cabin was a Jayco Eagle fifth-wheel trailer.

CHAPTER 37

On Crow Point that morning, Jenny walked Daniel to his truck. "Take care of yourself. And good luck with the hunt today."

"You take care of Waaboo," Daniel told her. "Mathias Paavola is still out there."

"Between Prophet and Henry and me, we'll keep him safe, I promise."

She kissed him goodbye, and in his rearview mirror as he drove away he saw her standing there, waving, struck with sunlight in a way that made it seem as if her blond hair had been spun from pure gold. Then she turned back to the cabin where Waaboo was still sleeping.

Daniel headed to Allouette along a rugged track mostly used by Prophet in the ATV on those rare occasions when Meloux wanted to go into the reservation town. It led along the northern shore of Iron Lake, which, through the broken wall of trees, was cobalt blue under the morning sky. As he jostled over the rough ground, he thought about what might be ahead that morning. Events had been unpredictable for so long now, he desperately wanted a day in which he could grasp something solid, put all the upheaval to rest. Along with Monte Bonhomme and Agent Danette Shirley, he hoped he might be able to do just that.

The tragic history of Fawn Blacksmith had led them to the speculation that human trafficking was at the heart of the events in Tamarack County. They were looking for a connection between Fawn Blacksmith, Adrian Lewis, and Mathias Paavola. Billy Bones seemed the most likely candidate.

When he arrived at the tribal police office, Daniel found Monte, Agent Shirley, and Officer LuJean Desjardins in conversation over coffee. Monte looked up and smiled. "Ready to roll?"

"Whenever you are."

"Zippy could hold down the fort," LuJean said.

Monte shook his head. "I need you here."

"Do me a favor, then," LuJean said.

"What?" Monte replied.

"You get this Billy Bones, you bring him here. I want to personally kick him in the balls."

Agent Shirley said, "I understand the feeling, but we'll let the law do that. You'll get a visit from BCA today. They'll be following up on a discussion I had with them last night about what's gone on out here, the shot at Waaboo and the shooting of Lewis. Be helpful."

"Always am with our fellow law enforcement agencies."

"Feel free to tell them where we've gone," Monte said. "But don't say anything about kicking Billy Bones in the balls, okay? If we get him, I don't want any claim of police brutality."

Desjardins shrugged, then said unconvincingly, "You're the boss."

They took Monte's cruiser and headed south toward Bixby and Sizemore School. As they drove, they went over what they knew and what they suspected.

Mathias Paavola was the most likely link to the blueberry patch and old cabin. Paavola and Lewis were connected at the very least through their drinking together at the Howling Wolf, but probably also through their work on the pipeline. If Fawn Blacksmith was being trafficked, it might well be that she was being used to service the men working the pipeline, a common circumstance in places and on projects that involved a lot of manpower. If someone had been grooming her for trafficking, Billy Bones seemed to be the likely candidate. The most promising lead on how he'd managed that seemed, at the moment, to be Sizemore School.

There was another wrinkle. Irene Paavola was still missing.

"Maybe her brother was afraid of what she knew and that she might talk to the police," Daniel said.

"Cork and Marsha Dross questioned her," Agent Shirley pointed out. "She didn't seem to be able tell them much that was helpful except how to track down her brother."

"That doesn't mean she didn't know more," Monte said.

"If her brother grabbed her, what are the chances she's still alive?" Daniel asked.

"We don't really know Mathias Paavola or what he's capable of," Monte said. "If he was involved in the death of Fawn Blacksmith and Olivia Hamilton, he could be capable of anything."

The day before, they'd been directed to talk to Candyce Osterkamp, who, apparently, was close to Irene Paavola. She'd been gone picking blueberries that day, but she was at work at the school when Daniel and the others arrived. They tracked her down to a flower bed filled with an array of blossoms.

"My butterfly garden," she explained, rising from where she'd been at work on her knees, a little trowel in her gloved hands. She wore a broad-brimmed straw hat that shaded her face. She was sixtyish, slender, smiling. "What can I help you with?"

They introduced themselves and showed their IDs. "We're trying to track down a man who may have worked here at one time," Agent Shirley explained. "Does the name Billy Bones mean anything to you?"

Osterkamp furrowed her brow and thought, then shook her head. "I can't say that it does."

"What can you tell us then about Irene Paavola?"

A darkness crossed her face that had nothing to do with the shade from her hat. "She's still missing, isn't she?"

"Yes," Agent Shirley said.

"Liam," Osterkamp said, as if the name were foul.

"Liam?" Monte said.

"Liam Boyle. Her ex-husband. There's a snake who'll charm your panties off."

"Tell me about him."

"Dark, handsome, smart. Devious. Mixed heritage."

"Mixed?"

"Ojibwe and Irish. He doesn't talk much about his Ojibwe side, but Irene's told me he's kind of superstitious in that he believes in signs and portents and spirits and such."

"We were given to understand that they divorced because of his drinking."

"That's not why they divorced. Well, maybe part of it. But mostly it was because he could be cruel. Abusive. There's something dark and scary at the heart of that man. I told her to stay away from him."

"But she continued to see him?"

"Irene is a pretty smart cookie, but some women have a weakness for a certain kind of man. She couldn't live with him, but she couldn't live completely without him either. So, yes, she still sees him from time to time."

"Any idea how we might contact Mr. Boyle?"

"You could check with Edie in the office. She's in charge of personnel. She might have an address or phone number for him."

In response to their questioning looks, she said, "Liam worked here for a while. He was down on his luck. Uber driver or something. Irene gave him a job. Groundskeeper, facility maintenance, that kind of thing." She thought a moment and added, "There's another possibility, I suppose."

"What's that?" Daniel asked.

"She still owns the house she grew up in. Never goes there, but she hasn't sold it, as far as I know. If she's afraid of Liam, I suppose it's possible she's hiding there."

"Where is it?"

"In Aitkin."

"Do you have an address?"

"I don't. But when you find her, will you let me know?" Osterkamp said. "I'd like to be sure she's safe."

They promised they would, thanked her, and as they headed toward the administration building, Daniel said, "Liam Boyle. Liam is Cork's middle name, a shortened version of William."

Agent Shirley said, "Billy is, too."

Monte said, "I think we've found our Billy Bones."

The address on file for William Boyle at the Sizemore School was in Duluth, a nondescript apartment building on the West End, not far from the run-down house in Lincoln Park where Fawn Blacksmith had once stayed. There was a sign planted in the dead grass of the lawn: APARTMENT FOR RENT. The mailbox associated with the apartment number they'd been given had no name on it.

They were standing at the doorway, discussing options, when a car pulled into the apartment lot. A woman got out, reached into the backseat for a bag of groceries, then approached, looking at them warily.

They identified themselves, flashed their IDs, and explained that they needed access. "For law enforcement reasons," Monte said, keeping it vague.

The woman, who looked to be of retirement age, let them in.

"Do you know anything about the man who lives in apartment 3B?" Agent Shirley asked.

"That's third floor. I don't know anybody up there. What did he do?"

"Thanks for your help, ma'am," Monte said. "We'll take it from here."

There was, as Daniel expected, no answer to their knock. The door was locked.

"We could contact the company on the sign, see if Boyle is still renting the place," Daniel suggested.

But Agent Shirley said, "Monte, give me your car keys." When he'd done so, she said, "Stay here. And Daniel, you come with me."

He followed her down the flights of stairs to the building entrance. "Wait here and keep the door open." She went to Monte's Tahoe, unlocked the door on the passenger side, and bent in for a few moments. Then she closed and locked the door, and she and Daniel returned to the apartment.

"Stand back," she said to the other two.

Daniel saw that she'd brought up a set of picks, and she began to work on the door lock.

"You carry those with you everywhere?" he asked.

"Pretty much."

"Not in any law enforcement manual I ever read," Monte said.

"I learned a long time ago to think outside the box. Et voilà." She pushed the door open.

The apartment was empty, not a stick of furniture in the place.

"Cleared out a while ago," Monte said. "Even before he might have been worried that we were looking for him."

"We could check on a forwarding address," Daniel suggested.

"Something tells me he probably didn't leave one," Monte said.

"What now?" Agent Shirley asked.

"Let's check in with Cork and Marsha Dross, see if they've got any kind of lead on Lewis's fifth wheel," Monte said. "If Liam Boyle is connected with all this, that might be a likely place for him to be hiding. And Mathias Paavola as well."

Which brought Daniel a jolting realization, one that made his gut draw taut. "If that's true, when they locate the trailer, they may be walking into a nest of vipers."

CHAPTER 38

"Paavola's Jeep isn't here," Dross said.

They stood in front of the kind of cabin Cork was very familiar with. There were so many fishing cabins just like it nestled among the trees on the shoreline of Iron Lake. It was small, probably only two or three rooms, built decades ago and showing its age.

"Doesn't mean the place is empty," Cork said.

"Let's put on those vests I brought," Dross said. "And by the way, I'm officially deputizing you."

After he donned a Kevlar vest, Cork took his Winchester from the lockbox in the back of his Expedition. He slid in five cartridges and fed one of them into the chamber. Dross had already drawn her service weapon.

"Cabin or trailer first?" Cork asked.

"Trailer," Dross said. "I'll approach, you cover me."

Dross had her weapon up and readied as she walked slowly toward the Jayco. Cork watched for any movement at the windows, the rustle of a curtain, the peek of a face. Dross knocked on the trailer door and shouted, "Police! Open up!"

Nothing happened. Dross reached out and tried the knob on

the door. She glanced back at Cork, then waved him over. He joined her.

"Unlocked," she said. "Ready?"

"Let's do this," Cork said.

The place was deserted and in mild disarray. Bottles of alcohol sat on the kitchen counter in various degrees of emptiness, along with several glasses. Dishes were piled in the sink, and flies buzzed over the crusted food. Magazines, some of them pornographic, were scattered on the dining table. A red tank top and shorts lay thrown on a chair. Cork opened the refrigerator.

"Pretty full," he said.

They went through the trailer slowly. There was one bedroom, the sheets on the queen bed a rumpled mess and in need of washing. A box of Trojan BareSkin Raw condoms was on the nightstand along with a vibrator.

They opened the door to the closet, which was empty, except for a number of hangers fallen to the floor.

"Looks like someone grabbed things quick and flipped those hangers off the rack," Dross said.

They checked the drawers of the dresser. Empty. In the bathroom, they found cosmetics and hairbrushes and toothbrushes. Towels hung on the racks, still slightly damp to the touch.

"Gone, but not all that long ago," Dross said.

"Cabin next?" Cork asked.

"Same as before. You cover me."

They stepped down from the camper and Dross approached the cabin, Cork covering her. She didn't knock this time, just tried the knob. The door opened. She stepped to the side and waved Cork to join her. They entered together.

It was small and smelled of old cabin, not an unpleasant smell to Cork. He'd been in so many Northwoods cabins filled with the same scent, a combination of damp and must and woodsmoke.

There was a table with a Formica top and three chairs, the padded seats covered in plastic that matched the Formica. There was a sofa with thin cushions. A cast-iron stove stood against one wall, and along the wall opposite it was a sink flanked by wooden counters. Thin checkered fabric curtained the windows.

A big muskie mounted on a lacquered board hung on the wall along with some framed photographs, mostly pictures of a man holding various fish, but a couple in which he stood with a kid. Cork looked closely to see if he could spot the kid's damaged ear but he couldn't. The place wasn't in disarray in the same way as the Jayco, but there were beer cans and bottles on the counter next to the sink. Playing cards were on the table, laid out in three hands, as if someone had been in the middle of a game.

Off the one main room were a small bedroom and a bathroom. They checked the bedroom. A single bed with unmade sheets. A box of condoms on the nightstand. In the top drawer of the old dresser were some articles of lingerie, frilly bras and lacy underwear. In the drawers beneath were additional linens and blankets. Cork sifted through and found a pad of drawing paper slipped beneath the folded blankets. He pulled out the pad and flipped through the pencil sketches while Dross looked over his shoulder.

"Quite an artist," she noted.

There were sketches of the lake, of the Jayco, of several young women. Then Cork stopped flipping. "Look familiar?"

"Mathias Paavola," Dross said.

Cork flipped a couple more pages. "Adrian Lewis."

There was only one other sketch of a male, unfamiliar to Cork. He was drawn in a way that made him appear both handsome and dark.

"Look at those eyes," Dross said. "They're like . . ."

"The eyes of a predator," Cork finished.

"Billy Bones, you think?"

"It's not Paavola or Lewis. So could be him."

Cork's cell phone rang. When he answered, Daniel told him, "If you locate Lewis's trailer, be careful. Paavola and Billy Bones might be there."

"We've found the trailer at a cabin Lewis owned on Little Trout Lake. No one's here. But they were. It looks like this is where they did their trafficking. What did you find out?"

"Billy Bones is probably William Boyle, Irene Boyle's ex-husband."

Cork told Daniel about the pencil sketches and the one that he and Dross speculated might be Billy Bones.

"Fawn Blacksmith was quite a talented artist," Daniel said.

"So she was probably here before she was killed," Cork said.

"Any sign of any other girls?"

"Whoever was here, it appears that they cleared out pretty quick."

"We checked the address for Boyle on file at Sizemore School," Daniel said. "It's clear that he flew the coop a while ago. But we spoke with Candyce Osterkamp, Irene Boyle's friend at the school. She said it's possible Irene is hiding out at the place where she grew up in Aitkin. You told me you tracked it down when Erno Paavola hired you to find his niece and nephew. You wouldn't happen to have the address? We're not that far away, and it might be worth checking out."

"Not off the top of my head, but it's in the files I keep at Sam's Place. Annie's at home. Give her a call and see if she can pop over and check it out."

Dross had wandered to the front door of the cabin and stood looking out into the morning sun. She suddenly called, "Cork, someone's in the woods!"

"Gotta go," Cork said and slipped his cell phone into his pocket.

He joined Dross at the door. She'd holstered her weapon earlier, but now it was out again.

"Where?" he said.

"See that sumac? In there."

The stand of sumac was fifty yards to the south, between a grove of birch near the shoreline and the mixed hardwood and evergreen that ran up to the main road. Although it was only July, some of the sumac leaves were already showing the blood red that usually came in late August. The stand was thick, and though Cork didn't see anything, he had no doubt that Dross had spotted someone.

"How do you want play this?" he said.

"Let's try being reasonable first." She leveled her weapon at the sumac. "You in the woods. This is Sheriff Marsha Dross. Come out now with your hands up."

There was sudden movement, a shiver among the sumac bushes, then everything went still again.

"They've run," Cork said.

Dross holstered her weapon. "Let's go."

Although the undergrowth along the shoreline was dense, they broke through at a sprint. Branches slapped at Cork's face and arms, and vines tugged at his legs. As he leapt over the trunk of a storm-toppled tree, his trailing foot caught in a dense tangle of brush and he went down. It took him a few moments to disentangle himself and to grab his rifle from where it had fallen. When he came up, he could no longer see Dross. He could, however, hear a woman screaming.

It took him nearly another minute to work his way to the source of the screams. He came out of the trees at the edge of the water, where the ground dropped suddenly a half dozen feet into the lake. Dross was already there, shedding her Kevlar vest. Twenty yards out, amid a great splashing of water, a young woman fought against going under. Dross divested herself of her belt and holster, knelt, and in a blaze of finger wizardry, unlaced and removed her boots in a flash. Then she leapt into the water feet first and swam toward the struggling woman.

Cork watched from the shoreline, ready if help was needed. But it was clear to him that Dross was handling the situation. She approached the woman from behind, grabbed her in a cross-chest carry, and despite the woman's flailing arms, managed to swim her back to shore. Cork grabbed the belt Dross had shed, leaned over the lip of the drop-off, and let the belt dangle.

"Grab it!" he called to the young woman.

Which she did, with both hands. Cork hauled her up, and she fell, wet and exhausted, on the wild grass near his feet. He let the belt dangle for Dross and helped her up as well. She sat breathing heavily next to the young woman, who lay with her face to the sun, her eyes closed. Except for the rapid rise and fall of her chest, she looked very much like a drowned kitten.

"Nice work," Cork said to Dross. "Where'd you learn lifesaving?"

"Three summers as a lifeguard on Gull Lake in high school," she said between gasps.

Cork assessed the young woman. She seemed to him more child than adult. She was clearly Native, her black hair short and tinted blue, and she wore only a halter top and shorts. Her feet were bare and were bleeding from her dash through the woods.

"What's your name?" Cork asked.

She opened her eyes, stared at him defiantly, and made no reply.

Dross sat up. "Why did you run?"

"You were going to arrest me."

"If you were being trafficked, no," Dross said. "You're the victim in this."

"Right," the girl said, clearly not buying it.

"How old are you?" Cork asked.

She only glared at him.

"Sixteen? Seventeen?" Dross said. She spoke gently.

"Eighteen come August."

Dross nodded toward the girl's bleeding feet. "Can you walk?"

"I been hurt worse than this."

"Let's go back then," Dross said.

"Rather not."

"It's all right. No one's there who'll hurt you."

"You don't know who you're dealing with, lady."

"Are you afraid of Adrian Lewis?" Cork asked.

The name made her flinch.

"He's dead," Cork told her.

"Good," the girl said.

"Okay to go back now?" Dross said. "Our vehicle's there."

The girl thought about it, then nodded. She stood up, but when she tried to walk, it was clear she was in pain.

Cork handed Dross his rifle, turned his back to the girl, and crouched. "I'll piggyback you."

The girl hesitated.

"Go on," Dross said. "He's one of the good ones."

The girl must have believed this, because in the next instant, Cork felt the weight of her settle onto him.

CHAPTER 39

"You said Toad was dead, right? How?"

Cork had retrieved the first aid kit from his Expedition. They were in the cabin now. The girl sat on the thin cushions of the sofa with her legs propped on a stool. Dross knelt in front of her, tending to the girl's injured feet.

"Toad?" Dross said.

"Adrian. That's what we called him."

"Someone shot him," Cork said.

"Not you?"

"We think it was Mathias Paavola."

The girl nodded as if that made sense. "He said he'd kill Toad if he ever hurt any of us again. Where are the others?"

"Others?" Dross said.

"Girls like me. Brandi and Coral."

"We don't know. We're here investigating the death of Fawn Blacksmith."

"Toad killed her. Probably would've killed the rest of us eventually if it hadn't been for Matt."

"Mathias Paavola?"

"Matt," she said with a nod.

"What's your name?" Dross asked, wrapping sterile gauze around the girl's right foot.

"Jade. At least that's what I'm called here."

"What's your real name?"

The girl hesitated. "You gonna send me to jail?"

"As I told you, if you were being trafficked, no. You aren't the criminal here."

"You're not lying?"

"I'm not lying."

"Margot Lachance."

"Why aren't you with the other girls?" Cork asked. "Brandi and Coral."

"We were playing cards when Billy came. Something was wrong. He was acting crazy. I mean, I've seen him mad before, but this was something else. He was screaming, waving a rifle around."

"Matt wasn't with him?"

"No."

"When you say Billy, is that Billy Bones?" Cork asked.

"Yeah."

Dross said, "And did he take the other girls away?"

"Yeah, last night. He just kept hollering. I mean, he was out of control. This was scary like I never seen before. Told us to get our things, that we were leaving. Didn't say where. Just"—and her voice dropped, imitating Boyle—"*get your damn stuff together now!*"

"Why didn't he take you?"

"Like I said, he was out of his mind. I told Brandi and Coral we needed to get away, but they wouldn't go."

"Too scared of Billy?" Cork said.

"Probably. And probably still a little in love with him. That's how we all felt, at least at first. They wouldn't go, but I hid out in the woods."

Dross said, "You indicated Adrian Lewis killed Fawn. Tell me about that."

"Owww!" Margot said and pulled her foot from Dross's grasp.

Dross was seeing to the girl's other foot now. "You've got a bad cut here."

"Sorry," Margot said, and let Dross resume her care.

"Tell us about Fawn," Cork said.

"Nobody called her Fawn. She was Ruby here. But we got close, and she told me her real name. She was Lakota. Me, I'm White Earth Ojibwe. She came after me."

"Here to the cabin?"

"That was before the cabin. We were outside Thief River Falls then, working out of the trailer. Brandi and Coral came after Fawn and Sapphire, when we got down here."

"Sapphire?"

"Yeah. She didn't last long. Billy told us she ran away. Which was strange. None of us got anywhere to run. Me, I always thought Toad might've had something to do with that."

"What happened to Fawn?" Dross said.

"We all had to take turns with Toad. Part of the bargain with him and Billy. None of us liked it, but nobody said no to Billy. There was something wrong with Toad. He liked to hurt you. He was with Brandi, there in the back room, and he was going to burn her with a cigarette. She screamed and Fawn ran in and pulled him away. He grabbed her by the throat and . . ." She didn't finish but instead closed her eyes as if replaying the scene in her mind. "He called Matt, and him and Adrian took her body away. That's all I know."

"This was when?"

"Couple of months ago, maybe. I don't remember exactly."

"What about Billy?"

"Was he ever pissed. I thought he'd kill Toad. He just told Matt to make sure Toad never hurt any of us. Christ, like that was going to stop Toad."

"You're from White Earth," Cork said. "How'd Billy Bones get his hands on you?"

"I ran away. Ended up in Duluth. Had no money, no nothing. Billy kind of rescued me. Or that's how I thought of it." She gave a grim laugh and shook her head. "Rescued."

"Why didn't you leave?" Dross asked.

"And go where? Back to my uncle? That pervert was worse than Toad. Girls like me and Brandi and Coral, we don't have anywhere else to go. That's why we stay."

Cork said, "Do you have any idea where Billy Bones took the other girls?"

"Nope."

"What about Matt?"

"I haven't seen him for a while. He came three or four days ago, really freaked out. Something to do with Fawn. Somebody found her body, I guess. He went away, then a day or so later, Billy got a call from him and went ballistic. Something about another dead girl. Billy left us here alone for a whole day. When he came back, he was acting crazy. I don't know. He could've killed Matt, I suppose. He sure seemed crazy enough. Screaming, hollering. Shouting about taking care of loose ends. I'm lucky he didn't shoot me."

Cork looked at this girl, who was thin, tired, scared, bitter, lost, abandoned. At that moment, she seemed to him the most ancient seventeen-year-old he'd ever seen.

Dross finished tending to the girl's injured feet and stood up. "I need to call this in."

CHAPTER 40

That morning, Stephen and Belle had asked Maria if she would be willing to return to Spirit Crossing, to help in the protest. They believed there was going to be another clash that might involve injuries.

"Will you come?" Maria had asked Annie.

"I'm too tired," Annie had said. It was more about her spirits than her body. "But go. You're needed. I'll be all right here."

They'd headed off in Stephen's Jeep. But Rainy left her Bronco in case Annie needed transport. So when Daniel called and asked her to check the files in Cork's office at Sam's Place, Annie grabbed the keys from the hook beside the mudroom door and took off.

She pulled into the gravel lot at the old Quonset hut and killed the engine. It wasn't yet opening time, 11:00 A.M., and there was only one other car in the lot. She knew it belonged to Sylvia Villebrun, who was in charge of opening and managing that day. Annie had performed these duties when she was a teenager, as had her brother and sister and so many other kids in Aurora. Sam's Place was often their first experience in a real job.

She sat a little while, recalling her time working for her father, recalling all the friends who'd worked with her, recalling so many sweet moments in the town of her birth. Although she'd left years ago to follow her own path, she'd never lost her love of this place and the people she'd left behind.

When she stepped inside, she greeted Sylvia, who was bustling around in the prep area, getting ready to open.

"Working alone?" Annie asked.

"Augie Treuer was supposed to be here to give me a hand. He's running late. Again."

"Happy to help," Annie offered. And she did, falling into a routine that was still as familiar to her as breathing.

Augie showed up fifteen minutes later, panting hard. "I still don't have a motorcycle license, so I borrowed my auntie's car," he explained. "It broke down."

"Can you get it fixed?" Sylvia asked.

"Needs a new carburetor, I guess. I got a friend who said he'll fix it for a hundred bucks. Costs money to get around. That's why I'm working here." He looked at Annie. "Who are you?"

She told him.

"I thought you were in South America or someplace."

"Home for my brother's wedding. You better get to work. You open pretty soon."

She left them to their duties and went to the file cabinet in the area of the Quonset hut that her father set aside for his private security work. She found the file for Erno Paavola and the address for the house in Aitkin where his sister had lived and had raised Irene and Mathias. She called Daniel and gave him the information.

Gwen Lytle, another teenager Annie's father had hired, came in for her shift. Annie thought about sticking around to give a hand, but there was something bittersweet in watching the kids in whom her father had put his trust do what he'd trained them to do.

She didn't particularly want to return to an empty house. Instead she decided to head to Crow Point, where Jenny and Waaboo were still under the watchful eyes of Prophet and Henry Meloux.

As so often in her life, the moment she'd stepped from the trees into the meadow on Crow Point, her mood had brightened. Henry Meloux had told her that there were places where the spirit of the Creator was especially profound, where the sense of peace was especially healing. Annie had understood all her life that Crow Point was one of those places. Still, that didn't keep Henry's sanctuary from being violated by those who cared little about what was sacred, as had been demonstrated so pointedly the day before, when Adrian Lewis had tried to kill her there.

In Guatemala, in the chaos of the barrio, she'd often held to the memory of Crow Point, used it to help center herself. But this day, she didn't feel the peace of the place. There was still so much in her that struggled with the truth of what lay ahead for her, a wall of fear and anger and regret that blocked the peace Crow Point promised.

Even when Henry Meloux came from his cabin and she saw the smile break wide on his ancient face, she didn't feel the welcome of all that he and that sacred place offered.

"*Boozhoo*, Granddaughter."

"*Boozhoo*, Henry. Where is everyone?"

"Swimming. At least your sister and the little rabbit are. Prophet is keeping watch."

She heard Waaboo's cries of delight coming from beyond the rock outcrops that sheltered Meloux's fire ring.

"When I told our little rabbit that you would be coming, he wanted to speak with you alone."

She didn't ask how the old Mide understood that she would be visiting. If she did, she knew he would simply say something like "The woods whispered it to me." Which, Annie accepted, was probably true.

"Go on," Meloux said. "If he wants to speak to you, he must have something important to share."

When she reached the fire ring, Annie found Prophet sitting on one of the long sections of sawed log around the ring that reminded her of church pews. Through a broad gap in the birch trees that lined the shore of Iron Lake, Jenny and Waaboo were clearly visible, splashing in the water. Prophet held a book in his hands, which he closed when Annie appeared. She saw that it was *A House Made of Dawn*. She also saw Meloux's old Remington leaning next to him on the log.

"He likes to spend a lot of time in the lake," Prophet said. "Instead of Waaboo, he should be called Nigig."

Which Annie knew meant Otter.

"Henry said Waaboo wanted to talk to me."

"He's been troubled lately."

"That's pretty understandable. He's been shot at."

Prophet shook his head. "Something else."

"Any idea what?"

"He keeps it to himself. There's a lot going on in that young brain of his. Sit." Prophet nodded at the place beside him. When she was seated, he said, "What is good is also a kind of magnet for what is not."

She gave him a confused look.

"Two poles attracting. Crow Point, for example."

"What do you mean?"

"I've wondered how a place like this, where the spirit of the Creator is so strong, can also be a place where things like yesterday occur. That man almost killed you. I know there have been other incidents here. I was a part of one. And I've been thinking how these things could be in a place like this. Henry, in his way, seemed to understand my question. He was the one who told me that what is good is also a kind of magnet for what is not."

"Ah," Annie said. "That sounds like Henry."

"Waaboo is like that," Prophet said. "I suspect that until he's a grown-up, he'll need protection from what isn't good. I think he's beginning to understand that."

Annie watched the child playing, and her heart went out to him. *Poor kid,* she thought.

And poor Jenny.

They came from the water, Waaboo running, his skin wet and tanned and glistening with droplets under the morning sun as if he were wearing diamonds. He was smiling broadly, but when he saw Annie, his face changed, grew serious.

Jenny was right behind him. "Henry said you'd be coming," she told her sister. Two towels had been laid out on one of the trunk sections. Jenny gave a towel to her son and took the other for herself.

"Everyone else has gone somewhere. It felt pretty lonely in the house. I thought I'd hang out here for a while." Annie smiled at Waaboo. "I have it on good authority that you'd like to talk with me."

Waaboo had toweled off, and now he nodded. "Alone," he said.

"Come on, Prophet," Jenny said. "I'll head back and start putting together some lunch for us all."

Prophet stood and lifted his rifle. "I won't be far," he promised Waaboo, then he followed Jenny.

"Come and sit," Annie said, patting the log beside her. When the boy was seated, she said, "So, what is it you want to talk to me about?"

He said, almost apologetically, "You're dying."

She was surprised. "Did Henry tell you that?"

"No. But it's true."

"Yes."

"And you're scared." He closed his eyes for a few moments.

When he opened them, he said, "And mad. Is it because you're dying?"

"Because there's nothing I can do about it. And because it makes me doubt."

"Doubt what?"

"God. Or rather God's love."

"Mishomis says we walk the path we were always supposed to walk."

"And I want to know why."

"I see things other people don't. Mishomis tells me why isn't important." He gave a shrug. "But I still wonder."

"Maybe someday you'll understand."

"You, too."

"Before it's too late, I hope."

With his bare toe, he drew a little circle in the dirt under his feet. "If I was dying, know what I'd want?"

"What?"

"To see Disney World."

She laughed. "Really?"

"What about you?"

She thought that over and finally smiled. "It's not what I want to see *before* I die. It's what I want to see *when* I die."

"What is it?"

"A face. Just a face."

He nodded, as if accepting that vague reply. "I haven't told Mom."

"Thanks. I'd like to do that myself. In my own time."

"Have you ever been to Disney World?"

"I can't say that I have. But it sounds pretty great. What do you say we head back to Henry's cabin?"

Waaboo reached out and gently touched her arm. "Her face," he said. "It will be there."

* * *

It was after lunch when Annie headed back to the double-trunk birch where she'd parked Rainy's Bronco. She felt much lighter than she had on her arrival. Some of that was probably the powerful spirit of the place itself, of being in the uplifting company of Jenny and Prophet, and certainly Henry Meloux, but it was also her conversation with Waaboo. Although it was brief, it had left her feeling less weighted. If a seven-year-old boy could bear the burden of what the Creator had put on his little shoulders, she could handle her own situation. Anger did no good. The why was unimportant. And she had the promise now that the face she wanted to see as she closed her eyes at the end would be there. Maria would be there.

She reached the double-trunk birch and took the keys to the Bronco from her pocket. Before she could unlock the door, a man appeared, coming around from the far side of the vehicle, startling her.

"Oh!" She took a step back.

He was handsome in a dark way, Native, and carried a rifle. The sense she got from him immediately made her think of Prophet's comment about what was good attracting that which was not.

"Let's take a walk," Liam Boyle said.

CHAPTER 41

The address Annie had given Daniel was for a house in Aitkin, a town with the only stoplight in the entire county. From the street, the place appeared badly neglected—peeling paint, torn screen door, sagging porch, dead lawn. But to be fair, the other houses on the block had not been cared for much better. Still, they seemed to be lived in. The house where Irene Boyle and Mathias Paavola had grown up did not.

Daniel, Monte, and Agent Shirley sat parked in Monte's Tahoe on the other side of the street and several houses down from the Paavola property.

"Cork told me Mathias Paavola drives a Wrangler," Daniel said. "I don't see one."

"If I were him, I sure as hell wouldn't advertise my presence by parking it out front," Agent Shirley said.

"There's an alley," Monte said. "Let's see what the place looks like from behind."

They cruised slowly up the street, around the corner, and into the alley. It was gravel, lined with tired-looking garages and battered garbage cans and a big tabby cat that eyed them menacingly from the top of an overturned wooden crate. The Paavola house had a garage in worse shape than most of the others. Monte rolled past and stopped a few houses away.

"I'll check it out," Daniel said and opened his door.

"Good luck seeing anything through those windows," Agent Shirley said. "There's years of dirt on them."

"If I were Paavola, that's exactly what I'd want," Daniel said.

Monte got out from the driver's side. "While you check the garage, I'll scope out the house."

There was no backyard fence, and Monte went straight to the house. Daniel found that Agent Shirley had been right. He couldn't see a thing through either of the garage windows. He tried lifting the garage door, but it wouldn't budge. He couldn't tell if it was stuck from rust or was locked. He was armed, and he took his Glock from its holster and used it to break a pane of glass on one of the windows. In the slender shaft of light that angled through the open square, he saw the wheel well of a vehicle. The tire looked new. He bent and took a better look. In the dim illumination the light gave to the rest of the garage, he saw clearly that the vehicle parked there was a Jeep Wrangler.

Monte came back. "Shades over some windows. They're old and yellowed. Sheets over others. They look new."

"The Wrangler's in there," Daniel said, tapping the side of the garage.

He waved to Agent Shirley, who joined them, and they stepped behind the garage, out of view of the house.

"How do we want to play this?" Daniel asked.

Monte said, "A couple of us up front while one of us covers the back." He eyed Agent Shirley. "Are you looking for more Jesus in your life?"

*   *   *

Cork and Dross put Margot Lachance in the backseat of the Expedition.

"Where are you taking me now?" she asked.

"To the sheriff's office, in Hibbing," Dross said.

"Juvie." Margot said the word as if it were a four-letter expletive.

"You'll be taken care of, your feet treated properly."

"You've never been in juvie."

"I'm very familiar with juvenile detention," Dross said.

"Not from the other side. Ever been in foster care?"

"I can't say that I have."

"Shit. You privileged white people. You don't know anything."

"You've been trafficked, Margot. You're the victim, not the perpetrator. You cooperate in the investigation of what Adrian Lewis, Liam Boyle, and Mathias Paavola have been doing, and I guarantee you won't go to jail. Protective custody, yes, for a bit, while we get all this sorted out and we figure what's best for you next."

"I got no next. None of us got a next. That's why we stuck with Toad and Billy and Matt. What do you care anyway?"

"Let's take this one step at a time, Margot. We'll figure out a next for you, I promise."

"Yeah. Billy was full of promises, too."

"I'm not like Liam Boyle."

"He'll kill me. That's what's next for me. I'll bet he killed Toad. He's probably already killed Brandi and Coral. He was screaming about killing Matt, too. And some damn kid."

Cork had said nothing during the exchange between Dross and the girl. Now he asked, "What kid?"

"Some kid Billy said talks to dead people. Said it was all his fault."

Cork's jaw went tight. "The guy who took a shot at Waaboo,"

he said to Dross. "We figured it might have been Adrian Lewis, except for the ball cap with the Thunderbird on it, a Native symbol. What if it was Boyle trying to silence Waaboo?"

"Makes sense now," Dross agreed.

Cork stepped away from the Expedition and punched in Jenny's cell phone number. He got no answer. Next he tried Prophet's cell phone, a number very few people had. Same result.

"Damn," he said.

"What is it?" Dross asked.

"Jenny's on Crow Point with Waaboo. I'm not getting an answer."

"Reception's iffy out there. You know that."

"I'd just as soon be sure." He punched in the number for the Iron Lake Ojibwe Tribal Police. LuJean Desjardins answered, and he explained his concern.

"I'll get out there and make sure everything's okay," she promised. "I'll keep you informed."

He thanked her and ended the call. But he wasn't comforted.

Monte Bonhomme took the rear of the house. Daniel went with Agent Shirley up front. They mounted the rickety steps, and Daniel moved to the side of the door, out of sight. Agent Shirley opened the torn screen door and knocked hard on the peeling paint of the inside door. There was no response. She knocked again, then glanced at Daniel, who gave a nod.

"Jesus loves you! I'm here to spread the word of his everlasting love! Praise God!" she sang out. She paused a moment, then knocked again and said, "You can hide from men, but you can't hide from God. He sees all. He knows the sin in your heart. He sent his son to suffer for those sins and to redeem you, praise the Lord!" Still nothing. She knocked a third time and cried out, "I will not leave this house until I have prayed the sin out of it and done the work mighty Jehovah has called me to!" In the voice of a banshee she cried out, "Dear God, hear my prayer!"

At which point the door swung open and a woman said, "Please move on. We don't want whatever religious crap you're selling."

Agent Shirley pushed into the open doorway, Daniel with her, his Glock drawn. "Police!" he shouted as the woman inside stumbled back.

To the right was the living room, empty of furniture except for an old table where a large laptop computer sat open, displaying a paused image from a video game. To the left, a bare dining room. Ahead, a flight of stairs leading directly to the second floor. The place smelled of mildew, dank air, and wood rot.

The woman held up her hands. "Don't shoot. Please."

"Irene Boyle?" Agent Shirley said.

"Yes."

"Where's your brother?" Daniel said.

She didn't answer, but her eyes shot up toward the ceiling. Voicelessly she mouthed, *He has a gun.*

Cork was driving well over the speed limit. "An hour to Aurora, another half an hour to Crow Point."

Dross was on her cell phone. "I'll get a couple of deputies out there to help."

"No," Cork said. He was thinking of Prophet and the need to keep him off the official radar. "Let the tribal police handle it."

"This man's dangerous, Cork."

"Keep trying Jenny's number." He glanced in the rearview mirror and could see the face of Margot Lachance, who looked exhausted. "Does the name Crystal Two Knives mean anything to you?"

"Never heard of her."

"She might have been using a different name." He described her.

"Not ringing any bells. Who is she?"

"A girl who disappeared."

"Hell, there's lots of those."

He thought about what Margot had told them, that she and the other girls stayed with their tormentors because they had no other option. And he thought about Crystal Two Knives, who'd seemed to have found a way to avoid falling into the hands of someone like Boyle and Toad and Paavola. He thought he'd helped her in this. But maybe he was wrong. What did he really know about desperation? In the rearview mirror, Margot Lachance looked so small. She'd crossed her arms over her chest and was staring out her window. What was she looking for, he wondered. Here he was, speeding east because of his concern for those he loved. As nearly as he could tell, Margot had no one concerned for her safety.

"You said you're White Earth."

"Yeah."

"Have you done ceremonies?" he asked.

"Did some powwows when I was a little kid. Long time ago. Before my mom died. Then I lived with my uncle in Fargo. Was that ever fucked up."

"Ceremonies are different. They can help," he said.

"Help what?"

"Feeling connected."

"To what?"

"Your people. I'm talking about healing ceremonies."

"I never even been to a doctor."

"I know someone I believe could help you."

"Not unless they got a million bucks to give me."

Dross glanced at Cork. "Henry?"

Cork nodded. "Would you let her spend time on Crow Point?"

"Let's see how things play out first."

"Mathias, my name is Monte Bonhomme. I'm a police officer."

Monte and Daniel flanked the bottom of the stairs, their weapons drawn. Agent Shirley had moved Irene Paavola away from any line of fire.

"I'm advising you to surrender your gun and come down so that we can talk," Monte said.

"I didn't do anything," Paavola yelled from upstairs.

"Then there's no reason not to come down."

Irene Boyle called out, "Just come down and talk, Matt. It's not them you're afraid of."

Agent Shirley said quietly, "Liam?"

Irene nodded.

"We can protect you from Liam Boyle," Monte called up the stairs.

"The same way you protected Adrian?" Paavola replied.

"We didn't know about Boyle then," Monte said. "You'll be safer in our custody than on your own, I guarantee it. And if you don't come down now, I'll make a call and this place will be surrounded by a sea of cops. There's no way out of this."

"Matt, please," Irene said. "It's over."

The house lapsed into a few long moments of silence, then Paavola said, "I'm coming down."

CHAPTER 42

They walked the path that Annie had walked so often in her life, through the woods heading toward Crow Point. The grass of the trail was strewn with sunlight broken into shards by overhanging tree branches. She could hear the song of birds, the buzz of insects. With each breath, she took in the scent of evergreen and wildflowers. With each step she felt the kiss of the summer air against her cheeks.

It was odd that she was so present in this moment with a man who held a rifle at her back.

"Who are you?" she asked.

"Doesn't matter."

"Why the gun?"

"What do you think?"

She stopped then and turned to face him. "I've been threatened with guns before."

"Is that so?"

"Rifles to be exact. Soldiers."

"I don't care. Get moving."

"Or you'll shoot me?"

"I wouldn't hesitate, believe me, bitch."

"Bitch?" She cocked her head and studied him. "Do you hate women?"

"Just shut up and keep moving."

"Is this about the dead girls?"

"This is about a kid who ruined everything."

"Did you kill those girls?"

"No. But I could have."

"Who did kill them?"

He slapped her hard. "I told you to shut up."

The blow had a strange effect on Annie. It served to quiet her spirit even more. "Forgiveness is possible," she said.

"For what?"

"What you've already done and what you're thinking of doing."

"You have no idea what I'm thinking."

"I believe I do. You want to kill my nephew. I believe it must be because he has a gift that's complicated your life."

"Complicated? He's fucking ruined it."

"Did he really do that? Or was it someone else a long time ago?"

When he hit her again, this time with the butt of his rifle, she went down. She lay on the path for a few moments while her head cleared. She touched the side of her face where the blow had landed. Her hand came away bloodied. She looked up at him. The rifle was leveled on her.

"All right," she said. "I'll walk."

They came out of the woods onto Crow Point. A thread of wood-smoke rose from the stovepipe of the cabin that Jenny and Waaboo were sharing. Annie stopped.

"What are you waiting for?" he snapped.

"Don't you feel it?" Annie said.

"What?"

"The power of this place."

"I'm sick of your talk. Just shut up."

Annie turned to the man. It was late afternoon now, the sun at her back, and her shadow fell across him. "Who was it?" she asked.

"Who was it who what?"

"Hurt you."

"Goddamn, I won't say it again. Just keep walking or I swear I'll shoot you."

"It will alert them that we're here. Anyway, I'm already dead."

"What the hell are you talking about?"

"You can shoot me if you want, but I'm already dead."

He looked at her as if she were the crazy one.

"Cancer," she said. "Here." She pointed to her head. "I'll be gone in a few months. Killing me now will just speed things up. So, who hurt you when you were a kid?"

"What are you, a goddamned psychiatrist?"

"A nun. Or I almost was." She smiled then. "Do you know what an epiphany is?"

"I don't care."

"It's a realization. For me a spiritual one. I've had an epiphany, and I have you to thank."

"Lewis should have killed you."

"But he didn't. And I think I know why."

"Yeah? Why?"

"You."

"What are you talking about?"

"I think this was meant to be, our meeting."

"You're nuts, bitch."

"No, I think I'm finally clearheaded. I'm going to die and that's the truth and there's no why about it that I'm going to understand. You're going to die, too, and you'll never understand the why of it either, no more than you can understand the why of the sun coming up. Acceptance. Embrace. Giving over to the Great Mystery without struggle." Her smiled broadened, but it was not meant for this man. "Giving over completely, that's the whole point. It makes it all so much easier."

"I've had enough of your bullshit. Go now or you're dead." The hollow black eye at the end of his gun barrel stared her in the face.

"I told you," she said, still smiling. "I'm already dead."

He stepped forward so that the barrel of his gun was less than a foot from her forehead.

The shot that came next shattered the stillness of the afternoon and sent a covey of grouse flapping noisily up from the meadow grass.

CHAPTER 43

Mathias Paavola began to descend the stairs.

"Hands on the top of your head!" Monte Bonhomme ordered.

Paavola laced his fingers over his scalp.

"Where's your weapon?" Monte demanded.

"I left it upstairs. I have a permit," he said.

"Don't move your hands from your head."

"I understand."

"Keep coming."

Paavola continued slowly down. When he stepped from the last stair, Daniel turned him and patted him down. "Nothing," he said to Monte, then he used a plastic restraint to secure the man.

"Are you arresting me?" Paavola asked.

"For the moment, just detaining you," Monte said. "Just to talk. What happens after that depends on you."

"I want a lawyer."

"You haven't been arrested. Not yet, anyway."

"I got nothing to say."

"All right, but just in case," Monte said, then gave him the Miranda warning.

Agent Shirley turned to Irene Paavola. "Why are you hiding here?"

"Matt was afraid my ex-husband was going to kill us."

"Why?"

"Because we could tie him to the deaths of Olivia Hamilton and the Indian girl. When we were married, I told Liam about Uncle Erno and his crazy belief in the end of the world and about that room under his cabin."

"Did Liam kill them?" Daniel asked. When she didn't reply, he directed his next question to Paavola. "Did you?"

"I had nothing to do with it. That was Adrian."

"Adrian Lewis?" Daniel asked.

"Yeah."

"Why did he kill them?"

"I told you, I got nothing to say."

"What do you know about this, Irene?" Agent Shirley said.

"Only what Matt told me."

"And what was that?"

"That Lewis went into a rage and killed the Indian girl. Liam told Matt and Lewis to get rid of her body. Matt thought nobody would ever find her in that clearing with the blueberries."

"Shut up!" Paavola snarled.

"It's over, Matt. You have to face up to it."

"What about Olivia Hamilton?" Daniel said.

Irene Paavola took a deep breath, as if what she was about to say wasn't easy. "Matt told me that this Lewis drugged her and took her to the cabin. He killed her there. He told Matt and Matt told Liam and they tried to clean up the mess. Then that boy who apparently has ESP or something got involved and Liam got scared. He was afraid he'd get connected to everything, so he was going to kill the boy before he, I don't know, before he sensed everything or whatever. Matt thought Liam was losing it and maybe would come after me."

"Because you knew that Liam knew about the room under the cabin and might talk to the police?"

Irene nodded. "That's when Matt brought me here. Forced me to come, really."

"For your own good," Paavola snapped. "Hell, he was on his way to kill you. That's why he set up that little rendezvous at your place. You were all decked out for him and hot to trot. You're lucky I got to you before he did."

"Were you helping Liam Boyle traffic young women?" Agent Shirley asked Paavola.

The man didn't say anything.

"He was," Irene said. "I'm so ashamed."

"You had no idea?"

"Of course not. I've spent my life trying to keep kids from falling into the hands of predators like Liam. And Matt. Jesus, Matt, how could you?"

"I did my best to keep them from getting hurt," he shot back. "Without me around, Adrian would've been a monster with them. And some of the pipeline guys, they could get rough. I swear to God, I tried my best."

"How did it all happen?" Monte asked.

Again, Paavola was mute.

"It was Liam," Irene said with obvious distaste. "He groomed the girls. I had no idea, I swear it. As nearly as I can tell from what Matt's told me, he was trafficking in Duluth first. Then the pipeline project began, my brother got a job, and Liam recruited him. Matt let his coworkers know about the service Liam was providing. And Matt knew this Lewis person, who kept the company from bothering the operation. According to Matt, he also provided a trailer or something where the girls were kept and did their work."

"And you had no idea?" Agent Shirley said. It was obvious that she had trouble believing this.

"Matt and I haven't communicated much in recent years."

"What about your ex-husband?" Daniel asked.

"Liam . . . well." She looked down at the old floorboards. "He's hard to explain."

"Candyce Osterkamp gave us a pretty good idea of his particular kind of charm," Agent Shirley said.

"I swear to you, I never had any idea he was involved in something like this."

"Somebody shot and killed Adrian Lewis yesterday," Monte said.

"That had to be Liam," Irene said. "Matt was here with me."

"You own a Remington thirty-aught-six," Monte said to Paavola.

"What of it?"

"Lewis was killed with a Remington thirty-aught-six round. Earlier today, an empty box of that same caliber cartridge was found in trash from your apartment."

"Boyle," Paavola said, his voice hard. "He took the rifle from my place in Dahlbert. I went back for my PlayStation and my rifle, but it was gone. My police scanner, too. That son of a bitch. I'll bet he was going to try to frame me for whatever he had in mind, then kill me and Irene so we couldn't talk."

"My colleagues found Lewis's trailer and cabin," Daniel said. "No sign of Boyle or the girls. Any idea where he might've taken them? Or do you think he might have eliminated them, too, in a way that would point the blame at you?"

"Matt?" Irene said.

His lips went into a hard line.

"Please, Matt. You said you did your best to protect them. Help them now."

The man breathed deeply, let out a sigh, and said, "There's a dump of a motel outside Dahlbert. He's kept some girls there on occasion."

"Name of the motel?"

"The Wander Inn."

"Let's hope they're there," Agent Shirley said.

"Does Boyle know where this kid with ESP might be staying?" Daniel asked.

"I don't know," Paavola said. "Probably. He's like a weasel, smart and mean."

Daniel's heart was racing. "I need to make some calls," he said.

CHAPTER 44

Annie's face was a mask of horror. Blood dripped from her cheeks like tears. The sound of the rifle shot reverberated in her head. When she opened her eyes, the world was veiled in red.

Then she saw him. He stepped in front of her, said gently, "You okay?"

Annie had trouble finding words. "I'm . . . not . . . dead?"

"You almost were," Prophet said. "A second or two away, I'd guess."

Annie lowered her gaze to the man who lay in the meadow grass. The side of his head was a mass of blood and exploded bone. She lifted her eyes to Prophet. "You?"

"I didn't have a choice. He was going to kill you, wasn't he?"

She thought a moment, gave one nod.

"Come on," Prophet said. He took her hand. "Let's get you to Henry and get you cleaned up."

Jenny had washed her sister's face of the blood and other matter that came from the bullet's backsplash as it exited Liam Boyle's skull. Because Annie's T-shirt was spattered with blood as well, Jenny had loaned her another. Prophet had taken Waaboo away for a while, but now that Annie was cleaned up, he'd brought the boy back. They sat at the table in Henry Meloux's cabin, with Prophet standing guard at the door.

Meloux said, "The woods are safe again, Prophet."

"A little insurance never hurt, Henry."

"How . . . ?" Annie asked. She didn't exactly recall what had happened. She remembered the rifle barrel inches from her forehead. She remembered her full embrace of what she believed was to come. She thought maybe she'd had her eyes closed, waiting for the bullet to do its work, but she couldn't say for sure. She would never be able to say for sure.

"Mishomis warned us," Waaboo said. "He told us a darkness had come to the woods. We hid."

Annie looked at Prophet, who stood in the doorway, silhouetted against the afternoon light. "And you . . . ?"

"I went to check things out."

"Did you have to kill him?" Annie said.

"When he put his rifle to your head, I figured I had no choice."

Annie frowned a moment, then said, "Thank you." She looked beyond him to the light outside. "He's just lying there."

"His body," Meloux said. "His spirit has already begun its next journey. Do not weep for this man, Anne O'Connor. This life was not kind to him. In the next, he will find peace."

"I hope he goes to hell," Waaboo said.

"Hush, Waaboo," Jenny said.

"There is no hell, Little Rabbit," Meloux offered. "Except what we create for ourselves here or others create for us. Better that this man's spirit has moved on."

"I need to pray for him," Annie said.

"Even after what he intended to do to you?" There was a note of anger in Jenny's voice. "And Waaboo?"

"It's just like Henry said. Someone created a hell for him here that misshaped his life. We aren't born with spirits bent on evil. I've seen firsthand the hearts of children warped by cruelty. I've spent years trying to do what I could to help. With that man, all that's left to me is to offer prayers that his soul finds rest."

"I can't be that forgiving," Jenny said.

Annie smiled just a little. "You'd make a terrible nun."

Her cell phone rang. When she answered, Daniel said, "I've been trying to reach Jenny or Prophet. No one's answering. I need to get word to them. Waaboo may be in great danger."

"Waaboo's fine," Annie said. "I'm with him and Jenny now. And Henry and Prophet. We're all fine."

"Not necessarily," Daniel said in a tight voice. "A man named Liam Boyle wants Waaboo dead. He may try to get at him on Crow Point."

"Liam Boyle," Annie said. "So that was his name."

"Was?"

"You don't have to worry about him, Daniel. Would you like to talk to Jenny?"

"Sure."

She handed the phone over and listened as her sister spoke.

"I'm sorry, Daniel. We had to silence our phones here for a while. We didn't mean to scare you." She listened. "We have a lot to tell you. Best we do that when you get here." She listened again and nodded. "All right. I'll see you then. But don't worry. We're not in danger anymore, I promise."

She handed the cell phone back to Annie.

The distant wail of a siren crept into the cabin, and Meloux said, "I will take my rifle now, Prophet. It is best if you stay in the forest for a while."

Prophet handed the Winchester to the old man. "What will you say, Henry?"

"That although my eyes are not as keen as they used to be, I still have a warrior's instinct." Meloux looked at the others and asked, "Who was it that sent the intruder on the Path of Souls?"

"You, Mishomis," Waaboo said.

"You," Jenny said.

Annie didn't answer immediately, and Meloux offered, "If the truth is what you need to hold to, you can always say that your eyes were closed and you did not see who fired the bullet. That will not be a lie."

Annie shook her head. "It's not that. I'm just thinking that I've been lying to myself and others for too long. It's time I told a few truths. This won't be one of them, however. You fired the shot, Henry." She turned to her sister and said, "But there's a truth I need to tell you."

CHAPTER 45

Daniel had called Cork and let him know that something had gone down on Crow Point but he wasn't sure what, only that everyone was safe. Liam Boyle, apparently, was no longer a threat. Cork was already near Aurora, so he cruised on through town. Instead of heading to the double-trunk birch and walking to Crow Point, he drove to the Iron Lake Reservation and followed the rough track from Allouette directly to Meloux's cabin, the same route the tribal police had undoubtedly followed. Sheriff Marsha Dross had insisted on staying with him. Margot Lachance was still in the backseat.

Cork parked behind the vehicle Officer LuJean Desjardins had driven. He saw Desjardins standing far out in the meadow, near the edge of the woods. Henry Meloux was with her.

Jenny came from Meloux's cabin to greet her father and Dross, and let them know that Daniel was on his way with Monte Bonhomme and the BIA agent.

"What's happened?" Cork asked.

"The man who tried to kill Waaboo is dead."

"Liam Boyle?" Dross was clearly surprised.

"Officer Desjardins said that was the name on the driver's license she found in his wallet."

"How did he die?" Dross pressed.

"He was going to kill Annie, then Waaboo. Probably the rest of us, too. Henry shot him before that could happen."

"Henry?" Dross seemed incredulous.

"He may be old," Jenny said, "but he still has the instincts of a warrior."

It was a phrase Cork would hear often thereafter.

"The body's out there." Jenny waved toward Meloux and Desjardins.

"I need to see about this." Dross headed immediately in that direction.

"Waaboo?" Cork asked.

"In Henry's cabin with Annie."

"Prophet?"

Jenny raised her eyebrows and said, "In the woods."

Cork nodded, catching all her hidden meaning.

"Annie told me, Dad."

Her face melted into sadness, and Cork saw tears gathering along the rims of her eyes. He took her into his arms. "I know." He felt her press against him as if trying to draw some of his strength into her own body. "We can't change what will happen, Jenny, but we can surround her with our love and our comfort and our prayers. We'll be beside her all the way in this."

"She's been gone so long. And now . . ."

"I know," Cork said again. Because he understood exactly how Jenny felt.

The rear door of the Expedition opened, and Margot Lachance stepped out. "Okay if I stretch my legs?"

Jenny drew away from her father's arms and wiped at the tears that rolled down her cheeks. She eyed the girl, then glanced at her father.

"I'll explain later," he said.

"I haven't eaten all day," Margot said. "You got any food around here?"

Jenny looked at Cork again, and he said, "See what you can rustle up, okay?"

She wiped once more at her tears. "This way," she said to the girl and headed toward the cabin she'd been sharing with Waaboo.

Cork went to Meloux's cabin. Inside, his grandson and Annie sat together at the table. Cork had the sense that he was interrupting an important conversation.

"Everybody okay here?" he asked.

"I wouldn't say that," his daughter replied. "But we're all alive."

"He was going to kill Annie," Waaboo said. "But Prophet shot him."

"Henry shot him," Annie corrected.

"The truth is safe with me, Annie," Cork said. "I'm just grateful no one was hurt." He studied them again. "I have a sense I've interrupted something."

"I told them, Dad," Annie said.

"She's dying, Baa-baa."

That was what Waaboo had called him ever since the boy was old enough to talk. But he seldom used that name for Cork anymore. Usually only when he was in need of comfort.

"I know," Cork said. He sat down with them and took Annie's hand. "But she didn't die today. And every day we have left, I intend to celebrate her life." He looked deeply into his beloved daughter's eyes. "We will all celebrate your life."

Annie squeezed his hand and smiled. Cork felt the calm that came from her now. It was something he often felt in the presence of Henry Meloux, the open embrace of the Great Mystery. And he was not afraid of what lay ahead. What lay ahead for them all.

EPILOGUE

Stephen and Belle were married on a Saturday afternoon in late August. The wedding was supposed to be held outdoors, on the grounds of a lovely old lodge called Burntside on the shore of Iron Lake, where the view from beneath the pines was postcard perfect. But an hour before the ceremony, it began to rain, a heavy downpour. So the guests found themselves inside a big ancient barn that had been reconfigured into a space for just such an emergency. It wasn't a large gathering, only the closest of Belle's and Stephen's families, forty guests in all. It was presided over by Anton Morriseau, Belle's brother, who was duly licensed by the state of Minnesota and was a pipe carrier. The two young people each put tobacco into the pipe, and the smoke went upward to the *manidoog* to be blessed by those spirits. With the drum of rain on the barn roof and the occasional crack of thunder in the distance, Belle and Stephen exchanged the vows they'd written, and Anton Morriseau gave his blessing. Belle's mother and Jenny draped a colorful blanket around the shoulders of the couple in the traditional way. And last of all, Henry Meloux was asked to give his own blessing.

He spoke first in Ojibwemowin, the language of the Anishinaabeg. Then he spoke again in English for those who didn't understand.

"You are two minds, two hearts, two souls. But this day you begin a journey of one. Where it will lead, I cannot tell you. Only the Creator knows. But I can tell you this. On your journey, you will never be alone. In the cold, you will have another body for warmth. In times of uncertainty, you will have a hand to hold for comfort. In the dark, you will have the whisper of love to assure you that the light will return." He took their hands and placed them between his own. "Go in peace, Grandchildren. May you find the way to *bimaadiziwin*, the good life. And know that the love of all the hearts here today goes with you."

Then, as if Kitchimanidoo, the Creator, the Great Mystery, was pleased, the rain ceased, the sun broke through the clouds, and its bright rays poured into the broad doorway of the barn and illuminated the gathering.

Stephen and Belle chose to delay their honeymoon. There was still the protest at Spirit Crossing. They worked together until Stephen left to begin law school in the Twin Cities, and soon thereafter, Belle joined him. Within a few weeks, greed and the insatiable hunger for oil moved the pipeline forward across the Jiibay River and on to its inevitable completion.

Still, life can be quite generous in the blessings it offers. Many weeks after the wedding, there was a surprise for those in Tamarack County who'd feared the worst for the missing young woman named Crystal Two Knives. A few days before Thanksgiving, she came home, bringing with her a young man she called her soul mate. She told the story of how she'd met him by accident when the old jalopy she was driving to the Twin Cities broke down and he stopped to help. He was an acrobat, on his way to Las Vegas to join Cirque du Soleil. On a whim, or as Henry Meloux might have said, blown by the breath of the Great Mystery, she'd gone with him. She was sheepish and apologetic when questioned about not communicating with anyone. She explained that she was afraid Red LaGrange, her abusive ex-boyfriend, might track her down and do harm to her and her new love. But she'd been keeping tabs on things back home, checking out the *Aurora Sentinel* online, and when she read that LaGrange had been arrested in Duluth and was facing significant jail time, she decided to return home. In the end, she was forgiven because she was no longer one of the missing.

Annie O'Connor stayed in Aurora, eventually in hospice care in the house where she'd grown up. Maria was always at her side, tending to her needs with loving hands. In that same way, all the O'Connors ministered to her. For what little time Annie had left, she was surrounded by an aura of love. Then one snowy winter morning, she took quietly to the Path of Souls. Maria's face was the last beautiful thing of this earth her eyes beheld before she closed them forever. She was laid to rest next to the grave of her mother, Jo O'Connor, in a lovely spot beneath a linden tree. Cork complied with her last wish, that on her headstone be written these three words: BE NOT AFRAID.

AUTHOR'S NOTE

In my story, the chief of the Iron Lake Tribal Police force is Monte Bonhomme. Bonhomme is modeled after a good friend in the Anishinaabe community, an *ininiwag* named Monte "Awan" Fronk of the Makwa (Bear) Clan. Monte, a member of the Red Lake Nation, has been a tribal first responder for thirty-five years with the Mille Lacs Band of Ojibwe and currently oversees tribal emergency management operations. At fourteen years of age, his adopted daughter, Nada, whose Ojibwe name is Aakwaadizi Neshkaadizishkid Ikwe (She Is a Fierce Passionate Woman), went missing.

Early in her life, Nada was diagnosed with second-generation fetal alcohol spectrum disorder. The situation became apparent as Nada grew older and her behavior became more erratic. Her lack of impulse control was due in large measure to permanent frontal lobe damage caused by the disorder. This led to frequent outbursts, eventually reaching the point of requiring out of home placement for her own safety. Because of the lack of services for children who suffer from the syndrome, Nada experienced multiple placements, and eventually she began to run away. At first, she was gone for

short periods but was located with the help of the exceptional resources provided by the National Center for Missing and Exploited
Children, or NCMEC. Then, in 2013, she disappeared completely.

Her non-Native social worker made little effort to locate the
missing girl. Monte reached out to his brothers and sisters in the
public safety community in the Twin Cities. Eventually, Monte
received word that his daughter's photograph had been seen cir-
culating on adult websites, and the devastating realization hit him
that Nada was being trafficked. When the photographs suddenly
dropped off the internet, Monte feared the worst. But one day, a
human trafficking investigator with the Saint Paul Police Department reached out to him. Thanks to a NCMEC poster, a possible
sighting of his daughter had been reported. In an extreme rarity
within the epidemic of missing and murdered Indigenous women
(MMIW), the police conducted a search of the suspected house and
located Monte's daughter. She was alive.

Nada was placed in a group home for older teens in Bemidji,
but she refused to talk about her experience, which is not at all un-
common for victims of human trafficking. She became more stable.
Eventually, she reached out to a sensitive resource officer at the al-
ternative school she attended, who arranged for a properly trained
investigator to take Nada to an advocacy center, where she was
finally able to tell the truth of her traumatic two-year experience.

At eighteen, Nada aged out of the system. She moved to the
Twin Cities, where she completed the work for her high school di-
ploma, got a job, and lived independently. She was in a long-term
relationship and was planning to marry. But the effects of being
trafficked still haunted her, evidenced in periods of extreme anger
or heavy drinking. Eventually, she and her fiancé broke up.

On May 26, 2021, Monte received the devastating news that
Nada had been killed by another boyfriend, a murder-suicide in her
Twin Cities apartment.

Monte arranged a traditional four-day Ojibwe funeral. Through the spiritual guidance of a respected Ojibwe elder named Baabiitaw Boyd, and with the support of family, community members, and Monte's uniformed brothers and sisters in public safety, all of whom had gathered to grieve with him, Nada's spirit began her journey to the place the Ojibwe call *Gaagige-minawaanigoziwining*, a place of everlasting peace.

According to a 2018 study undertaken by the Urban Indian Health Institute, homicide is the third-leading cause of death for Indigenous girls and teens.[*] More than half of American Indian or Alaska Native women (56.1 percent) have experienced sexual violence in their lifetime. The murder rate of AI/AN women is almost three times that of non-Hispanic White women.[**] In 2020, there were 1,496 American Indian or Alaska Native people recorded as missing in the FBI's National Crime Information Center, 578 of whom were female. Because of reporting difficulties or omissions, this is probably a gross underreporting of the actual number.[***]

These are statistics, horrible in their implications of the threat to Native women in this country. But the numbers often mask the tragic individual stories of the women who have been victims of violence or who have gone missing. And the numbers say nothing about the grief suffered by their families and their communities.

After Nada's death, Monte was approached by members of the

---

[*]   "Missing and Murdered Indigenous Women and Girls," Urban Indian Health Institute, 2018.

[**] "Research Policy Update: Violence Against American Indian and Alaska Native Women," Policy Research Center, National Congress of American Indians, 2018.

[***] "2020 Missing American Indian and Alaska Native Persons Data," U.S. Department of Justice, Office of Justice Programs, 2021.

MMIW movement and asked to speak about his daughter's situation from the perspective of a Native father. He speaks openly now and publicly about the tragedy of his daughter's life. Along with others whose loved ones have gone missing or been murdered, Monte continues to give voice to the victims, to seek justice, to do his best to open the eyes of people who refuse to see the enormity of the situation for those who live in Indian Country.

The horrific treatment of the Indigenous people on this continent goes back centuries, beginning with the perception of those earliest of our European ancestors who viewed the Native people here as savages and who, from the very beginning, treated them in savage ways. Ignorant misconceptions, destructive stereotypes, human avarice, persistent prejudices, all have contributed to the ongoing struggle of Native people to preserve their cultures, their languages, and their right to the freedoms that both our Constitution and lawful treaties are supposed to ensure.

The violence against Native people continues, as the statistics demonstrate. But the statistics are only part of the story. Another important part is the perception that still lingers in the hearts of so many Americans of European ancestry that somehow Native people are different from us.

I have no Native blood running through my veins. I'm aware every time I sit down to write a novel in my Cork O'Connor series that I'm intruding on a culture that is not my own. If I err in my evocation of the Anishinaabeg, it's not intentional and, I hope, not detrimental. My wish is that in writing stories like this one, I may in some small way open the hearts and minds of readers to the enormous struggles our Native brothers and sisters face every day.

ACKNOWLEDGMENTS

I'm grateful to my friend Sergeant Chet Carlson of the Polk County Sheriff's Office in northern Minnesota. Chet has been both supportive and helpful over a lot of years. I'm especially appreciative of the help he gave me in writing this story. Not only was his advice regarding specific law enforcement details invaluable but he aided a good deal in my understanding of the complicated issues surrounding crimes that involve the interface of local, federal, and reservation jurisdictions. If I've made any errors in the story I've told, the blame lies fully on my shoulders. Chet did his best.

Thanks also to my many Anishinaabe friends who, when I broached the idea of writing a story about missing and murdered Indigenous people, encouraged me to go forward. I'm grateful and honored to have their trust.

And finally, to the Anishinaabeg here in Minnesota, I owe a deep debt of gratitude for the inspiration that comes from their continued courage and determination in the face of so many obstacles. *Chi miigwech.*

RESOURCES

If you're willing to enlighten yourself even more about the issue of missing and murdered Indigenous people, here are a few resources that may prove helpful:

Melanie Florence and François Thisdale. *Missing Nimama*. Clockwise Press, 2015. (This is a children's book, a sensitive approach to a difficult topic.)

Mona Gable. *Searching for Savanna: The Murder of One Native American Woman and the Violence Against the Many*. Atria Books, 2023.

Jessica McDiarmid. *Highway of Tears: A True Story of Racism, Indifference, and the Pursuit of Justice for Missing and Murdered Indigenous Women and Girls*. Atria Books, 2019.

Missing and Murdered Indigenous Women Task Force: A Report to the Minnesota Legislature. December 2020.